Magebound

Magebound

Katica Locke

P.D. Publishing, Inc.
Clayton, North Carolina

ISBN-13: 978-1-933720-65-4
ISBN-10: 1-933720-65-4

9 8 7 6 5 4 3 2 1

Cover art by Boulevard Photografica
Edited by: Day Petersen / Georgia Beers

Published by:

P.D. Publishing, Inc.
P.O. Box 70
Clayton, NC 27528

http://www.pdpublishing.com

To Penny, for everything;
to Rayne Adams, for all your help;
to my sister, for being my wall;
to my mother, for supporting me unconditionally

I've never seen such a pathetic slave market, and I've been to some real ass-end of the universe places. This one is just a rotting wooden platform in a field of mud and yellow grass, with us slaves corralled off to one side. There are six of us, down from the eight that left Ventia a week ago. The old man died at sea, and the girl was bought up before we even stepped off the ship, by a whorehouse, I think. The woman who bought her looked like a madam; I saw too much ankle and bosom at either end of her dress for her to have been a Lady. She spent some time looking at the teenage boy with us, but finally left without him. Erion was probably asking too much. The girl kicked one of the slavers as she left, so I think she'll be okay. I hope so. I'd rather be worked to death in the fields than suffer her fate any day.

As we wait for the inevitable, I stand silently with the others: the boy; two broken looking men in their late thirties; a big, brooding fellow a few years older than me; and a sour woman not quite old enough to be my mother. All of us have our hair sheared down to the scalp. It marks us as slaves and keeps the crawlies off our heads. It's better than branding, which I've heard still happens on some planets. We're under *tight* security, our hands bound loosely in front of us and a single sleeping slaver sitting guard outside the corral. The fact that no one, not even the kid, has tried to make a run for it just shows how dismal Traxen is — even if we did escape, there isn't anywhere to go.

The auctioneer is a fat man with a big nose, one of those fat, red noses that looks like it hurts all the time, not like mine, which is just too large for my face. He must drink a lot. I would, if I had a nose like that. He's over in the shade of a canvas tent, talking with Erion, the slave trader in charge of our ragged asses. They seem to be waiting for the slave owners and potential slave owners to gather, but I think the dozen or so men sitting impatiently on the overturned wooden crates in front of the platform is all the crowd we're going to draw.

As we all wait, I scan the faces of the men and then I take a good look at their shoes. Most of the time, you can tell an off-worlder by his shoes. Not always, but both times I was dragged through a world gate, it was by men wearing strange shoes.

I rest my bound wrists on the weathered fence rail and bite the inside of my lower lip. I don't want to be taken off Ashael again. I was born here; this planet is my home. It might not be much, compared to more advanced worlds, but I'd rather till the land here with just a mule and a plow than stitch someone's strange, weightless shoes together, or wash out the bilges on their space freighters. I don't think I have to worry about it, this time. Traxen is a long way from Greater Kormunae. Erion steps out into the sun and strides in our direction.

They start with the kid, of course, the auctioneer lying through his teeth to try and push the bidding up. Strong as an ox, my foot. He sells for more than I had guessed, to a weary looking farmer in a battered straw hat. Scratch that as non-definitive — they're all weary looking farmers in battered straw hats. This one has a drooping mustache and a knife tucked into his belt.

I watch the farmer lead his new slave down the road. I'm pretty good at judging what kind of master a man will be by the way he leads his slave. Mean ones jerk on the rope. Nice ones leave some slack. Horrible ones make you run along behind their wagons. This guy leaves slack, so maybe the kid'll be okay. I don't have time to worry about it, though — I'm up next.

"Great Maele, would you look at this fine young man!" I slouch and look down at my bare feet, caked in thick, black mud. "At seventeen years, he's just entering the prime of his life..." Who're they kidding? I'm six months shy of twenty-one, though I suppose I hardly look over eighteen. That's what happens when you never get enough to eat. "...an educated man, learned in reading and writing..." Educated, ha! I can write my name and read a little. I guess for a slave, that *is* educated. "...but strong and hard-working. He can plow, sow, reap, slaughter, woodwork, millwork, stonework." Yeah, but I'm not very good at any of them. "If his master hadn't taken ill and died, this man would not be standing before you today."

If I hadn't beaten my master with a rake and run away, and then been dumb enough to get caught by Erion, I wouldn't be standing here. I'd probably be dead, considering my master was trying to pour lamp oil on me and light me on fire when I took off. Said I looked at his daughter funny. Well, she was pretty funny looking, a long-necked goose of a girl with buggy green eyes, but I never looked at her like *he* meant.

"This is a once in a lifetime opportunity," the auctioneer continues. "Now, who'll give me a half-coin for this fine specimen?"

I roll my eyes. I'm worth at least three coins, but none of the farmers seem to realize it. Maybe I look like I eat a lot. One of them, a lean man with a scar across his left cheek, finally raises his hand, making a bid. His clothes are mostly leather, worn slick and shiny, and he's got spurs and a rope, so I'm guessing he's a rancher, probably from a fair distance, since this isn't exactly cattle country. I hate cows.

"If I let this fellow go for less than a coin, it would be highway robbery," the auctioneer says, stepping closer to me. He reaches up toward my face and I open my mouth before he has a chance to touch me, showing the crowd my teeth. I know the drill, and I hate being touched. "Look at those fine teeth!" He turns me around and lifts my shirt, showing them my back. "Not an ounce of fat on him." There's a muttering in the crowd and I scowl down at my feet. I'd like to see one of them live my life and look better. It's not like I asked to be beaten, and whipped, and cut, and burned.

The auctioneer steps away from me and I turn around. The few gathered farmers have moved to one side of the market. I guess it wasn't me they were muttering about. A horse and rider have come right up to the platform. My heart begins to pound in my chest as I take a second look. It's a unicorn, a black unicorn, with a hooded and cloaked rider, his face hidden in shadow. He raises a hand and points at me, and I can feel the color drain from my face, because it's not a hand, it's a claw — like a hawk's or a dragon's — slim, black, curved, and gleaming. I try to swallow, but my mouth has gone dry.

He tosses a small sack at the auctioneer's feet. It clinks like money and several gold coins spill out. It's probably three times what they'd get for me, even in a big city. "Sold," the auctioneer says, his voice barely more than a whisper as he brings his gavel down, missing the podium completely. He doesn't seem to notice. He's shaking as he hands the end of my lead to my new master. I want to ask him, *What the hell are you afraid of? He didn't just buy you*, but I bite my tongue.

As I step down from the platform, I glance over at the other slaves. They've crowded the rail and I can see it in their eyes, that intense relief that it's me instead of them. I've seen that look many times, worn it occasionally, so I can't blame them. I turn away and trot alongside the unicorn as my master heads out of town.

I've never been this close to such a beautiful beast. The only unicorns I ever had contact with were the worn pair of brown mares one of my richer masters kept to pull his carriage. It was my job to muck out their stalls, but I was never allowed to get this close. This big, black stallion gleams from horn tip to tail tip, and carries himself with such fierce pride I have to wonder how anyone could even manage to get a saddle on him, let alone mount up. But then I raise my eyes to my new master, to the claws holding the reins. I guess that explains it.

It's not easy to run with your hands bound in front of you, but my master seems in no hurry, lucky for me. Still, I'm hurting by the time he turns off the main road, my legs and back and every breath burning as we begin to climb a well-worn mountain path. Grassy hills rise up on my left, with a handful of fat brown sheep scattered near the top, and slope down to a patchwork of farmland on the right. The unicorn blocks most of the view to that side, though. I glance up at my monster of a new master, seeing nothing but darkness inside his hood. He hasn't said a word to me, and I'm not much of a talker anyway, even when I can breathe, so the journey is a silent one. I'm starting to wish the rancher had bought me.

We come around a bend in the trail and I can see a single pointed, slate-shingled roof silhouetted against the sky. Another few steps and more of the tower comes into view — a single arched window looking sightlessly out over the village and the sea. A castle. I hate castles. A castle means a lord, someone you have to bow and scrape to, and wash and dress and clean up after. I've belonged to several lords, none of them with towers as tall as this, and the ones who *just* beat and kicked me were the nice ones. It seemed that the richer and more powerful they were, the more cruel and perverse they felt they could be. If my master's castle is any indication of his wealth, I'm probably better off running for it. Hell, I'm probably better off dead.

I should have made a break for it back when the hills were gentle and covered in grass. Now it's just dirt and gravel rising up beside me and, beyond the unicorn, it looks like the ground just drops away. It could be a fall of five feet, or five hundred, and I'm not going to chance it unless I have to, because there's quite a range between short enough to walk away from and far enough to kill you, and I'd rather not lie broken and bleeding at the bottom of some cliff until something hungry finds me and finishes me off. So I guess I'm going up. Unicorns are nimble and quick, and I'll probably end up being stabbed in the back by that dark, spiral horn, but the closer we draw to the castle, the more I can't allow myself to be taken inside. Better a quick death than a slow one.

I grab the lead rope in my hands and jerk on it. It slips from the taloned hand easier than I expect and, for a second, I just stumble along beside the unicorn, the rope slithering along under my feet. Then I turn and scramble up the hill, but it's a lot looser than it looks, and I have to fight a slide of scree and dirt. It's worse than running up a hill of sand, because these rocks are sharp, and the dust rises up, choking me. I'm not getting anywhere and I glance over my shoulder to see how close my master is, but he's just sitting astride the unicorn, that blank, empty hood turned up toward me.

I lose my footing and hit my knees, my hands digging deep into the hillside as I start to slide, but I just pull more dirt and rocks down after me. Eyes closed, I roll down the hill and slam into the legs of the unicorn, which feels like being thrown into an iron fence post. I would know. I lay on the trail, half buried in debris, holding my side as I cough and choke and try to breathe. I can't get up. I may have broken a rib. Wouldn't be the first time. Squinting up at my master, silhouetted against the pale afternoon sky, I wait for him to decide what to do with me. Hopefully, he'll just throw me over the cliff and be done with me.

After several moments, he swings down from the back of the unicorn and grabs me by the arm. I wince, expecting those talons to cut right through my flesh, but his claws don't feel any different from human hands. He pulls me to my feet and I cry out, leaning into the pain as if that will somehow make it go away. It doesn't. I grit my teeth and straighten up. I am taller than him by nearly half a head. He pushes back his hood and scowls at me. He's just a man, for some reason reminding me of my uncle Asrard, who I've not seen in nearly fifteen years, his eyebrows full and beginning to gray, his eyes dark, but his face not unkind, even as he frowns at me. He beats the dirt off my shoulders, his hands just hands now.

"Idiot," he mutters, pulling a small knife out of his belt. I flinch, but he just cuts the rope that binds my hands. I rub at my wrists, the skin red and raw, and glance down the trail, the urge to run so very strong, even with my side screaming with every breath I take.

"Run if you want, but there's nowhere to go," he tells me.

My eyes dart from the village, half a mile away, to the scattered farmhouses in the valley below, to the sparkling ribbon of river winding through the valley and down to the bay, and then to the wide dirt road heading east along the edge of a rocky headland. He's right. I'm hundreds of miles from any place I would even begin to call familiar, in the middle of a damn fishing village and farm country. Why the hell did Erion even bring us here? I turn back to my master.

"Give me a hand, will you?" he asks, putting the knife away. He grabs a handful of the unicorn's mane and I help him up into the saddle, drawing a sharp breath between my teeth as the pain cuts through me. I lean one hand against the unicorn's flank to keep from doubling over and he swats me a stinging blow across my face with his tail. "Hey, are you okay?"

I step back and look up at my master. "Yes, M'Lord," I answer automatically, pulling my hand away from my side. No sense letting him know where to aim if he wants to kick me, though he doesn't strike me as the kicking type. "Please, M'Lord, what is going on?" I ask. He nudges the unicorn in the ribs, heading toward the castle as he begins to speak. I have to follow if I want to hear.

"I'm not your lord, nor anybody else's. My name's Thadyn. I'm — I *was* Lord Sactaren's assistant, but I've gotten too old for the job, which is why you're here."

"Lord Sactaren?" I ask.

"Yes," Thadyn says. "He's Traxen's resident mage."

I stop short and swallow hard. Mages. I've never been owned by one, but I've met people who had been. At least, I'd assumed that they'd once been people. I glance up at the castle. Money and power and magic. Is there a worse combination?

"Hey, you coming?"

I want to tell him no, but I've really got nowhere else to go. And he looks none the worse for wear, as far as I can tell. I sigh and follow him.

"What's he like, if I might ask?"

"Sactaren? Well..." Thadyn squints up at the castle, "you won't meet another man like him. What he's like, exactly, depends a lot on you." I start to ask him what he means, but he doesn't let me. "So they said you can read and write. Is that true?"

"Yes," I say after a moment's hesitation. "But not very well. I read better than I write."

"Good enough," he says. "If you don't know something, ask Schaff — that's what he's there for." We reach the end of our climb, crossing an open table of stone toward the main gate.

"Who's Schaff?"

"He's a pain in the ass, but he's supposed to help in the shop. That's what you'll be doing during the day, selling potions and charms to the villagers. And don't worry — it's mostly love stones to witless girls and colic remedies to new mothers. Sometimes a cow will stop giving milk or a chicken become ensorcelled by a pegwitch, but it's been years since anything really exciting happened around here."

We pass under the gate and into the inner courtyard. Some castles make grand gardens of their courtyards, with trees and flowers and fountains, or training grounds for guards and soldiers. This one is just empty flagstone from one wall to the other. I glance up at the blank, barren walls, not a banner or pennant to be seen. Two corners of the castle are low battlements, the third is the high tower, and the fourth is a lower, blocky tower with what looks like plants growing on top of it.

"What is that?" I ask, gesturing toward the greenery.

"Her Ladyship's garden," Thadyn says, scowling in that general direction.

He dismounts and I follow him as he leads the unicorn to a dark doorway cut into the northern wall. I jump back as something with pitch black skin and too many arms leans through the doorway and takes the reins from him.

"What the hell was that?" I ask.

"That's Qito — he looks after the animals. Come on, I'll show you around the shop."

He takes me through a door in the south wall, into the castle proper, and I'm surprised by how empty it is. The corridors are wide, but the floors are bare stone, lit by flickering torches that dance in the chill draughts. My hopes rise. Maybe he's not so wealthy after all.

We enter a room that looks exactly like a general store, with shelves on each wall and a long wooden counter. There's so much stuff in here, I can't make out anything specific for a moment, and then my eye falls upon a neat stack of bones sitting between bottles of pickled snakeheads and a box of shriveled roots. Now I see feathers, fur, scales, stones, sticks, leaves, all sorted and labeled and priced, just waiting to be bought. I make a slow circle of the room, my mouth dropping open anew as each strange thing comes to my attention.

"He looks like a grouper."

I turn, but it wasn't Thadyn's voice, and I see no one else in the room.

"Do you have to walk around with your mouth flapping open?"

I step toward the counter, toward the strangest cat I have ever seen sitting beside a basket of pink, heart-shaped stones. He's a deep red color, a bit more rusty than blood, and nearly black down his back and across his shoulders, with a more pointed muzzle than most cats, more like a fox, and very large ears. His eyes are a dark, glittery gold, and his tail is full and bushy, tipped with white, very much like a fox. I begin to wonder if he's really a cat at all.

"At least you're quick," the cat-fox says, though he sounds a bit sarcastic to me.

"You must be Schaff," I say, reaching out to scratch between his ears. He growls and bats my hand away with a surprisingly heavy paw.

"Do that again and there will be claws," he tells me, jumping down from the counter and stalking out of the room. Thadyn beckons me into the back room.

"I would try to stay on his good side, if I were you," he says, and then shows me the more powerful and expensive potions and charms. I scan the labels, picking out a word or two here and there, and hope I haven't insulted Schaff too much. I'm really going to need his help.

At the rear of the back room is a staircase leading upward. Thadyn motions for me to go up. The stairs are dark and I go cautiously, one hand on the outside wall as the steps spiral around a center post. The air grows warm, with a slightly smoky, musky smell, and I begin to see a faint light filtering down from above. The stairs open suddenly into a room crowded with tables and shelves, cages of small animals, and strange instruments I can't begin to describe, nor guess what they do.

"Where are we?" I ask, my voice barely louder than a whisper. Thadyn clears his throat.

"My Lord Sactaren?"

I swallow loudly. I'm filthy, my feet black with mud, clothes dirty and torn and stinking of sweat. Not exactly how I want to meet my new master.

"Yes, Thadyn?"

His voice is soft, slippery, and I can't tell where it's coming from. For a round room, this place has a lot of shadowy corners. Actually, it's not all that round, I notice, as my eyes sweep the walls. It's more of a half-circle, with a flat wall of shelves to my left, beginning at the stairwell and ending at a fireplace.

"M'Lord, this is..." He nudges me in the ribs with his elbow, making me wince.

"Lark," I say through gritted teeth.

"This is Lark, M'Lord."

"Lark, like the songbird." I don't like that voice; it moves from shadow to shadow, seeming everywhere, or right behind me. "Thank you, Thadyn, you may wait downstairs." I want to grab him, beg him not to leave me alone with the mage, but can't move as he disappears down the stairs. Sactaren's voice draws my attention back to the room. "Can you sing, Lark?"

"Not very well, M'Lord," I reply, trying to still my shifting eyes. He has to be in the room, but I cannot find him.

"How old are you?"

"Nearly twenty-one, M'Lord."

"And you can read?"

"Yes, M'Lord."

"On the table near the window is a book bound in red leather. Read from it."

I walk to the table, my hand shaking as I pick up the book and open to a random page. My stomach is tight and trembling. I don't know what he will do with me if I fail his test; I don't want to find out, either. For a moment, the writing swims on the page, so many squiggles that mean nothing, but I take as deep a breath as I can manage with my hurt rib and start at the top of the page.

"'... of my own. Let me help you find your way,' the wo- wolf said." It's a children's story! I start to sigh in relief, but wince as my side gives another twinge. Definitely broken. "Sana sh-ook her head. She...knew not to tr-tr-trust a wolf. The wolf—"

"Enough."

I quickly set the book down. I'm sweating, and not just because it's hotter than the fires of Hell in here.

"Lark, catch."

I turn as an egg flies through the air toward me from out of nowhere. Quick reflexes are all that save me as I cradle the egg to my chest, my heart thumping loud in my ears.

"Put it in the bowl on the table." I do as I'm told. "Now, look out the window." Night has fallen and the faint lights in the village and the ships in the bay wink up at me. "Look at the sky, Lark, and tell me how many stars you can see. If you see more than two, you may go."

It's a cloudy night, but patches of deep navy sky show through here and there. Still, I count but a single star. I wait as long as I dare before I answer, begging the clouds to open up, but that one star continues to gleam coldly at me.

"I see one, M'Lord."

"Very good, Lark. Now come here."

His voice creeps across my skin, surrounding me, and I don't know where to go, so I walk to the center of the room. I wait, looking all around the room for him, and then he's suddenly standing beside me, close enough to touch. I jump, drawing a sharp breath and wincing as my side screams in protest.

He's about my height, but thin, so he seems taller, his skin a warm, rich golden color, not like anyone I've ever seen before. His eyes are exotic, too — large and wide, veiled by thick, dark lashes, and a pale blue to rival the clearest winter sky. They make his other features seem small and delicate. I am captivated by his hair, the way it falls straight down his back to his waist, sliding off his shoulders like a curtain of black silk streaked with locks of silver and turquoise. He has several thin braids woven through with bones and stones and feathers and carved charms. Several charms and amulets hang on cords around his neck. He is wearing a simple, thin white shirt, the laces undone down to his navel, and his skin glistens in the firelight, damp with sweat. His pants are dark blue suede, and his feet are bare. He's frighteningly beautiful.

"I am Lord Naeven Sactaren," he says, his voice making the hair on my neck prickle as he devours me with his eyes. He suddenly reaches for me and I stiffen, but force myself not to move as his hand slides up under my shirt, his fingers pressing into the sore spot on my side. It hurts. I bite down hard, but a small sound slips out anyway and I cast my eyes down as he looks at me.

"It's not broken, I think, just bruised," he says, walking past me to a table crowded with jars and vials. As he picks through them, he speaks. "So, Lark, you are a brave young man, and intelligent, and quick, and honest. I value these traits quite highly." He selects a jar and returns to my side. "Now, tell me what you would consider to be your greatest faults."

I swallow hard. "M'Lord, I..." He opens the jar and dabs his fingertips into the pale lavender salve inside. "I'm stubborn and willful, and I'm not worth near what you paid for me."

He regards me for a moment, then reaches under my shirt again and rubs the salve into my side, making me wince and my breath catch in my throat.

"Tell me one thing you have done that you are ashamed of."

I lower my eyes, my four-year-old sister's cries echoing through my mind as if mere days had passed, and not thirteen years. I'd been eight, and she'd been bugging me, so I told her if she didn't leave me alone, I was going to sell her. A few days later the government took our farm and the slavers took us away. My father and I were loaded onto one wagon, my mother and sister on another. I can still hear her crying, over and over, "I sorry, Lark, I sorry." That was the last time I saw them.

"I-I beat my master with a rake and ran away," I say. My sister, my parents, my memories, they are all I have that is *mine*, and I can't — I won't share them with him. I feel the weight of his gaze upon me and I swallow hard. After a moment, he takes his hand out from under my shirt and lets me breathe.

"Will you run away from me?"

I keep my eyes fixed on the floor as I answer softly, "I don't know, M'Lord." He is frightening, but his demeanor does not seem at all cruel or perverse, though I do have a painful habit of looking for the good in people and missing the bad. "I don't think I will."

"And if I must 'discipline' you, will you beat *me* with a rake?" I don't look up, but he sounds almost amused by the thought.

"I will try to never give you cause to discipline me, M'Lord," I say. I want to add that the paranoid old bastard had been trying to kill me, but that would sound like I'm trying to make excuses. I'm not. There is no excuse for what I did. A master has every right to do with his property as he pleases, from painting his shutters red to setting his slaves on fire. I reacted without thinking — more evidence of my willful streak.

"Then I'm sure I won't have to," he says, stepping past me and taking a small wooden box down off one shelf. From the box he pulls a round, black stone about the size of an acorn. "Hold out your hand," he commands. He sets the stone on my palm and I jump as it starts to flash red, yellow, gray, green, brown, orange — so many colors I can't keep track of them. Lord Sactaren raises his eyebrows. "You have more diseases than a third-rate whorehouse," he says, and his gaze turns appraising once again. I look back down at the floor. It's not *my* fault.

I glance up as he steps back over to his table of potions under the window. He picks up a little bottle and an old silver spoon. "Come here, Lark," he says as he fills the spoon with a thick, pink potion. He holds it up and I hesitate, then open my mouth. The potion is sickly sweet, clinging to the inside of my mouth and making me want to gag. He glances at the stone, still flashing in the palm of my hand, and then sets the bottle down. Next, he has me eat a piece of bitter root, and then drink something that looks a lot like watery pus. Luckily, it just tastes like dirty water.

He keeps glancing down at my hand, and I finally realize that every time he gives me some new potion or herb, another color disappears from the flashing stone. He's curing me.

"You're very lucky," Lord Sactaren says after a moment. He hands me another glass of some bitter smelling brew. "Many of these infections have been in your body for years. A few more years, and they would have killed you." He takes the empty glass and hands me a small, pale blue pill. "Last one," he says. I swallow the pill and look down at the stone, now just a dull red color, and watch as the red slowly fades to white. Lord Sactaren picks up the stone and it turns black again before he returns it to its box. Does that mean he's sick?

I watch him place the box back on its shelf. He doesn't look sick. He turns and catches me looking at him. "I'm not ill," he says quietly, and I drop my gaze back to the floor. "You're very intelligent, Lark. I think you'll do quite well here." He turns away and takes a seat at his desk, the old wooden chair creaking under his weight. "I think you'll find I'm not a difficult man to please, just be polite to the customers and don't let them steal anything."

He picks up a stack of papers and begins leafing through them. I hesitate a moment, wondering if that means I'm dismissed. I hope so; beads of sweat are beginning to trickle under my arms and down my back from the heat. Before I can take a step toward the stairs, though, he says, "Oh, and try and stay away from my wife."

"M'Lord," I say quickly, my mouth suddenly very dry, "I-I would never—"

He laughs, a soft, whispery sound. "I'm worried about your safety, not hers. The Lady Sactaren can be cold and spiteful, and I would not have you run afoul of her. Luckily, she rarely leaves her part of the castle. Now, go back downstairs and Thadyn can finish instructing you. Good night, Lark."

"Good night, Lord Sactaren," I say, bowing low as I back toward the stairwell. I'm halfway down the stairs when I realize that my rib has stopped hurting. I can even draw a deep breath, though I quickly find out that it still hurts to touch. I pause and glance over my shoulder. A raw, flickering golden light is playing across the inside of the stairwell above my head. For a master, he doesn't seem that bad.

Chapter 2

When I enter the shop, Thadyn is counting small blue stones into little leather pouches, which he sets aside immediately.

"I guess you'll be finishing that later," he says, motioning for me to follow him into the hall. He shows me to the kitchen and the larder, both well stocked but with no cook in sight. "I hope you can prepare your own food," Thadyn says. "The master rarely eats a regular meal, so there's no cook. Help yourself, but don't be a pig." He takes me down a long hall, stopping short and pointing to the floor, to the hacked off edge of a midnight blue carpet. "You see this? Never go beyond this point. Beyond here, Her Ladyship rules, and her servants can get ugly if they catch you where you're not supposed to be."

"The master did warn me of her," I say.

"Did he now?" An elegant young woman steps out of the nearest doorway, no more than a few years older than me, fair, with dark hair and eyes, wearing a wine colored dress. "How...thoughtful of him."

She clasps her hands behind her back, her eyes taking me in with a single, slow look. After a moment, she smiles, but it's not a friendly smile. "He's your replacement, I take it?"

"Yes, this is Lark," Thadyn says.

I almost breathe a sigh of relief as the weight of her gaze shifts to Thadyn.

"Well, aren't you the lucky one. So this is goodbye?"

"I truly hope so," Thadyn says, and Her Ladyship's lips turn white as she presses them into a thin line.

She glances at me again, her dark eyes flashing. "Whatever my *dear* husband told you about me, I'm not the one you need to worry about. Mark my words, he *will* hurt you." She turns and walks away without a backward glance.

Thadyn scowls after her. "Bitch," he mutters. My eyes widen. He glances up at me. "Well, she is. And don't let her scare you with her warning about Lord Sactaren. She's always trying to cause trouble." He leads me back down the hall and around the corner, to the second door on the right. "Here's where you'll sleep," Thadyn tells me as he opens the door.

I'm expecting a bare room with a straw mattress in the corner and a pot to piss in, and for a moment, all I can do is stand in the doorway and stare. There's a real bed, with a pillow and a quilt, not some rough-spun wool blanket. I have a table and chair, and a lamp, and a wardrobe, though I have no clothes to put in it. Next to the wardrobe is another doorway, and by the clear lamplight I can see a washstand and basin inside, and a pitcher for water. I step into the room and I see a shelf against the near wall, crowded with books and jars and crystals. I glance at Thadyn and he's wearing a crooked grin.

"You can tell how bad a person's had it by the disbelief in their face," he says. "It looks like you deserve a break. Goodbye, Lark."

"Goodbye," I whisper, "and thank you." He shuts the door behind him as he leaves, and I'm alone. Or so I think.

"Are you just going to stand there?" I jump as Schaff slinks out from under the bed. "You're a real mess, you know that?"

"I'm sorry," I stammer. "Can I help you?"

He rolls his golden eyes. "It's my job to help *you*, so pay attention, for the love of Arin. I hate repeating myself." He leaps up onto the table and sits primly, his tail draped across his feet. "First of all, those clothes will have to go. We can't let the customers see you looking like a slave."

"But, I have nothing else to wear."

He pulls his lips back in what can only be described as a smirk. "Look in there." He flicks his tail at the wardrobe.

I open the doors, gaping like a fish again at the sight of all the shirts and tunics and pants and trousers and belts and shoes, and articles of clothing that I'm not even sure how to wear. And the colors! For someone bound to shades of gray for the last decade, rich wine, plum, navy, and forest fabrics are almost too much to bear, as are the bright whites and pale blues. I know these are not expensive clothes — in my mind, I know — but in my heart, I feel too grateful for words.

I'm so filthy I can't even touch them. I dash into the washroom and pour water from the pitcher into the basin, splashing a little onto the flagstone floor in my haste. There's a mirror hanging on the wall, with real glass, and I cringe at my reflection. I can't believe I had to meet my master looking like a mudchild. I wash my face and hands, turning the water in the basin brown, but there's no window to throw the dirty water out of, so I stand there, wondering what to do.

"Step back," Schaff instructs from the doorway. I do, raising my eyebrows as the water begins to drain out, leaving a clean, empty basin.

"How?" I ask, running my hands along the porcelain. There are no holes or cracks in it whatsoever.

Schaff sighs. "I'm going to give you this one for free, since you're new, but from now on, think hard before you ask that question. *This is a mage's castle.* That is the answer to most questions of *How?* and *Why?*, okay?"

I nod and reach for the pitcher again. It's full. I open my mouth, and then close it again. It's a mage's castle. Of course. "And don't bother with that," he says, "you'll be here all night. There's only one way to clean up this big of a mess. Come with me."

He has me choose something to put on. I pick up a blue silk shirt and black suede trousers, running my hands over the fabric. "You're going to bed, not the ball," Schaff snidely points out. I grab a nightshirt and a robe. He suggests slippers, too, as the stone floors are very cold.

"Where are we going?" I ask as he leads me down a darkened hall, only half of the torches burning.

"In here," he says, stopping outside a door. I push it open and nearly choke on the steam that billows out. "This is Naeven's private bath. This is an emergency, so it should be allowed, but don't ever come here on your own. He shouldn't come down from his tower this late at night, but I'll stand guard at the door just to be safe. Now hurry up. And don't forget to wash behind your ears."

Feeling more than a little uneasy, I step inside and shut the door. The steam is so thick I can't see the other side of the room, but I place my clothes and slippers on a rack beside the door and quickly peel my slave rags off. I can hardly believe how much dirt spills out onto the floor around me.

In the center of the room is the bath, a bubbling pool large enough for four grown men, sunken into the floor. It's also the source of all the steam. It's almost too hot as I slip into the water, making me gasp as it touches my side, but then the heat seeps into my tired muscles and I groan quietly.

"It feels wonderful, doesn't it?"

I scramble to my feet, splashing water on the floor as Lord Sactaren steps out of the steam, naked and gleaming, his skin like wild honey, or the crust of fresh-baked bread, his hair silvered with tiny drops of moisture.

"M'Lord, forgive me," I beg, my eyes downcast, feet sliding on the wet stone as I try to get out of the bath, "Schaff said—"

"I heard him," the mage says. "Relax, you're in no trouble." I stop moving and stand there, my chest heaving, eyes fixed on the floor at his feet. "Perhaps I should have warned you about Schaff, as well." He sounds amused again, though I can see nothing funny about this. "He likes to play tricks, usually harmless ones, and he thinks himself very amusing. Others usually do not. This, for example. I think he had a feeling that I would be in here." I glance up to find him inspecting me with those ice blue eyes. "It seems he played a trick on both of us."

He walks toward me and I can't help but notice the lean, powerful way that he moves, like the hounds one of my noble masters kept. You could see their muscles working just under their skin, see their power and grace even when they were standing still. My master is like that. His skin is perfect, without a single blemish or scar, and I lower my eyes, wishing I were anywhere else. I can feel the weight of his gaze as he steps past me, and then his fingers trace the long, red scar high on my left shoulder, making me flinch. That is the most recent, inflicted by the scythe of another slave who thought he deserved my share of the water when the bucket was passed around. I'm not ashamed of the scars, but I do hate them, hate how they make me look, hate what they remind me of.

I try not to pull away, but I hate being touched, too. After a moment he walks away, toward the door.

"Enjoy your bath, Lark," he says, "and get some rest. Tomorrow's going to be busy."

I wait until I hear the door close before I take a single ragged breath, my legs suddenly shaking, and I practically collapse into the water. I draw my knees to my chest and shiver, cold from the inside out, the water taking forever to warm me again. He is so intense, and yet so restrained. When he speaks to me, I feel as if every word is deliberate, when he moves, every step, every look, every turn of his head is planned. I wonder what he would be like if he ever lost control. I don't think I ever want to find out. I slowly become aware of voices outside the door and I start to listen.

"You can't tell me he's not *exactly* what you were hoping for," Schaff says.

"That boy is...is..." Sactaren falls silent and I find myself leaning toward the door. What am I? "Did you *look* at him?" I cringe and sink back into the water.

"Yeah, so he's a little fucked up. So what?"

"So I requested someone to *assist* me. There is not enough of that boy left to be of any use to anyone, let alone to be my assistant."

"Oh, come on, Naeven. From your current condition, I'd say you can think of at least *one* use for him. Besides, I have a feeling he's going to surprise you."

Lord Sactaren doesn't answer, and after a minute of silence, I figure he's left. I stare across the room, into the clouds of steam, feeling hollow inside. Do I look that broken? And what "condition" was Schaff talking about? I sit a moment, worrying my lip between my teeth, then grab the bar of soap sitting on the edge of the bath. It smells like flowers and has sand mixed into it. I look at the brown scum already floating across the surface of the water to the overflow drain and hope one bar is going to be enough.

I scrub myself raw, but my hands and feet won't come clean. Dirt is ground so deeply into the calluses that I finally have to give up. It feels strange not to have mud between my toes and grit in the golden stubble that covers my scalp. I can't remember the last time I was even close to being clean. Perhaps the summer before last, when our master drove us into the livestock pond before taking us to market. The water was gray-green and smelled sour, so I don't think it helped much.

I walk across the room to dry and dress, and I notice that my rags are gone. Did someone else come into the room, or did Lord Sactaren throw them out? Both thoughts unnerve me — that I didn't hear someone come in, or that my master had to clean up after me. Perhaps there's an easier answer than that: it's a mage's castle. That I can accept. Warm, clean, and dry in my new nightshirt, robe, and slippers, I step out of the bath and nearly tread upon Schaff, curled up outside the door.

"About time," he grumbles, moving down the hall toward my room. "C'mon, I'll fill you in about tomorrow, and then we both need some sleep."

"Why would you do that to me?" I ask, fighting the urge to kick him right in his bushy tail.

He glances back, his eyes reflecting green in the torchlight. "Why not? It was funny. Besides, it's not like he's angry with you."

"No, just disappointed. Even better."

"What, were you listening at the keyhole?" he asks. He flicks his tail and starts down the hall again. "First rule of eavesdropping — don't assume you've heard the whole conversation. As for what he said..." He sighs and shakes his head. "He's just grumpy 'cause his wife isn't pregnant, *again*, and he's got a mages' conference in a couple of days he has to go to." He reaches my door first and waits for me to open it. I don't.

"Well, I would appreciate it if you wouldn't play jokes on me in the future," I say, trying to keep my tone reasonable, when all I really want to do is scream, *Don't ever do that to me again!*

He sits down and looks up at me. "Sorry, but I can't promise anything. I tend to do whatever I feel like when I feel like it. Always have, always will, and it won't do you any good to be mad at me.

Just learn to live with it; Thadyn did." I sigh and open the door. He bounds into the room and leaps onto the bed, taking a seat in the middle of the quilt. "Sometimes, customers will show up at dawn," he says, "but you're not expected to open shop until eight. You eat lunch around noon, in the shop and not around customers. We close at four. You should spend about an hour restocking shelves, sorting charms, whatever. ... Do you need an invitation to sit in your own room?"

I'm standing near the door, trying to make sure I remember everything he is telling me.

"Sorry," I say, walking to the table and pulling out the chair. "This doesn't feel like a place I'm supposed to be."

He laughs, a high-pitched yipping sound. "You're a lifer, aren't you?" I'm not sure what he means and just shrug. "Were you born a slave?"

"No, I was a farmer's son until I was eight."

He squints at me, one ear flicking up and down. "Eight...almost thirteen years... You're from the Bahndune area."

"That's right. How—"

"Horrible drought down there around then. A lot of farmers lost everything. So, the government took your farm, and when the proceeds didn't cover the balance owed, they sold you and your family to cover the bill." I nod. "You must really hate them."

"Who?"

"The government...the lords...the rich...the powerful. The men who think they can buy and sell you like a bruised turnip. You've spent most of your life serving them, and what have they ever given you? Scars, that's all I can see. And I would bet my tail that the scars on your hands and your face are nothing compared to the rest of you." I draw the collar of my robe tighter. "You have to hate them, you have to resent every man who's had the nerve to lay down a coin and think it makes you his."

I don't answer. Of course I hate being owned, but there's nothing I can do about it. I glance at him and he's nodding his head slowly.

"Yep, you're in this for life. They've beaten the man right out of you. You'll never be anything more than a slave." He jumps down from my bed and pads silently across the room. "Now go to sleep; I'll wake you around seven." He slips out into the hall and I walk over and close the door behind him.

I'll never be more than a slave. Is he right? Every time I ran away, I got caught because I couldn't fit in, couldn't take care of myself, couldn't walk through a town without casting my eyes to the ground every time I met someone on the street. Couldn't be anything other than a slave.

I put out the lamp and lie down on the bed, on top of the quilt. The pillow is soft and solid under my head, packed with feathers, not straw. I think the mattress is feathers, too. It doesn't crackle as I turn over. I draw a deep breath and let it out slow. Nothing but a slave. If I never get sold again, that might not be so hard to live with.

Chapter 3

I jerk awake, Schaff laughing as he jumps off my chest and onto the floor. It's morning, the sun lighting the ceiling above the door, pale and gray as it slides through the high, narrow windows. I roll out of bed, wash and dress, choosing a simple shirt of pale blue and gray trousers. The shirt has long sleeves and a high collar, which I like. It hides most of my scars. Schaff has to remind me to put on socks and shoes. I'm used to being barefoot, sometimes binding my feet with bark and strips of cloth in the winter to walk in the snow, but never real shoes, so this gives me some trouble. He laughs and rolls on the floor as I fight with the socks. They're trickier than they look.

We walk to the kitchen and eat a simple breakfast. I can't cook, so I eat bread and a little cheese, and drink some milk. Schaff has a dish of cream and a raw chicken liver. He tells me about some of the villagers that come to the shop regularly: an old woman with a gray shawl who always buys flea tonic for her cats; a young woman with brown hair and a pug nose who buys either love charms or cream to get rid of her freckles; a farmer and his wife who usually buy something for their cow. Once in a while, one of the local lords will stop by. I'm to be exceptionally respectful and courteous if they do.

As we enter the shop, Schaff leaps up onto the counter and hunkers down next to a vase of peacock feathers. My hands are sweating as I go to unlock the main door. I glance back at Schaff and he smirks at me.

"Good luck," he says. "And if you need help, don't ask me; I'm not supposed to talk in front of the customers." He closes his eyes and feigns sleep.

The clock on the wall strikes eight and I have to open the door. Just my luck, there's a woman standing outside already, her brown hair bound back into a simple bun and a gray shawl wrapped about her shoulders.

"Good morning," she says politely. I step back and allow her inside.

"Uh, how may I-I help you?" I ask.

She looks around the room as she walks over to stand before the counter, a new straw handbag hanging from her arm.

"Oh, just tell Thadyn Mrs. Herion is here."

I make my way back behind the counter. "Sorry, but Thadyn is...not here. He left."

Her face falls. "Oh. Will he be returning?"

Out of the corner of my eye, I see Schaff slowly shake his head, no. "I'm afraid not, ma'am. I'm Lord Sactaren's new assistant, Lark."

"Oh," she says again, finally taking a look at me. Her eyes are the same dark blue as her dress. "You're very young," she says at last. "Could you get me another jar of the lavender hand cream, three banishing stones, and a raven's feather? My cousin is expecting." *Expecting what?* I want to ask, but nod instead.

"Okay," I say, and flee into the back room. Jars, stones, feathers. There's hundreds of each. Hiding my face in my hands, I force myself to take a deep breath. It's not that difficult. Lavender begins with the letter L, just like Lark. It's a pale purple. I scan the labels, but there's a dozen that begin with L, and they're either a clear amber color or thick and white. Banishing stones. Not a clue. Ah, raven feathers — they're black. So are half a dozen other birds. I'm going to get turned into frogspawn, I just know it. I hear a sound behind me and turn as Schaff leaps down from the counter and pads into the room with me.

"She's getting impatient," he says under his breath. "You better hurry."

"I don't..." I drop my voice to a whisper. "I can't read these, the words are too big. Help me."

He leaps up onto the table at my elbow. "The hand cream is on the second shelf, third jar in. Banishing stones are in that basket. The raven feathers are right here."

He points with his paw and I quickly gather up the items. I start toward the shop, stop, come back. "What do I charge for these?" I ask.

He rolls his eyes. "Didn't Thadyn tell you about the book?" I shake my head. "There's a large, hidebound ledger out there. Open it to the most recent page, tell it what she's buying, and it will tell you how much."

I nod and return to the counter. Mrs. Herion is absently flipping through Lord Sactaren's catalogue of spells, and closes it as I set her items on the counter.

"Here we are," I say, forcing a smile as I glance around for the ledger. I find it on a shelf behind me. It's filled with pages of neat script, endless rows of products and prices. My printing is terrible, but it doesn't seem to matter. There's no pen.

"Let's see, one jar of lavender hand cream." I raise my eyebrows as that neat script appears upon the page as if written by an invisible hand: *Lavender hand cream - 3 laenes.* I study the words for a moment, trying to learn them. "And three banishing stones." *Banishing stone x3 - 6 laenes.* "And one raven feather." *Raven feather - 1 laene.* "That's all," I say. The book does nothing.

Am I supposed to add this up? They asked if I could read, not do mathematicals. I add worse than I write. Well, one more than three is four, that I know, but six more than four? One more than four is five, one more than five is eight... No... I smile sheepishly at Mrs. Herion.

"I think if you say, 'Total', it'll add it up," she says. I hear Schaff snicker from near my ankles.

"Total," I say, and the book obeys. "That'll be half a coin, please." She passes over the money and puts her hand cream, stones, and feather in her handbag.

"This is your first day, isn't it?" she asks. I nod. "You did very well, then. Thank you, Lark." Schaff leaps onto the counter and she gives him a stern look. "You could be a little more helpful, you know."

"Good day to you, too, Ascille," Schaff says. She shakes her head and leaves. I turn on Schaff.

"What is your problem?" I ask. "Why is everything a joke to you?"

"Try being me, slave," he says, a slight growl in his voice, "and if you don't throw yourself from the tower window, you might just find other people's discomfort a whole lot more entertaining, too. Now," he leaps back down from the counter and heads for the back room, "get in here and pay attention."

He spends the rest of the morning telling me the contents of every shelf, box, bin, basket, and jar — when he's not insulting me in front of customers, that is. He tells the girl buying love charms how dirty I was when I arrived. He tells the farmer with potato gnomes about my scars. He calls me an idiot in front of a fisherman looking for a charm to help him find where the red-fin are running. I want to ask him what makes his life so horrible, but I'm not sure I want to know.

I'm picking at my lunch and listening to him outline the many uses of moonstone, so that when someone comes in wanting protection on a long journey, or supplies for a fertility rite, I'll be able to help them, when I hear the hinges of the shop door squeak. I glance out. It's a boy of eight or ten, his homespun leggings too short, his thin tunic heavily patched. I would have taken him for a slave if not for the lank hair hanging in his eyes.

"I think I can get this one," I tell Schaff, setting down my sandwich and brushing crumbs off my shirt as I step out behind the counter. "How can I help you, little man?" I ask. He steps up and lays three laenes on the counter, one of the little silver coins bent nearly in half.

"Please, sir," he says, his voice hoarse, each breath wet and raspy, "our cow is sick. She won't give milk anymore."

I'm suddenly reminded of a little boy, barely able to lift his father's rifle, sitting in the rain for an entire night, waiting for the fox that kept sneaking into the hen house. My brother died of pneumonia, but not before he shot that damn fox. When the chickens, or the cow, is all you have, there isn't anything you won't do to protect them.

"Has she eaten any toadstools lately?" I ask. He shakes his head. "Has she been coughing?" No. "Do you live near a grove of rowan trees?" He nods. "Have you ever found flowers in the stall?" Another nod. "Sounds like pixies. Hang on a minute."

I return to the back room to find the meat missing from my sandwich and Schaff licking his lips.

"Where did you learn so much about cows?" he asks, ignoring the dirty look I give him.

"I spent most of a year on a dairy farm," I say, trying to figure out where the sabaka beans are kept. Schaff flicks his tail toward the proper shelf, over above the baskets of feathers, and I pour a generous amount into a small envelope. I head out into the shop, but stop as I hear the kid cough, a deep, thick hacking that makes my chest hurt just to listen. I turn to Schaff. "Hey, lunch thief, do we have anything that'll treat pneumonia?"

"Yeah, why?"

"The boy is sick."

"Did he ask to be cured?"

"No, but...he'll probably die if—"

"Not our problem." I can't believe he's serious, but he just stares at me.

"You would let that kid walk out of here, knowing that he will probably not live out the week?" He doesn't answer. He doesn't have to. "Well, I can't. Now, where is it?"

"Naeven will not be pleased."

I swallow hard. Displeased masters leave scars. Oh, to hell with them both. "I'll answer to him later. Where is it?"

He points to several small bottles of tonic. "Have him mix two drops of that in a cup of water and drink it twice a day for two weeks. Two drops, twice a day, two weeks."

"Got it." I step out behind the counter and set the envelope and bottle next to the book. "Okay, one dose of sabaka beans. That's...five laenes." He frantically searches his pockets, but he has no more. "You know what," I say, handing him the beans, "don't worry about it right now. You can pay the rest later."

"Maele bless you, sir," he says, and starts coughing again.

"Take this, too. No charge." I give him the tonic and make sure he understands the directions before I let him leave. I stand at the door and watch him head down the mountain. Is the life of one poor farm boy worth my master's displeasure? Yeah. I was once a poor farm boy, after all.

The afternoon passes uneventfully. It begins to rain shortly after one, just a light drizzle, but enough to keep the villagers off the mountain, apparently. I keep glancing at the ledger, at the nine laene loss written in red ink — seven for the tonic and two for the rest of the beans — and wonder what nine laenes will cost me. A beating? No meals? Extra work? Those I would not mind, not even the beating, but my master is a mage — I'm making myself sick, imagining what he might do to me. Finally, I close the ledger with a thump and turn to Schaff, seated on the corner of the counter. "So, where did Thadyn go?" I ask, tired of the silence.

He stands, stretches, and then pads over and curls up on top of the thick book.

"Hmm, comfy," he mutters, then closes his eyes. "He ran off with some fisherman's widow from down south," he says after a moment. "Got a nice little farm. I heard her smart-assed kid even warmed up to him."

I raise my eyebrows. "Lord Sactaren let him buy his freedom?" I ask. Some masters won't. I guess I figured the mage would be one of them.

Schaff cracks an eye and squints at me. "Sure," he says, the tip of his tail twitching. "Naeven's a real nice guy...if you give him what he wants."

I lick dry lips, run my fingers back and forth along the edge of the counter. "And-and what does he want?" I ask.

"From you?" Schaff asks with a chuckle. "I can't imagine."

I jump as the shop door flies open, five figures in damp, tattered cloaks spilling through the doorway. "Good afternoon, gent—" I choke as three of the figures turn toward me, none of them gentlemen. "I mean, ladies. How can I—"

"Schaff, I need that favor you owe me," one of the women says, pushing back the hood of her cloak. Her skin is a lustrous dark brown, almost black, making her pale hazel eyes gleam like stars in the night sky, and her long, black hair is pulled back and knotted around a pair of bone picks. A long, pink scar runs from the bridge of her nose down under her left eye and then turns sharply to slice down her upper lip, making her the scariest woman I've ever seen.

"What's wrong, Erryn?" Schaff asks, sitting up, his large ears pricked forward.

"Demarcus," she replies.

"How long?"

"Five minutes. Maybe." Her eyes shift to me. "Who's this? Where's Thadyn?"

"Later," Schaff says, leaping down from the counter. He heads for the main hallway. "This way. Quickly."

The woman in charge, Erryn, motions for three of the others to follow Schaff. "Watch him," she says to the fourth, and points at me. I swallow hard as the fourth woman, her face hidden in the shadow of her tattered black hood, slips around the end of the counter, so close I can smell tar and sour alcohol on her.

"Don't worry about him, he's the mage's slave," Schaff calls from the doorway. "Lark, mop up these footprints, will you?"

I glance over the edge of the counter at the mud they tracked in with them. I don't understand what's going on, but I turn to fetch the bucket and mop from the back room anyway, and find the tip of a slim dagger pressed into my chest. Stepping back slowly, I raise my hands and look over at Schaff.

He clears his throat and sits down on his haunches, the tip of his tail twitching. "There's no point in hiding you if your fiancé can just follow the footprints," he says.

Erryn bares her teeth at him, then turns to the woman holding me at knifepoint. "Put it away, Stingray. Give the boy a hand." She glares down at Schaff. "And he is *not* my fiancé."

Schaff just stands up and leads them down the hall. I glance at the remaining woman. The dagger has disappeared. "Your name's Stingray?" I ask, slipping past her. She doesn't answer, just watches from the doorway as I fill a bucket with water from another of Sactaren's enchanted pitchers and grab a mop out of the corner. "Who is Demarcus? Why are you running from him?" I carry the bucket past her. I start mopping at the hallway and head toward the shop door. Stingray makes no move to help me, though really, there's nothing she can do. Stingray...that's an unusual name for a woman. It sounds more like a— "Are you pirates?" I ask, frowning at her.

"You gonna swab that floor, or do I have to come over there and slit your throat?" she asks, her voice startlingly rough and raspy.

That's a good enough answer for me. I push the bucket across the flagstones with my foot as I wash away the evidence of our cutthroat guests. Pirates. What the hell is Schaff doing owing a favor to a pirate? A female pirate — I stop dead and raise my eyes to Stingray, standing motionless behind the counter. "You're from the *Iris*, aren't you? That was Captain Erryn Marr, wasn't it?"

She doesn't respond, but she doesn't have to. I've never heard of an all female pirate crew, save one. I quickly go back to my mopping before I find myself with a slit throat. The barest sound of a footstep outside is all the warning I have before the shop door flies open again. The handle of the mop slips from my fingers and hits the floor with a sharp *crack*, making me jump. I glance toward Stingray, but she's vanished.

"Where are they?"

I turn to the man in the doorway as he shakes his wet, stringy brown hair out of his eyes. He's maybe twice my age and half a head taller, but thin, practically skin and bones, his dark brown eyes sunken and wild as they dart around the room.

"Who?" I ask, keeping my eyes on him as I bend down and pick up the mop. "Those women?" His attention snaps to me, his intensity making my skin crawl. There is something not entirely sane about this man. "I-I chased them out," I tell him, resisting the urge to glance toward the counter again. "Look at the mess they—"

"Is there another way down this mountain?"

I shrug. "Not that I know of, but I suppose you could go around that hill out there and meet back up with the road... Hey, where are you going?" I ask as he dashes back through the door, leaving it standing wide open. I walk over and shut it, and turn to find Stingray standing just a few feet away.

"Nice work," she rasps. "For a second, I thought I was going to have to kill you both." She glances over her shoulder and whistles, imitating some kind of sea bird. "Is your name really Lark?" she asks suddenly.

"Is your name really Stingray?" If she won't answer my questions, I'm certainly not going to answer hers.

"You got that floor scrubbed yet?" Schaff asks as he trots into the shop, alone. He glances around, then at Stingray, and finally calls back over his shoulder, "Okay, c'mon in, he's gone."

Captain Marr and her lady pirates file into the shop, their cloaks off and being carried by the last woman in line. They're dressed like pirates, all right — all but the captain barefoot, in canvas pants stained with tar and blood, and torn tunics belted with rope. Each one is armed with at least one dagger, some with cutlasses as well. Captain Marr looks more like a disillusioned gentleman, in scuffed boots, faded black suede trousers and a billowy black silk shirt, with a blood red sash tied at her waist. Two pistols are stuck through the sash, as well as a fancy hilted rapier. Wide ivory bracelets cover her wrists and silver hoops hang from her ears, not quite round anymore.

Schaff leaps up onto the counter and takes a seat on the ledger. "So, Erryn, what brings you to Traxen?"

"The same thing that brings anyone to this gods forsaken little rat hole," Erryn replies. "Your charming personality."

Schaff grins, showing needle-sharp teeth. "Same shit as last time?"

"Yeah. And something to get rid of crabs. Squall picked them up in Jexlen and the little whore has spread them to half the crew."

"Nice," Schaff says, then glances at me. "Haven't you finished with that yet?" he asks. I glance down at the bucket of dirty water and the muddy footprints still in front of the door. "Forget it. Get over here, will you?"

I shove the bucket out of the way and lean the mop against the wall, then start to step past the pirates, but Erryn reaches out, making me wince as she digs her fingers into my upper arm.

"So where *is* Thadyn?" she asks.

Schaff sighs. "You know how Lord Sactaren is," he says, sounding disgusted. "He grew tired of Thadyn ages ago and as soon as I was able to find a suitable replacement, Sactaren threw Thadyn out on his ass. I don't know where he went."

I glance at Schaff, but keep my mouth shut. He must have a reason for lying.

"And this..." Erryn lets go of my arm. "...is the best you could find?"

I hurry back behind the counter, looking down at the floor so I won't get my throat slit for scowling at them. Damn, I'm just a disappointment to everybody, aren't I?

"He's a bit of a fixer-upper," Schaff says, "but he's got a great ass. Lark, turn around, let 'em have a look." My scowl deepens as I turn my back to them. "He's also very obedient," Schaff says, and they all start laughing.

The back of my neck burning, I shove my hands in my pockets and stride into the back room, away from them. I don't care. I don't care what they think about me. They don't know what I've been though, the shit I've survived that made me look this way. Do they think getting these scars was fun? I lean back against the shelves of merchandise and hang my head, my eyes burning with hot, unshed tears. I see a flicker of movement out of the corner of my eye and glance toward the doorway, quickly turning my face away as Schaff pads in.

"What're you doing over there?" he asks, leaping up onto the low worktable. "Help me get their stuff together before Demarcus comes back." I blink hard, trying to drive the wetness from my eyes before I shove myself away from the shelf with my elbows. "There's empty crates in that cupboard and... Hey, what's wrong with you?" I scowl down at the floor. "Did I say something?" he asks after a moment and I clench my fists in my pockets.

"What did I do to you?" I ask, my voice quiet, but trembling. "Why do you have to say those things about me?"

"Damn, you're almost as sensitive as N...evermind." I look at him, seated upon the table, his tail curled around over his feet. "I was kidding...or maybe I wasn't. Nothing personal, either way." Nothing personal. That's easy for him to say. "Hey," he says after a moment, and I glance over at him, "I'm sorry, okay?"

"Really?"

He squints up at the ceiling, like he's thinking about it. "Yeah...well, maybe a little. Actually, no, not really. You gonna get that crate now?"

With a sigh, I fetch an empty crate and start to set it beside him on the table, but then turn it upside down and drop it over him. He glares at me from between the slats. "Not funny," he growls. I fight a smirk and let him out. He lashes his tail, his big ears flattened against his head as he barks out what I need to take off the shelves: six jars of heavy duty seamen's hand cream, six bottles of concentrated lemon tonic, six jars of lavender and willow salve, two dozen packets of contraceptive tea, and eleven anti-lice charms.

"Can they pay for all this?" I ask as Schaff jumps off the table.

"The question isn't 'Can they', it's 'Will they'," Schaff says as he heads back out into the shop.

I carry the heavy crate out and set it beside him on the counter, quickly tallying up the items in the ledger. "That'll be...twenty-seven coins, six laenes," I say, biting the edge of my lip as Erryn crosses her arms over her chest.

"That's a pretty steep price there, Schaff," she says. "What do you say we just slit both your throats and take the stuff?" I swallow hard.

"Do you really think Lord Sactaren would let any of you off this mountain alive if you did?" Schaff says with a laugh. "Just hand over the money, you greedy pirate, and get the hell out of here."

Erryn laughs, her teeth very white against her dark skin, and motions to the other women. Two of them step forward and grab the crate, one on each end, and a third drops a fat, battered leather bag on the counter. "Twenty-seven, you said?" she says.

"And-and six laenes," I add. She opens the bag and digs around until she finds one platinum ilae, seven gold coins, and six silver laenes. Most are stained with blood, and two of the coins are stuck together by it.

"Thank you," I say, dropping the money in the cash box and then wiping my hand on the leg of my trousers.

"See you 'round, Schaff," Erryn says as she and her lady pirates file through door, slipping into their cloaks as they head back out into the wet afternoon.

"Hey, so we're even now, right?" Schaff calls after her.

"Not hardly," she replies with a laugh, and pulls the door shut behind her.

I turn slowly to look at Schaff. "Why do you owe a pirate a favor?" I ask.

He snorts and hunkers down on the counter, his ears flattened. "None of your business," he growls. "Now finish mopping the floor."

We close at four and Schaff helps me clean up. I kick off the heavy shoes as soon as the bolt has been thrown, my feet hot and aching from being bound in leather all day. The cold stone feels good. We're almost out of relaxation tea, so he shows me where the bulk tea leaves are kept and how much of each to put into the packets. I'm finishing these when I hear footsteps coming down the tower stairs. My hands start to shake and I spill leaves on the table.

"I hope you're good at groveling," Schaff mutters as he slinks out of the back room, leaving me alone as Lord Sactaren steps out of the stairwell, a small wooden crate in his hands. I drop what I'm doing and rush to take it from him.

"M'Lord, allow me," I say.

Inside the crate are several jars of lavender hand cream, seamen's hand cream, a few fish locator charms, potato gnome powder, and another bottle of pneumonia tonic. I open my mouth to ask how he knew, but close it with a snap. It's a mage's castle. Of course he knows. He probably knows everything that happens within his walls. I silently put the items away. I guess he didn't have time to get to all of it. There's no lemon tonic, or anti-lice charms.

He has something to say to me or he wouldn't be standing in the entrance to the stairwell, watching me with his winter blue eyes. I finish my work and stand at the table, rubbing my calloused fingers over the rough wood slats of the crate. I feel drawn to look at him but I'm afraid, so I stare down at the table.

"How did you enjoy working in my shop?"

His voice slithers around me, making me shiver. For a moment, I don't understand what he's asking. I've never been allowed to enjoy or not enjoy my work. Even now, I'm not sure how I feel about it. It's better than summer in the fields, or winter in the mines, I guess.

"Very well, M'Lord," I answer, hoping it's what he wants to hear.

"Did Schaff give you any trouble?"

"None worth mentioning, M'Lord."

He makes an amused sound, almost a laugh. "Did he explain how a shop is supposed to function? You see, Lark," his tone is easy, almost friendly as he walks across the room toward me, but I feel like a rabbit being eyed by a wolf, "this is a business, not a charity. Customers come here to buy things. They give us money and we give them what they want. If they don't have the money," he stops behind me, close enough that I can feel his breath on my neck, "they don't get anything. Understand?"

I nod. "Y-yes, master."

"Good."

He reaches around me with one arm, his hand overlapping mine for a moment as he picks up the crate. His skin is soft and warm. My heart races as he stands there, not saying or doing anything, just standing there, scaring me. He knows it, and I hate him. He finally steps away and heads toward the tower stairs. I lean against the table, my chest heaving as I try to catch my breath.

"Today's mistake better not happen again, because if it does, there will be consequences." I glance up to find him watching me from the stairway. "Am I understood?"

I hang my head. "Yes, Lord Sactaren."

I wait until his footsteps have faded completely away before I sink down onto the little wooden stool beside me. It could have gone worse, I suppose. Few masters will let you off with just a warning. So why am I shaking like a leaf? I don't know. I've been beaten unconscious and felt better afterward. It has to be a spell, some dark curse he's put upon me. All I know is, I don't want to displease him again.

I find Schaff in the kitchen, tearing into the body of a young rabbit, his muzzle dark with blood. The room reeks of death, turning my already nervous stomach. He looks up as I enter, licking his chops.

"You survived, I see," he says. I can think of nothing in the ice box or pantry that I would be able to keep down, nor anything to say to Schaff, so I turn to leave. "Hang on," he says, and I pause in the doorway. "Why did you do it, give that boy the tonic?"

"I used to be him," I say with a shrug. I don't talk about my brother to anyone.

"So, what happens next time some kid who used to be you walks in?"

I shake my head. "Lord Sactaren is right — this is a business, not a charity."

"So, that's all it takes to change who you are, one word from your master?"

"Yes," I say, scowling at the floor. "He owns me."

"Only if you let him."

He goes back to devouring the rabbit and I leave, stalking down the hall to my room. What does he know about being a slave? He's a glorified pet. He calls the master by his given name. No one who has ever served a day, worked an hour, or received a single lash would ever do that. I shut myself in my room for the remainder of the evening, pacing, brooding, but eventually sitting down at the table with one of the books from the shelf to practice reading. I will not be dependent on Schaff a single day longer than I need to be. It's late when I finally put out the lamp and lie down. I forget to change out of my clothes — it wasn't so long ago that I had but one set of clothes — and fall asleep.

Chapter 4

I am determined to run the shop as Lord Sactaren wishes, and for a few days, it's easy. The customers pay their bills in full and go on their way. Two of those days I don't even see him; he's off at his mages' conference. It's not until afternoon of my fifth day as Lord Sactaren's assistant that the trouble starts. Schaff and I are discussing the uses of carum roots when the shop door opens and a man strides in, his chin jutting out and eyes narrowed as he looks at us. He's wearing black suede boots that come halfway up his thighs, white trousers, a dark blue shirt with fancy silver buttons, a white jacket, and a midnight blue cloak trimmed with silver fur thrown over one shoulder. He's no more than ten years older than me, but everything about him screams Lord. I snap to attention and bow my head.

"Good afternoon, Lord Drumar," Schaff says, nodding respectfully. "Is there anything we can help you find?"

"I doubt it," he says. He turns and begins browsing, picking up random items and turning them over in his hands before setting them back down, making a mess of the neat displays. He glances at me. "Where's Thadyn?"

I'm not sure if I should answer, or let Schaff. There's an awkward pause. "Lord Sactaren decided to let him go," Schaff says finally. "He was growing old."

Lord Drumar doesn't respond, but goes back to his shopping. Moments later, the door flies open and a young woman stumbles in, her face pale and streaked with tears. In her arms she cradles a small, pink blanket. Thick, black stains spatter the front of her dress and a viscous goo drips from one corner of the blanket onto the floor.

"Please help," she cries, nearly hysterical. "She's choking!"

I step out from behind the counter as she holds the blanket out to me, revealing a tiny baby girl inside, her face smeared with the same black goop. The first two inches of several large, grayish worms squirm in her gaping mouth. Horrified, I recoil, then reach out to clean the revolting things off of her.

"Don't!" Schaff barks, leaping from the counter to my shoulder, his claws digging into my flesh through my shirt. "Those are kairon worms. If you try to remove them, it could kill her."

I fight the urge to vomit as one of the worms stretches itself out, leaving more of that black ooze on her skin, and begins to crawl into her nose. She chokes, the most horrible sound, and tries to cry, but each tiny breath is thick and labored.

"What do I do?" I ask Schaff. I've never seen anything like this before.

"Get sulfur, almond oil, and a drakling skin, quickly."

I stand and turn to run to the back room, but Lord Drumar is standing between me and the counter. "I believe I was here first," he says, looking disdainfully at the woman and child.

I'm not sure what to say. I know what I want to say, "Get out of my way, you pompous ass," but luckily, Schaff steps in.

"We'll be right with you, Lord Drumar. This is a rather life or death situation." He nudges me in the head with his paw and I step around Drumar. Once we're in the back room, he growls, "May Arin strike that man with lightning."

I tuck the jar of sulfur under one arm and grab a bottle of oil off the shelf. "Is he always..." I'm pulling open drawers; I can't remember where the drakling skins are.

"Yes," Schaff answers, and adds, "The third one."

I pull out a thin, scaly white skin and rush back out into the shop. The mother has placed her baby on the counter and is weeping silently as the little one weakly kicks at the blanket and flails her tiny arms.

"Now," Schaff says, "we can save your daughter, but it's going to cost a coin and a half, up front."

I crane my neck around to stare at him. I just want to shake him and scream, *How could you?* He jumps onto the counter and glances up at me, then turns back to the woman. "Our master is not a forgiving man." She digs into her pockets, coming up with a mere half coin and three laenes — not even half of the stated cost.

"I-I can get more," she says, laying the money on the counter. "Please, don't let her die." She turns to run out the door, but I reach across the counter and catch her by the arm.

"It's all right," I tell her. "Stay. We'll help your daughter."

"You sure about this?" Schaff asks under his breath. "Naeven said—"

"I'm sure," I say, but I'm not. I'm just hoping to Maele that Sactaren's not really the monster I'm starting to see. "Even he couldn't be this heartless."

"Wanna bet?" Schaff mutters.

I bite the edge of my lip and glance down at the child. Can my master really do worse to me than this, than making me watch her die? I don't think so. "What do I do?" I ask.

Schaff shakes his head, but sits down and instructs me. "Put a drop of oil on her chest and rub it around." I pull back the blanket and find more of that black goo on her chest. "Don't worry, that won't hurt anything. Next, sprinkle the sulfur lightly over the oil."

She's breathing hard as I run my fingertips across her chest, but her lips are turning blue, her skin going gray.

"Okay, now what?" I ask as I set the sulfur aside.

"Wipe your hands," Schaff barks and I grab a rag from under the counter. "Now, lay the drakling skin over the oil and sulfur." He looks up at the mother. "Step back, please, and whatever you do, don't interfere. This won't do any permanent damage." He nods at me.

The baby has stopped fighting, her tiny chest jerking, but no air seems to be getting to her lungs. Her mouth is full of squirming gray worms. The drakling skin is about the size of my hand held flat, and covers her chest completely.

I jerk back as it crackles and spits blue-white sparks into the air. The baby thrashes and screams, thick white smoke boiling up toward the ceiling. The mother shrieks and turns away, covering her ears with her hands as her daughter chokes, gasps, and screams again. I can only stand back and watch in horror as the sparks rain down, scorching the counter and pink blanket.

"Schaff! What the hell is this?" I shout. We were supposed to help her, not burn her alive.

"There's a tin bucket just inside the back room," he tells me. "Get it." I cringe at the thought of sending the mother home with a bucket of ashes, but do as I'm told. "The skin will burn up in a moment," he says, and as I watch, the sparks fizzle and die. I fight not to turn away — the last thing I want to see is a baby with her skin burnt off. "Now, quickly, clear her mouth." I step up to the counter and wave the smoke away, amazed to find her flecked with bits of soot and ash, but otherwise unharmed by the fireworks. The worms are fleeing her body, crawling out onto the counter. I hesitate for just an instant, then grab them in both hands and pull.

They slide out of her easily, but I have to drop the ends I have in my hands in the bucket and grab again, pulling out nearly five feet of worms before they slip free. I throw the slimy mass down and wipe my hands on the rag, shaking from the inside out. The mother has approached the counter and stands weeping, her trembling hands hovering over her daughter's still form.

"Schaff, she's not breathing," I say quietly.

He pads over from the far end of the counter and sniffs her face. "Roll her over onto your hand," he tells me.

She's fragile and light as I hold her, so warm, but so still. Black ooze drips from her mouth as I hold her, face toward the floor. "Thump her on the back — she needs to clear her lungs." I do, but carefully — she's so little. "Harder." Closing my eyes, I pound on her back, the blow forcing a flood of slime to splatter at my feet. She jerks, coughs, chokes, and begins to cry. I laugh, tears stinging my eyes. It's an angry cry, not that horrible strangled sound. I turn her over and wipe her mouth with my fingers, then hand her to her mother. She's sobbing with relief and holds her child to her chest.

"Thank you," she sobs, "thank you both."

"Don't thank me," Schaff mutters, just for me to hear. "I didn't have *anything* to do with this."

"I know," I whisper, but I'm smiling as she takes her baby out into the afternoon sunshine. There isn't a damn thing Sactaren can do that will make me regret this decision, though I'm sure he's going to try.

Lord Drumar clears his throat from the corner. I'd completely forgotten he was there. Or maybe I was hoping he'd left. I nod courteously. "I'm sorry, sir; can I help you now?" At first, I think he's ignoring me — he wanders toward the counter, turning a circle as he scans the shelves around him — but then he answers.

"I have to travel in the sun, wind, and rain," he says, "and it's ruining my skin. I look more like my father every day. I need something to get rid of these lines and wrinkles."

"Of course," Schaff says with an obviously false smile. He leaps back on my shoulder and we step into the back room. "Oh, if only I could slip him some dragon bile instead," Schaff hisses. "I would almost bear Naeven's wrath just to watch the skin melt off that bastard's face. No, give him the lily, milk, and aloe cream. That ought to make his vain ass happy."

I take the cream back to the counter, stepping wide to avoid the puddle of black slime. The ledger has several scorch marks on the cover and a nasty black spatter along the edge of the pages, but works fine when I ring up Drumar's wrinkle vanishing cream.

"That'll be a half coin and two laenes," I tell him. He drops a stack of laenes on the counter and reaches for the jar. Schaff leaps down from my shoulder, landing next to the jar.

"I'm sorry, Lord Drumar, but you're six laenes short," Schaff says, placing his paws on top of the jar, claws out.

Drumar scowls at him, then at me. "The peasant woman didn't have to pay," he says.

I grit my teeth, trying to keep a civil tone as I speak. "She could not afford the treatment, or afford not to have it," I tell him.

"You, sir, can do both. Six laenes, please, or take your business somewhere else."

He puffs up his chest in indignation, then throws the six coins down. Schaff removes his paws from the lid of the jar and Drumar leaves, slamming the door behind him. Schaff looks up at me with a crooked smile. "There's no where else *to* take his business. We're the only magic shop within two hundred miles, or three days on rough seas. Unfortunately," his grin fades, "that means he'll be back."

"Does he come here a lot?" I ask.

Schaff flicks his tail, a gesture I'm starting to recognize as his version of a shrug.

"Twice a week, maybe, but with the personality of a swamp toad, twice a year would be too often to see that man."

He peers over the edge of the counter, laying his large ears back along his head, looking from the bucket of worms to the black puddle oozing along the cracks between the flagstones. "Well...I guess we better get that cleaned up."

By "we" he means "I". Luckily, I'm as good with a stiff brush and bucket of water as I am with a pick or a hoe. Still, it's nearly time to close shop when I finish. We haven't had a customer since Drumar left, so I'm not worried as I leave Schaff dozing on the counter to carry the buckets of dirty water and writhing gray worms outside and heave the contents over the edge of the cliff.

The view out over the valley is beautiful, with the crowded village nestled between the rocky hills and the wild, gray sea beyond, the waves capped with white foam. I can see fishing boats braving the rough waters out beyond the jetty. I never worked on a fishing boat, never want to. It looks very wet. The sun is hanging low over the hills, pale behind high clouds, and the wind blowing off the mountain peak behind the castle is bitterly cold.

I turn to go back into the shop and something near the castle catches my eye. It's just a small patch of color against the formidable gray of the mountain castle, a tannish ball about as big as a head of lettuce, but I would swear it's moving.

I make my way carefully across the uneven ground. It's not very big, but neither are wolfmice, and I've seen what's left after a pack has finished with a man. Bones, mostly. This creature is covered in tan fur, with darker patches and streaks. I make out a stubby tail at one end and small, round ears at the other. A huge black eye is fixed on me, the entire creature trembling. As I draw near, it leaps forward, a frantic, desperate movement, all its limbs scrabbling over the jagged rocks — and I mean *all* of them. It has six legs. It's also covered in blood. It leaves thick, wet smears on the rocks as it scrambles away from me. I drop the buckets and chase after it, not sure what I'm going to do when I catch it, but I can't just let it crawl off somewhere and die.

Instead of heading for open ground, or up the mountain, it dashes at the side of the castle and scrambles up the wall several feet before losing its grip and falling into a heap on the rocks. I slide to a stop, ready to grab it, but it doesn't move. Its little body is limp as I carefully lift it up, but I can feel its heart pattering in its chest. Cradling it in one arm, I fetch the buckets and hurry back to the shop, hot blood running down my wrist.

"What took so long?" Schaff asks as I enter. He notices the creature in my arms and stands up, his ears flicking back. "Great Maele, what are you doing? Get that thing out of here, it's probably diseased."

"It's hurt," I say, laying it on the counter.

Schaff jumps down and growls at me. "It's a kholdra," he says. "There's a thousand more just like it all over the mountain. Throw it out for the owls."

I ignore him, rolling the kholdra over and searching through the matted fur for the source of the blood.

"Looks like the owls already had a go at it," I say. It has several deep scratches down its back and bites on its head. "What do we have to treat open wounds?"

Schaff makes a disgusted sound from down near my feet. "You can't quit, can you? Naeven won't be—"

"I'm already in trouble for the woman and her baby. At least I can do one more decent thing before I'm rendered into hand cream, or whatever." I glance down at Schaff. "What's he going to do, kill me twice?"

"Yeah," he says, his pointed face dead serious, "he could." I step over him and go into the back room, digging through cupboards until I find an old wooden crate and some packing straw in a burlap bag. "You're doing this anyway? You can't save everyone, you know."

"So, because I can't help them all, I shouldn't help any, is that what you're saying?" I glance at him over my shoulder. He's standing in the doorway. "What I do may not matter to you, or to Lord Sactaren, or to anyone else, but to that little creature, it matters, okay? Now what cream or powder or potion do I use?"

Schaff sighs. "I've never met anyone as altruistic as you, Lark. I'd put the aloe salve on the cuts and give it a little chamomile-catnip tea, to keep it calm and restore the lost blood. And just in case I don't see you again, or I don't recognize you when I do, it's been an honor knowing you."

He smiles and disappears; I sigh and finish filling the crate with straw. Schaff might just be tormenting me for the fun of it, but I don't think so. I wish he were. I find the salve and fill a little copper kettle with water from the pitcher. Using tongs, I lift a small firestone out of a marble bowl and drop it into the kettle, then go out into the shop.

The kholdra hasn't moved, but its breathing has eased and I see only a little fresh blood in the wounds. I wait for the water to heat, then pour some onto a clean cloth and wash the matted blood away. The aloe salve is cool and has a clean smell as I gently apply it to each of the wounds. When I finish, I wipe my hands and stand a moment, looking down at the creature. It's only slightly smaller than the baby girl. Its middle and hind limbs end in stubby paws, but the front pair appear much more nimble, more like furry little hands. Its head is very round, nose small and pink, its eyes set high on the sides of its head. Its fur is so thick and silky. I reach out and stroke its cheek, smiling to myself. My smile vanishes as I realize that I'm not alone.

Lord Sactaren is standing in the doorway of the back room when I turn, his arms crossed over his chest, leaning against the door frame. I quickly bow my head, my mouth gone dry when I try to speak. "M'Lord, I-I did not hear you. Forgive me."

"For what, Lark, for not hearing me, or for disobeying me?" I swallow hard. "You did not hear me because I did not wish you to, so there is nothing there to forgive."

He steps out of the doorway and walks toward me. I fight the urge to back away, my whole body going stiff and cold. If he yelled or beat me, I don't think I would be this frightened, but his voice is so calm and he has yet to raise a hand to me. I don't know what to do.

"I'm sorry, M'Lord," I say. He stands so close I can smell the smoky, musky odor of the tower room upon him. He makes my heart race.

"Are you?" he asks softly. "And if today's events were to repeat tomorrow, what would you do differently?"

I want to lie. I'm scared and I want to save my neck, but even the thought of letting that baby die makes *me* feel dead inside. I can only answer the truth. "Nothing, M'Lord."

"Then you are not sorry. Not yet." I shudder, and I think he notices. He steps past me and looks down at the kholdra on the counter. "I see I can add compassion to your list of attributes.

Perhaps there is a good reason, then, why my books are in the red again?"

"No, M'Lord. Nothing excuses my disobedience." That's the bottom line. I disobeyed.

"Yet you did it anyway. You knew you would be punished, and you did it anyway." He leans close again, breathing on my neck, his hair touching my face. "I can feel the fear pouring out of you, I can see it in every tiny tremble of your body. You are *terrified* of me, yet something caused you to deliberately disobey my wishes. I am greatly intrigued." He steps back and leans against the counter. "Tell me what happened today."

I lick my dry lips and describe the events of the day as factually as I can. I keep stealing glances at him, looking for some spark of compassion, of understanding, but his expression never changes. I'm doomed. When I finish, I bow my head again and wait for his verdict. After a moment, he makes a small sound in his throat.

"Hold out your hands," he says. Trembling, I hold them out, palms up. He takes my right hand in both of his, his fingers pressing into my flesh, feeling the bones inside. "You have good hands," he says. He runs his fingers down mine, over the rows of hard calluses. "A bit rough, but," he trails his fingertips across the soft hollow in the center of my palm, causing my breath to catch in my throat, "perhaps I can find use for them after all." He lets go and sweeps past me, and I'm once again overcome by the power of him as he pauses in the doorway, his hair a shining curtain flowing down his back and rippling like water as he turns his head, revealing a glimpse of golden throat and delicately curved jaw, one wild blue eye fixing on me. "See to your new friend, and eat something," he says. "I shall expect you upstairs at sunset."

"Yes, M'Lord," I whisper.

He is beauty; he is perfection; he is terrifying — and I can't look away. The corner of his mouth lifts in a smile, then he steps out of sight and my sanity returns. I can hardly breathe as the realization hits me: I'm bewitched! I can still feel his hands upon mine, that warm, smooth skin, and his scent clings to me. I breathe deep and the pit of my stomach trembles, sending a shiver through my body. What am I to do?

I prepare tea for the kholdra. The fragrant steam replaces Lord Sactaren's musky odor and calms my nerves, but it can't stop my mind from racing. I have never felt like this. Never. I've been abused, and raped, but I've never been seduced before. When he looks at me, I know he wants me, I can see the lust in his eyes, the longing. I don't know why he hasn't just taken me. None of the others ever waited this long. Should I just let him, just get it over with, so he'll stop gliding and posing and teasing me with his magical voice? For a second, I wonder if it would be worth it, but then I shudder and wrap my arms around myself. Nothing could be worth that pain.

I coax a few drops of warm tea down the kholdra's throat. It swallows, but does not wake. I hope it will live. If it does, I think I'll call it Khas. I place it in the crate of straw and pour myself a cup of the bitter tea. If tonight goes as I fear, I will need all the help I can get to stay calm. A little blood restoration probably won't hurt, either. I always bleed.

I stand at the counter and drink my tea, watching the kholdra lie still and quiet. Every now and again it will shift in its sleep, slowly burrowing down into the straw. A pest, Schaff had said, one in a thousand, fodder for the owls. Little Khas and I aren't so different then: expendable, replaceable, forgettable. At least I matter to him.

The thought of eating turns my stomach, so I stand in the doorway of the shop and watch the sun slip past the edge of the shadowy gray hills and kiss the rim of the sea. The rough water glows gold as it swallows the remaining moments of the day. With the sky fading to lavender, denim, and gray, I turn and lock the door, then make my way to the back room. I pause beside Khas's crate, stroke his furry side, and then begin the long climb to the mage's tower.

Chapter 5

The heat is almost smothering as I step into Lord Sactaren's workshop, and mingled with the smoke and musk is the sharp smell of sweat. I don't see him, but I know he is in the room — I can feel his presence, like a great storm drawing near.

"Lord Sactaren," I say, lowering my eyes to the floor, "I'm here as you ordered."

"So, you *can* follow directions." He doesn't bother with the voice tricks this time. I can tell he's somewhere to my right, though I don't dare to look up. "I expected you to run to escape your punishment, but you surprise me. Not many men can do that. So," he steps out of wherever he has hidden himself and crosses the room, his bare feet keeping to the edge of my vision, "what am I to do with you?" Now his voice reaches out and touches me, sending a chill down my spine, even in the sweltering heat of the fire.

"I doubt laying the whip across your back would make any difference. You probably wouldn't even feel it through all that scarring." I do have several large "dead" areas on my back, but I still feel the lash just fine. I almost tell him so. It would be better than— "I can think of only one thing that might make an impression upon you. Until the supplies you have given away are replaced, your evenings will be spent in my workshop, helping me prepare the ingredients for the creams and charms and tonics and spells we sell. Perhaps once you see how much effort must be put into them, you won't be so quick to give them away."

"Is that it?" I ask stupidly. I glance up, afraid he will be angry, but he just raises one eyebrow at me.

"Isn't that enough? Do you need to be beaten, as well?" He is shirtless, his skin gleaming with sweat, and I remember the sight of him in the bath, naked and beautiful, like a golden statue brought to life by the breath of Maele himself.

"No, M'Lord." I look back at the floor before the sight of him entrances me. I can feel the spell at work in my blood, hot under my skin, singing in my ears, but at least I can still think. "I have never had a master so merciful, M'Lord, I-I..." He is walking toward me and I can't think of what I was going to say. "Thank you, M'Lord," I say at last. I can feel his eyes sweeping over me as he steps past, moving to the fire grate instead. Sweat rolls down my face as he places another billet of wood onto the glowing bed of coals.

"Don't thank me yet," he says ominously. "One evening with me and you may beg for that beating."

I steal a glance at him as he pokes the fire with a length of iron, and my insides curl into a cold, tight ball until he leans the poker back against the wall. His beautiful hair falls over his shoulder in a thick braid, the turquoise and silver wound through like thin ribbons. The silver catches the firelight and glows like the last flash of the setting sun, his skin gleaming a rich red gold. As I watch, sweat beads up along his collarbone and rolls down his chest, over his smooth, flat stomach and soaks into the waistband of his light cotton trousers.

"Hot, isn't it?" he asks, and I realize that he's caught me. My face burns as I look back at the floor. "It has to be," he continues, not waiting for me to answer. "My draklings need the heat to incubate their eggs. Come here." I walk to his side and he shows me a long glass box on a shelf next to the stone wall of the fireplace. The bottom of the box is covered in fine white sand, and at first glance, appears empty.

"M'Lord, I don't..." At the sound of my voice, two bright, black points appear in the sand, right before my eyes. The tiny grains shift and a long, pearly white reptile raises itself up on stocky legs, the inside of its mouth a bright red as it hisses at me.

"That's the male, protecting his mate," Lord Sactaren says. The drakling is beautiful, his pebbly skin faintly iridescent. He snaps at me, his blunt nose thunking against the glass. I scan the rest of the tank. "She's in the far corner on their nest, but you won't see her." I spend a moment looking, and he's right; I see nothing but sand. "I have their last clutch over here."

He shows me another tank, one not so close to the fire, but the whole room is like an oven. I can feel the sweat trickling down my back, my thin shirt sticking to my skin. Sweat is starting to roll down my scalp, making my head itch. He may be right; I can't imagine spending an entire evening in this hell.

This tank is crawling with nearly a dozen little draklings, all of them scrambling over each other and trying to climb the glass. They're about half the size of their sire, and their skin has a more golden hue to it. My master hands me a small metal pail half full of damp sawdust. "Since drakling skin is one of the ingredients missing from my stores, you can have the honor of feeding these little demons from now on."

"They eat...wood chips?" I ask, looking into the pail.

Lord Sactaren laughs, a cool, silky sound, and reaches over to tap hard on the side of the pail. The sawdust begins to heave and squirm as several large, fat, ivory colored grubs rise to the surface. I draw back. I wasn't that fond of squirmy things before the kairon worms.

"You have to feed them by hand or they fight, and skins with scars are nearly useless. Drakling skins, that is." I glance at him and he's looking at me. I've never seen a face that could hide thoughts and emotions so completely. I have no idea what he's thinking, but I doubt it's anything I'd like. "When you're finished, I will find you something else to do to atone for your mistake." He starts to turn away.

"It wasn't a mistake." I almost drop the pail of grubs when I hear my own voice, barely louder than a whisper, but like a shout in the quiet workshop. I cringe and pray that he hasn't heard me, but apparently Maele has better things to do than save me a beating. My master pauses, then walks back to my side, as close as he can get without actually shoving me up against the wall. Still wearing these horrible shoes, I'm tall enough that he has to tilt his head back a little to look me in the eye.

"It wasn't, huh?" he says.

I'm already going to get it, so I don't bother trying to lie. He can only hit just so hard for just so long. "Forgive me, M'Lord," I say. "I will do whatever I have to, to make up for my...disobedience, but I can't call saving that little girl's life a mistake. Do what you must to me, but, short of killing me, nothing is going to make me regret doing it. Or stop me doing it again."

Lord Sactaren turns his head and sighs, his breath cooling the sweat on the side of my neck. "I was afraid of that," he says, and even in the stifling heat, I feel chilled to the bone. For all my stupid bravado, I don't want to die. "Well, I guess you'll just have to assist me from now on, then. With a competent assistant, I suppose I could afford to be a little more charitable."

Him using all his big words doesn't help any, but that isn't the only reason I take a moment to understand what he's said. He's not doing what I expect him to, and it's unnerving. Before I can do little more than blink stupidly, he has reached up and wiped a drop of sweat off the side of my face, his fingertips lingering on my cheek.

"You may even learn something," he says, and his voice pulls seductively at my body. He steps back and walks away, saying over his shoulder as he takes a seat at his worktable across the room, "But first, feed my draklings their grubs. And be careful — they bite."

I swallow hard and turn my attention to the scrambling, twisted pile of reptiles. They look like they want to eat me alive. Well, I've been bitten by worse. I push back the metal grate on top of their cage and reach into the pail for a grub. Several pair of heavy black pincers dig into my flesh and I jerk my hand back with a yelp.

"I warned you."

I set the pail on the shelf beside the tank and glance at his gleaming golden back, his thick braid hanging off to one side as he leans over his desk, a slim silver quill pen in hand, but he says nothing else to me. Wincing, I pick the grubs off my hand and drop them back in the pail. They leave angry red dents in the meaty part of my fingers but don't manage to draw blood, though not for lack of trying.

The tiny bites already stinging, I shake up the sawdust and dart my hand in as the fat, nasty crawlies wriggle around, trying to get their nasty little feet back under them. I hate bugs. I pinch one behind the head, feeling the gooey insides squish, and it squirms between my fingers. My upper lip curls as I hold it down for the draklings. They jump and crawl over each other, pushing and snapping, and I pull my hand back to keep from losing a finger. Pressing my lips together, I cast a sideways look at my master, but he offers no advice. He's not paying *any* attention, as far as I can tell.

With my empty hand, I reach into the tank and grab one of the hungry reptiles. It scratches at my fingers, but its claws aren't sharp enough to hurt. I offer the drakling the grub and it snaps it out of my hand, crushing the head with one powerful crunch and then gulping down the rest with a series of jerky head movements. I watch as it finishes swallowing and rubs the sides of its mouth on the back of its scaly hand. It blinks its beady black eyes at me and waits for more. I feed it two more grubs before it loses interest and turns its head away when I offer. Can't say I blame it. Three would be just about my limit, too. I place it back in the tank and it crawls into a corner and closes its eyes, leaving just a tannish lump in the white sand.

One at a time, I feed each of the draklings, until there is just one left, and I can't help but notice that he's a bit runty. The others are a good finger's length longer, and he has more of that golden color in his skin, like he's not maturing as fast. He wiggles just a fiercely when picked up, though, and bolts down grubs like there's no tomorrow. After he's eaten his three and turned away from a fourth, I take a moment to stroke the top of his head. The pebbly skin is surprisingly soft.

"Don't get attached." I jump at the sound of my master's voice and quickly place the little drakling back in the tank. He has turned in his chair and has one arm draped over the back. "I have to kill them in a week to make room for the new batch."

The draklings lounge in the sand, the runty one crawling over to rest his head on the back of another, and I find myself hating him more for saying that than for anything he's done to me yet. I've never been good at keeping my feelings to myself and they must show on my face, for he says, "Where did you think drakling skins came from?"

I look down at the floor. "I don't know, M'Lord. I guess I thought...reptiles shed their skins."

"True," he replies, and I hear the chair creak as he turns back around, "but unlike serpents, drakling skin does not peel off in one piece; it flakes off in a white powder, which has no value. Have you finished?"

"Yes, M'Lord," I say, sliding the grate back over the cage. I'm tempted to leave it slightly to one side, give them a chance to escape, at least, but I don't. Without drakling skin, that baby would have died. So, unfair as it might be, I do not meddle with this arrangement. I wipe my face with the back of my sleeve. My shirt is plastered to my body, and still I can feel the sweat rolling down my sides and trickling through my cropped hair.

"You may remove your shirt and your shoes, if you wish," Lord Sactaren says, setting the quill to one side and rising to his feet. "It makes the heat a little more bearable."

"Thank you, M'Lord," I say, "but it's not that bad." The last thing I want is to feel his eyes moving over my bare skin again, lingering on each scar. It's bad enough having to look at him, the very definition of perfection, without him studying the ruin that is my body. He pauses, then I hear him walk to the center of the room.

"As you like," he says, as if it doesn't matter to him one way or the other. I hope that's true. "Over here." I hurry to his side. "I would like you to process this lavender into a fine powder." He shows me a large burlap sack stuffed with dried lavender branches — the normally pleasant scent almost enough to choke on — a simple, gray soapstone mortar and pestle, and a clear glass bottle. "Just the leaves; the stems can be fed to the fire. Let me know when you're done."

It takes a lot of leaves to make just a little powder, and they don't crush up easily, brittle though they may be. My forearms begin to ache before I've gone though even a quarter of the bag, and the pestle keeps slipping in my sweaty hands, giving me blisters in places I didn't even know could get blisters. I take a moment to wipe the sweat from my stinging eyes, but my sleeves are as wet as the rest of my shirt. I'm dripping on the floor. I'm also dying of thirst, but I can't seem to work up the courage to ask for a drink of water. I keep imagining what it might cost me later.

I hear his chair slide back from the table and I get back to work, though he probably already noticed the silence. I lick at my dry lips and taste salt as he walks behind me, but doesn't stop or speak. I hear him shifting things on the shelves near the window, and then he steps over to my right and sets a small cask on the table next to the bag of lavender. I continue to grind, but my attention is on my master. I watch as he cracks the wax seal around the top of the cask and peels back the thick black skin. It's full of white cream. I turn quickly back to my work as he glances at me.

"Hand me one of the jars in that crate to your left," he says.

I hadn't even noticed the crate, on the floor by my feet, full of neatly stacked jars like the ones the hand cream is sold in. That's what's in the cask — hand cream, but before he puts the magic stuff in it. I give him a jar, and his fingers brush mine as he takes it. I almost jerk back. I'm trembling inside as I stare down into the mortar. I hope he's enjoying himself, enjoying this spell he's cast on me — I know I'm not.

He picks up the bottle that I've been dumping the powder into and gives it a slight shake, the larger pieces shifting to the surface. I pause, waiting for him to tell me it's not good enough, but he just measures out a spoonful and puts it in the empty jar. I let out the breath I'm holding and wipe my forehead with my dripping sleeve.

"Are you certain you wouldn't be more comfortable in less clothing?"

"Quite certain, M'Lord," I say, keeping my eyes on my hands as I fish more lavender from the bag and strip the leaves from the woody stems.

"You don't want me to see your scars, is that it?" he asks. I'm not certain he expects an answer, and I don't want to have to give him one, so I say nothing. "Is that it, Lark?" There is something so sensual about the way he says my name, as if he were speaking of far more intimate things.

"M'Lord," I say, trying to keep my voice from trembling or cracking, but it seems determined to do both, "if I were as-as beautiful and perfect as you, I wouldn't want to look at anything as ugly as me."

"You think you're ugly?" he asks.

My eyes shift to him and back to my hands. I know I am. Most days, it never bothered me, but since he became my master...

"M'Lord, I do not think myself anything but your slave. However, many former masters have told me that I am ugly." As well as slavers, fishermen, gypsies, and other slaves. He makes a disgusted sound in his throat and I tense, but it's what I said, not something I've done.

"I've never been one to hold to other men's opinions," he says. "I do not find you ugly, so if offending me is your only concern, you won't. If, however, you are uncomfortable for another reason..."

He waits, and it occurs to me what he's waiting for. I've already told him how beautiful I find him; does he really need to hear it again? Vain man. Or perhaps he's testing how effective his enchantment is, how completely bewitched I am. Well, I may be feeling the spell, but I'm not about to give in to it without a fight.

"I'm very *aware* of my scars when I'm around you," I tell him.

"Because I'm so...perfect."

He says the word slowly, carefully, and I raise my eyes to his face. He's looking past me, not at me, and for a moment I see a shadow of feeling in his eyes, a flicker of pain and sadness. Maybe he's human after all. As if he can hear my thought, his attention snaps back to me, and his eyes are hard as chips of blue topaz.

"I'm not perfect," he says, stepping around the end of the table toward me. I take a small, involuntary step backward and my heel taps the crate of empty jars, the brittle *clink* of glass making me jump. "The universe does not *allow* perfection; it strives for balance — an equal amount of good and evil, light and darkness, beauty and ugliness."

He reaches out and grabs my jaw, turning my head to one side. I watch him out of the corner of my eye as he studies the long, faded silver scar that runs from just into my hairline down my cheek. My heart races as he slides his fingertips across my skin, lightly tracing the scar. I can hardly breathe as his fingers trail down the side of my throat, settling over my fluttering pulse.

"Look at me." I'm trembling as I obey. "Do you know why you find me so beautiful?"

Because you bespelled me, I think to myself. "No," I whisper, feeling the lie betrayed by my pounding heart.

The corner of his mouth lifts in a secret smile. "Yes, you do."

He takes his hand from my neck and grabs my right hand, bringing it up toward his lips. I resist the urge to jerk away; fighting back will only make it worse. He touches the tips of my middle and index fingers to the corner of his mouth, just down from his lips, and I frown slightly. I can feel a thin, raised line, slick and hard under my fingers. It doesn't take a slave to recognize a scar, we're just better at it than free men. Forgetting myself, I lean toward him, trying to see the mark.

"You can see it in sunlight," he tells me, and I realize how forward I'm being. I step back, bowing my head, but he won't let go of my wrist.

"M'Lord...Master, please," I say. I'm shaking again, and he hasn't even done anything to me.

"It is our imperfections, Lark, that make us beautiful. Without this scar, even though you can barely see it, I wouldn't be half as interesting. I probably wouldn't merit a second look from you."

He's toying with me now. As if I would have given him a first look if he hadn't bewitched me. I am a good slave; I do not look at anyone in lust, especially not my master. It is not allowed. Yet I raise my gaze to him again.

"I have scars, too, you know, more than you do, probably."

I glance at his flawless golden skin. "I find that hard to believe, M'Lord," I say quietly.

"Not all scars are on the outside," he says, and his tone sends a chill down my spine. I don't want to know how you get scars on your insides. "Besides, I'm a mage; you should know by now that you can't always trust your eyes."

He lifts my hand back to his face, brushing my fingertips across his cheek and along his jaw, his skin hot and damp with sweat. It feels like I'm touching my own skin, a mess of thin, old lines and hard, knotted lumps, flat, slick burns and deep, rough craters. My eyes tell me it can't be, he's beautiful, but my hand tells a different story. I raise my left hand and hesitantly touch his throat, tracing a long knife wound I can't see down onto his chest. My fingers find a curved string of knotted scars and I follow it onto his side, just below his ribs. Teeth marks, is all I can think, but the creature would have to have been a—

"Dragon," he says, and I jerk back. "That one almost had me." He smiles at the recollection. "Being a mage is a dangerous profession. I don't know a single one of us who has faced death less than a dozen times, not if they've been practicing for more than a year, but just try convincing someone that all these scars mean you're good at your job. No, they want the mage who looks fresh out of his apprenticeship, and so we waste a little magic to cover them up." His eyes flicker over me, from head to toe and back again. "I could waste a little magic on you, I suppose. What do you say I hide one of your scars every time you...please me?"

My stomach knots up at the insinuation he puts into those last two words. "M'Lord, I-I—"

He raises his hand and I fall silent. His brow furrowed, he reaches toward me, placing his fingertips at my temple. I feel a sudden touch of ice against my skin and I gasp. He draws back, a smug smile on his lips. "You have pleased me today, Lark."

I don't know what I did, but if he says so... I raise my hand and feel my cheek where the cold touched me, but it's just the old knife scar, just as it has been for the last ten years.

"Look, over there," he tells me, pointing toward a cluttered shelf near the stairs.

I step over to it, seeing books and stacks of papers, several small animal skulls, scattered quills, stones, crystals, and burnt-down stubs of candles. I'm not sure what he wants me to look at. I glance over my shoulder and jump. He's standing behind me, so close his scent fills my senses — musky, spicy, thick, rich, wild, dangerous — a scent that conjures thoughts of blood and sex, birth and death. I swallow hard.

Lord Sactaren leans around me and I stiffen as he places his left hand on my waist, his right reaching up to pull a tarnished silver hand mirror down from between two old books, their leather covers cracked and scorched. He holds the mirror up for me to look into. My reflection looks as uncomfortable as I feel, and I force my face to relax, though I can't do anything to hide the fear in my eyes. Usually a dark rust brown, the pupils have nearly swallowed the color, making them almost black.

I try to figure out what he wants me to see — my large, chiseled nose, my thin, cracked lips, my square jaw, the uneven straw-colored stubble covering my head, the various scars marring my sun tanned skin... I blink and lean closer, turning my head slightly to one side. The long knife scar is gone. I run my fingers over my skin; I can still feel it, but I can't see it. I look at the others, the whip slash over my right eye, the burn on my jaw, the tiny cuts and scratches from beatings I can't even remember — I think about them gone and I tremble inside. All I have to do is...please him. It can't be such a great cost, can it?

"You like this?" he whispers, his lips next to my ear. I nod, barely. "I can hide them all," he continues, "all but...this one." His hand leaves my waist, his arm wrapping around my body as he touches a small scar at the corner of my mouth, almost identical to his. "Or maybe...this one." His hand glides down to the hollow of my throat, to a little crescent shaped scar I can't remember where I got. He leans closer. "I think you'll find I'm not so hard to please." I can see the side of his face in the mirror and he's smiling as he looks at me, a very *hungry* smile.

He places the mirror back on the shelf, his other hand lingering a moment at my throat before he steps away. I realize I'm holding my breath and let it out in a rush, my heart pounding in my chest. Still smiling, he moves back to his corner of the table and scoops the thick hand cream out of the cask with a large wooden spoon, scraping it into the small jar with the lavender powder in it. He returns the large spoon to the cask and picks up a thin stirring stick, his eyes fixed on the jar as he mixes the contents.

I swallow hard and make my way back to my place at the table. What is his game? What is he waiting for?

Lord Sactaren screws the lid on the jar and sets it aside, then wipes his hands on a rag and takes a little silver flask out of his pocket. I watch, my mouth tasting like the inside of a sand dune, as he pulls the cork and takes a sip, his eyes squinting up as he makes a sour face. He holds the flask out to me.

"M'Lord, I—"

"Just drink," he says, shaking his head. "You're no good to me if you die of thirst, so you needn't be afraid to ask for water." I take the flask and raise it to my lips. "Just a sip," he cautions me. "It's a little tart."

I don't know how much more of this torment I can take. My mouth is so dry, my lips cracked and stinging from the salt in my sweat, that I could empty an entire horse trough of week old bharg piss. What do I care about a little tartness?

I care a lot, I discover, as the liquid touches my lips. A sip is all I can manage as my lips pucker and tears spring to my eyes. This crap is like biting into a lemon, and it bites back as I try to swallow. I hand the flask back to my master and cover my mouth with my hands as I cough and choke. "What...is that?" I manage to ask.

"The one thing I never leave home without," he replies with a crooked smile as he slips it back into his trouser pocket. "I invented it myself. One sip cures even the most horrible thirst. You can live off this for up to two weeks."

"What happens after two weeks?"

"Your body breaks down into various elements, mainly salt." I stare at him and he shrugs. "Two weeks isn't bad, though. Plenty of time to get rescued if you're lost."

"Couldn't you have made it taste better?" I ask, wiping my mouth on the back of my hand. I'm salivating like crazy, that sour taste still clinging to the back of my tongue.

"It took a long time to get it to taste like that," Lord Sactaren says, and I realize I've overstepped my bounds.

"Forgive me, Master," I say, bowing my head, "I-I meant no offense."

His voice startles me, not the suddenness of him speaking, but the softness in his tone.

"Lark, stop."

I slowly raise my eyes, not sure what I'm supposed to stop doing. I'm not doing anything but breathing. He can't mean that, but I try to make each breath as shallow as possible, just in case.

He steps around the end of the table again. "If you were to be just my slave, I would not mind the bowing and cowering and flinching and 'Yes, Master, no, Master' crap, but I don't need *just* a slave." He steps a little closer and reaches out, placing his hand on my shoulder.

This is it, I realize, my insides curling into one cold lump; he's going to take me. He's going to turn me around, he's going to bend me over this table, he's going to—

"M-Master, please..." I whisper.

His grip on my shoulder tightens slightly. "Call me 'Master' again and I will *not* be pleased."

"I'm sorry, Lord Sactaren." I stare at the floor and wait for him to speak, but the silence drags on, until I can't stand it any longer and raise my head to find him just watching me.

"Schaff was right, there is no will left in you." He sighs. "That's too bad. You showed a lot of promise." His gaze lingers on my face a moment, then he turns away. "I'm sure you'll be much more comfortable with one of the nicer lords of this valley. I bet Irra would like to buy you; he mentioned needing help in the vineyard just last week."

"You're... Lord Sactaren, you're getting rid of me?" It feels like the bottom has been cut out of my stomach and my chest is tight when I draw breath.

He glances over his shoulder, then begins to gather up the supplies off the table. "I'm not angry with you, Lark, this just isn't working out. You're not what I need. When you told me you were stubborn and willful, I thought perhaps you would be perfect, but now I think you were just repeating what others had told you, when it wasn't the truth to begin with. Go back to your room and rest; tomorrow I'll find you a new home."

Stunned, I take a step toward the door, but only one. "I don't want a new home." He continues to clean up, ignoring me, and I feel the back of my neck grow hot, and it's not from the fire. A slave is never supposed to clench their fist in the presence of their master, but I come real close, grabbing the hem of my shirt and squeezing until sweat drips from between my fingers onto the floor. "What about the boy?" I ask, my voice loud enough that he can't pretend not to hear me. "What about the woman and her child? What about the kholdra?"

"What about them?" he replies.

"Isn't...isn't that stubborn enough. Isn't that willful enough?"

He sets down the bottle in his hand and turns toward me, his cold eyes flashing. "It's compassionate, I'll give you that, and shows a bit of courage, but you're just not strong enough to be of any use to me."

"But...I liked helping those people," I tell him. "I've been a useless, worthless, helpless slave most of my life, but in the last two days, I got to make a difference in someone else's life. I-I *mattered* to them." I feel tears stinging my eyes.

"You can make a difference somewhere else," the mage argues. "I'll sell you to the apothecary—"

"No." I swallow hard. I interrupted him. He looks surprised, but waits for me to continue, so I do. "I want to stay *here*. Schaff may be...Schaff, but he's the closest thing I've had to a friend since I was a child, and you may terrify me sometimes, but you have not once raised your voice or touched me in anger in the two days I've belonged to you, and that's two days longer than any master before you. And you'll have to pardon me if I bow and cower and flinch. I'm a *slave*. It's what I was trained to do. That's all I—"

My voice breaks and I stop, unable to continue. Now I know what he meant about scars on the inside. Some wounds linger forever, I guess. I bow my head, but just to keep him from seeing the hot tears that slip silently down my face.

"All right," Lord Sactaren says after a moment, "you can stay. But I want you to stop this flinching and groveling; it's unbecoming." He closes the distance between us and I raise my eyes to meet his. "My Lord, or Lord Sactaren will do, never Master, I hate that. You may argue a point should you disagree, but not in front of others, and from now on, when I order you to do something, you *will* obey." I nod to show I understand. "That being said, I will not often order you to do anything. I would like you to run my magic shop as you have been, and in the evenings, assist me up here. I would also like you to accompany me should I be called away from the castle on business."

"Yes, M'Lord," I say, wondering what sort of business trips mages make.

"Good. Then I believe there is only one thing left to say, and you may retire for the night." He reaches out and trails his fingertips along the curve of my jaw and I can't help but tense. "I am not a cruel or sadistic man," he says. "I did not enjoy making you fear me, but I had to know if there was enough spirit left in you to be useful. I suppose I can be too familiar at times," with a crooked smile, he takes his hand back, "but I will never hurt you."

"So...it-it was all just another test?"

He arches an eyebrow. "Every day we live is a test, Lark — a test of our courage, our kindness, our fortitude, our morality, our strength. I had to test you to see if you could withstand the tests that, as my assistant, you would face on a daily basis."

"Does that include your seducing me?" I ask, speaking before I think. My heart jumps into my throat as the corner of his mouth lifts in a faint smile.

"Don't take it personally," he says. "Seduction is what I know best." His gaze lingers on me for a moment, and I sense there is more that he's not saying. "Well, good night, then."

"Good night, M'Lord," I say and move toward the stairs. I pause in the doorway, then turn. He's watching me. "If it's all the same to you, Lord Sactaren," I say, glancing at the clock, "it's still early, and I didn't finish with the lavender."

"It's not all the same," he says, then his lips curve upward in the ghost of a smile. "I would be glad of the company."

I probably shouldn't press my luck, but there's something I have to ask. "M'Lord, I was wondering about the kholdra... If the creature lives, may I keep him?"

"It will live," he tells me, and his tone leaves no room for doubt. "I hope you're around when *I* need doctoring. You seem to have a talent for it. Have you given the kholdra a name?"

"Khas, M'Lord."

He smiles. "Then he already belongs to you. Be careful, though, a kholdra is not a dog or a cat. It is wild and will probably never make a good pet." I hadn't thought of that. "You could always return him to the wild when he is well. I would allow you a more suitable companion if you wished — a hamster, perhaps?"

"Thank you, M'Lord. I'll think about it." He pulls a couple of stools out of a dusty corner and sets out an array of supplies on the table. I linger near the doorway, watching him, my hands toying with the buttons on my cuffs. Finally, I set my jaw and slip out of the shirt, dropping it in a sodden, stinking heap next to the top stair. A breath of night air slinks through the window and cools the sweat on my back. I shiver, but that's not the only reason.

Lord Sactaren glances at me as I take a seat at the table, his expression unreadable, but the intensity in his eyes betrays him. He wants something, needs something, something he can't have, but looking at me, however briefly, eases that need, just a little, just enough. For now.

I shudder and set to work grinding lavender leaves. I should know by now that I can't trust my eyes, not around him, and I can't trust my gut, either. Both taunt me with promises of the wonders I would find in his bed, if I let him touch me, if I let him taste me, if I let him take me, but it's all just magic, and all spells wear off eventually.

Chapter 6

"And what are the common names for red, blue, and green corundum?" Schaff asks, his tail twitching as he quizzes me.

"Ruby, sapphire, and emerald," I say as I lean against the edge of the counter. He's been at me all morning, and I think he's running out of hard questions.

"And where do you find dragon's pearls?"

"Colossal oysters."

"And what is jasmine used for?"

"Love spells and charms."

"And for how—"

Crash! Both of us jump and I spin around, my heart pounding. "That came from the tower," I say, taking a step into the store room.

"I wouldn't go up there," Schaff says and I glance back at him. "Naeven does this all the time — throws fits and breaks things. It's best to just leave him alone. He'll be fine in a few days."

I swallow hard. "But I-I'm supposed to assist him this evening," I say.

Schaff frowns. "Well, he could get over it sooner, I suppose—" A sound like splintering wood echoes down the staircase. "There goes the furniture," Schaff says, shaking his head. "Sorry, sounds like it's going to be a long one. I wonder what pissed him off this time. Anyway, for how long can a lesser healing charm work?"

I look back at the stairs and then return to the counter. "Lesser healing...ah, willow or ash?"

Sometimes as much as an hour passes before I hear another thump, or bang, or crash, but it goes on all day. As I step over to lock the shop door, it sounds like something explodes up above. "That didn't sound like throwing a fit," I say as Schaff and I go down the hall toward the kitchen.

"Have you ever heard a mage throw a fit before?" he asks. "I didn't think so. You still going up there later?"

"I have to," I say. "I told Lord Sactaren I would."

"Yeah, but that was before he decided to break everything in sight. If you go up there, we may end up picking pieces of you up off the floor along with the chairs."

"Are you trying to scare me?" I ask, pushing open the kitchen door.

He chuckles. "More or less. I'm just making sure you know what you're getting into. Being Naeven's 'assistant' is a hell of a lot harder than you can ever imagine."

"What do you mean, his 'assistant'? Why did you say it like that?"

He leaps up onto the table and sniffs at the bread basket. "Rye — blech. All I meant was that the definition of assistant doesn't come close to describing the complex nature of your relationship with Naeven. *Assistants* tidy up and fetch things, run errands — that sort of stuff. They don't fuel your spells, or sleep in your bed, or keep you from losing your soul... Hey, is there any of that chicken left?"

"Forget the chicken," I say. "What the hell are you talking about? I'm supposed to do those things?"

He flits his tail in the air. "That's what his last 'assistant' did."

I turn and head for the door. "Where are you going?"

"I'm not hungry," I tell him as I jerk open the door.

"Well, I am!"

I hurry down the hall and through the shop, hesitating only a moment to peer in at the sleeping kholdra in the store room. He still hasn't woken up, though the cuts and scratches look like they're starting to heal. Another loud bang echoes down the stairwell and I see him twitch. Poor little Khas. I square my shoulders and head up to the tower, prepared to find the room in ruin, the table and desk and shelves reduced to rubble, books shredded and burned, jars broken and melted. I hope the draklings survived.

I step up into the tower and stop short. Barefoot, wearing black trousers and no shirt, Sactaren stands at the table, a measuring cup in one hand, a jar of dried flowers in the other, and arches an eyebrow at me as I glance around the cluttered room. Nothing's broken. My eyes stray back to him, his skin gleaming. It's hotter than Hell up here again, but I don't think that's the only reason why I'm suddenly dry-mouthed and sweaty.

"Is something wrong?" he asks.

I shake my head. "No, M'Lord. I'm here as you asked."

He glances at the clock. "I didn't expect you until later. Have you eaten?"

"I wasn't hungry. I-I..." I lower my eyes to the floor. "I wondered what the noises were."

"Has Schaff been telling stories again?" he asks, setting the jar down with a thump.

"He said you were angry, M'Lord. He said you were breaking things."

Sactaren sighs. "As you can see, Lark, I am neither angry nor breaking anything. I am, however, losing patience." I glance up as he measures out a quarter cup of flowers and dumps them into a shallow copper bowl. "I'm attempting to create a charm that will summon rain when activated. This summer's going to be long and dry, and the damn farmers are going to be knocking down my door, begging for me to bring rain to their fields. If I can get this stupid charm to work, they can use it themselves and I won't have to go down and perform a spell, like some carnival sideshow." He runs his finger down the page of the open book on the table beside the bowl, adds two tablespoons of heather, and then stirs the contents with a tarnished silver fork.

I take a hesitant step closer. "Is there anything I can do to help?" I ask.

"I don't know," he says, not looking up. "Can you find me a blank lilac charm in that chest over there?" He gestures toward a big wooden box with tarnished brass corners and a broken lock.

I hesitate, then shrug out of my shirt, and cross the room. Lifting the lid, the powerful scent of cedar wafts up into my face. Inside is a jumbled mess of wooden discs — cross-cut slices of branches — some only as big around as my little finger, others the size of my wrist.

"Does the size matter, M'Lord?" I ask, picking out several with pebbly bark and lavender heartwood. I glance over my shoulder and flinch back. He's standing less than a foot from me.

"Let's see what you found," he says. I hold out my hand, but his eyes linger on my face a moment before looking down at the charm blanks. "Very good," he says, a hint of surprise in his voice. "How did you know?"

"Schaff's been teaching me, M'Lord."

"About lilacs?"

"About all kinds of wood. And herbs. And stones."

He raises his eyebrows, regarding me with a whole different kind of look this time — slow, lazy, contemplative. "I think..." he reaches out, his fingers hovering over the discs of lilac wood before selecting one of medium size, "this one will do quite nicely." As he picks it up, his fingertips graze the soft hollow in the palm of my hand. I jump and drop several of the discs.

"Sorry, M'Lord," I say as I duck down and scramble to pick them up. When I climb back to my feet, he hasn't moved.

"No harm done," he says, and motions for me to put the rest of them back in the chest. As I lay them down on top of the pile, he reaches past me and picks up one of the wooden circles. "So what would this one be?"

I swallow hard and look down at the charm. Slightly pinkish wood, thin, rust-red bark...

"Madrone," I say.

The corner of his mouth quirks in a smile as he drops it back in the chest. "And this one?" He picks up a large circle with thick, cracked black bark, brilliant white wood, and a bluish heart.

"Shintan lua-kao."

He drops it and closes the chest with a thump, his eyes lingering on me before he turns away. "Over here, Lark," he says, walking to the work table. I follow and he pushes the bowl toward me. "Here I have fern, heather, and pansy, all of which have the power to summon rain, to pull the moisture out of the air. What I want to do is *create* water, not just draw what is already there, and *that* is what I simply cannot seem to do."

"M'Lord, you can't — I mean, I thought water was one of the four elements — it can't be created, because it is the basis of all creation."

Sactaren regards me for a moment, one hand absently sliding back and forth along the edge of the table. Finally, he leans toward me and my shoulders tense as I fight to not draw away.

"Very few people on Ashael know what I am about to tell you," he says. "This is classified information, and I could be charged with violating several technological quarantine laws if anyone finds out."

"I-I won't tell anyone," I whisper.

He nods and turns to the table, and I jump back with a gasp as his fingertips begin to glow red, filling me with a heavy, trembling chill. He glances at me, then draws a shimmering crimson circle on the tabletop.

"This circle represents magic and is based on the four elements — fire, water, earth, and air." He draws another circle beside it. "This circle is science, based on a different set of elements — hydrogen, helium, oxygen, carbon, lithium — a hundred and twenty-nine in all." Sactaren places a hand on the outside edge of each circle and pushes them together so that they overlap in the middle.

"Where magic meets science, you get alchemy," he says, pointing to the middle section. "I was never very good at alchemy." He waves a hand over the circles and they disappear. "I do know that water is made up of one part oxygen and two parts hydrogen. Both elements are quite common; they make up the very air we breathe. However, in its natural state, oxygen bonds with itself — two oxygens. I would have to break that bond in order to bond hydrogen to it, and," he sighs and throws his hands up in the air, "nothing I've tried has worked. So now I'm back to summoning rain like a primitive witchdoctor." He glances over at me. "You didn't understand a word of that, did you?"

I hang my head. "Not really, M'Lord."

He sighs. "I don't know why I thought... I'm lucky you can read at all, I guess. Just...just feed the draklings, okay?"

"Yes, M'Lord."

I don't know why I should feel so ashamed. I'm not a mage; there's no reason why I *would* understand him. That's not my fault. I stand at the tank and feed his scaly little beasts, stealing glances at my master as he reads from his spell book, absently tapping the edge of the lilac disc against the table. After a moment, he pushes the book aside and picks up a large silver quill from off the table. He dips it in a small bottle of ink and writes something on the wooden disc, then exchanges the feather for the bowl. I watch, a squirming drakling trying to escape from my grasp, as Sactaren's hands begin to glow again. I cringe as that cold weight pulls at me, low in my chest, rattling me like silent thunder.

Sliding the disc to the center of the table, he unceremoniously dumps the bowl of herbs and flowers onto it. Something explodes, red smoke boiling up into the air as the sound of shattering stone echoes through the tower. I scream and duck, pulling the drakling to my chest as I brace myself to be hit by debris.

"Son of a bitch," Sactaren mutters, and I hesitantly raise my head.

The table is still standing, not even scorched. The lilac disc is broken into half a dozen charred pieces, and the flower petals and fern leaves are just gray ash, but that's it. My eyes dart to Sactaren. Strands of his long, black hair hang in his eyes and his cheek is smudged with soot. He sighs and clears the ashes from the table with a swipe of his hand before glancing over at me. I quickly turn away and place the drakling back in its tank, my heart pounding in my throat.

"I guess that's enough of that," Sactaren says after a moment. "Now, what should I... Lark, could I get your help with something?"

"Of course, M'Lord," I say, sliding the cover back over the tank and hurrying over to the table. Sactaren pushes a dented tin bucket out of his way with his foot and steps over a tangle of antlers and heavy copper chain to reach the tall shelves behind the table. He takes down a wicker basket and sets it in front of me. Inside are pieces of dried orange peel, all hard and curled up. Next, he hands me the mortar and pestle. I don't have to be a mage to guess what he wants me to do. While I grind the dried peels into powder, he disappears down the stairs, leaving me alone in his workshop.

My eyes stray back to the cluttered shelves, filled with all kinds of containers and tools. He has no less than six iron cauldrons, all of them different sizes, and a whole tray of old, bent silverware. I see boxes of rocks, baskets of bones, jars of herbs, and bags filled with Maele-only-knows-what. What's on the shelves is neat enough, if a bit cluttered, but on the floor between the shelf and the table is a pile of tangled sticks and bones, books and scrolls, chains and cord, broken crates, ripped cloth, dented bowls. Half of it looks like garbage. I wonder if he ever has trouble finding things in that mess.

My eyes snap back to the mortar as I hear his soft footsteps on the stairs. He enters the room and moves to my side, placing a large handful of fresh aloe on the table. I tense as he leans toward me, my eyes darting up, but he's only looking into the mortar at the powder. After a moment, he glances at me, our eyes meeting briefly before I look back down at the table.

"Good job," he says, his voice quiet. "As fine as you can grind it, and then put it," he steps past me and drags one of the smaller cauldrons off the near side of the shelf, "in here." With a thump, he sets the cauldron on the table.

I continue to work while he takes a thin knife and slices the fat aloe spikes into strips, which he also adds to the cauldron. When all the aloe is cut up, he walks to the cupboard near the window, the top covered with jars and bottles. I stop to watch as he opens the cupboard doors and picks through nearly a dozen clay pitchers, each one with a stiff paper tag tied around the handle.

"What...what are those, M'Lord?" I ask.

He pulls one out of the back corner and carries it over to the table. "This pitcher draws water straight from the Rhoem Sea, one of the saltiest bodies of water on the planet."

I bite the edge of my lip as he fills the cauldron with saltwater. "Forgive me, M'Lord, but...why?" Saltwater isn't of any use — you can't drink it, you can't water your crops with it..."

The corner of his mouth twitches in a faint smirk. "Finished with that orange peel?" he asks and I duck my head.

"Almost, M'Lord." I shouldn't be asking stupid questions.

He reaches over and takes the pestle from my hand, his skin gliding across mine for a brief instant, and I feel my heart catch in my throat. "That looks fine enough, Lark," he says. "Go ahead and dump it in." The powered orange peel clumps on the surface of the water, then darkens as it gets wet and begins to sink to the bottom.

Sactaren walks around behind me, reaching over the pile of stuff to pull a long, silver spoon out of the box on the shelf. "Stir it, would you?" he asks, handing the spoon to me. The handle is wrapped tightly with scuffed and stained leather cord, and the spoon part has been beaten nearly flat. While I stir the salt and orange and aloe mixture, Sactaren searches the shelves, finally standing on a stack of books to reach a pair of tongs way up on the highest shelf.

"Watch yourself," he warns, picking up a large firestone out of its stone bowl. I draw back, flinching as he drops the stone into the cauldron with a hiss. He adds another, and then a third. Three stones? Why would he need to heat this that much? With three stones, the water will boil away in less than an hour.

As steam begins to rise from the surface, I glance over at him. "What should I do now?" I ask.

He gestures to the cauldron. "Keep stirring it. And if the level falls below two-thirds, *carefully* add more seawater." I frown slightly, looking back at the bubbling liquid as I dip the spoon into it. I know what he's doing...I think. As the water boils, it turns to steam, but the salt is left behind. If we keep adding more saltwater, it'll just get more and more salty, until—

"Bath salts," Sactaren says and I jerk my head up. He gives me a faint smile. "You looked like you were trying to figure out what we're making. Herbal bath salts."

"Oh. Yes, thank you, M'Lord." I had almost worked it out, too.

He drags the two wooden stools out from under the table and pushes one over to me.

"Have a seat, Lark; this takes hours. Let me know when you get tired and we'll trade."

"Yes, M'Lord," I say with a nod, but I'll be Cheyn's lover before I tell him I'm too tired to work.

He starts to walk past me, but then stops, reaches out, and catches my chin. I tense, fighting not to pull away from him, and slowly raise my eyes to his face.

"I mean it, Lark," he says. "I'll never ask you to do anything I'm not willing to do myself." He releases me and I nod again, my heart pounding as I look back down into the cauldron. How can he be so generous in what he says, and still so frightening in what he does?

While I stir, he pulls several books off his shelves and sits at the other end of the table to read, quill and paper beside him. Every now and then he makes some notes, but mostly he reads.

The tower is silent save for the bubbling cauldron and the occasional turn of a page or scratch of the quill. I keep a careful eye on the water, adding more as it boils away. I don't think an hour has passed when Sactaren shuts his book with a snap and stretches. "All right, Lark, my turn."

"M'Lord, I-I'm not tired," I say, rising hesitantly from the stool.

"But *I'm* tired of reading," he says, walking around the table and taking the spoon from my hand. "Why don't you..." He glances around. "Hmm. Ah, I know. That shelf there..." He points with the spoon, dripping water on the table. "I noticed someone has spilled something sticky on it. Do you mind washing the items and the shelf?"

"Not at all, M'Lord."

He has me fill a chipped porcelain basin with water and grab a rag. The "something sticky" is honey, I think, or some kind of tree sap. It smells sweet, whatever it is. I carefully remove each thing from the mess — bottles and jars, mostly, but several crystals and bones, too. A few items, papers and dried herbs, are ruined, and he has me drop those into the dented tin bucket on the floor. I wonder how long they'll stay in the bucket before it gets knocked over and spilled.

I'm scrubbing the shelf when Sactaren's voice makes me pause. He's speaking under his breath, too quietly for me to make out. I wait until he falls silent, and then ask, "Forgive me, M'Lord, but were you talking to me?"

He glances up from the cauldron, his eyebrows raised, and for a moment he looks puzzled. "What? Oh." He gives me a crooked smile. "No, Lark, that wasn't directed at you."

"Was-was it a spell, M'Lord?"

He shakes his head. "No, I was just singing." He adds more water to the cauldron, and then looks back up at me, a hint of a smirk on his lips. "Would you like to hear?"

I lower my eyes to the floor. "I-I... Whatever pleases you, M'Lord," I say. I think I hear him sigh, but a moment later, he begins to sing. The song isn't in Alau or Tirannish — the only two languages I know — so I don't understand the words, but the melody is pretty, and Sactaren has a good voice.

Ki ent zerh'et Sur mire
lred ujz'u Kan zh'ormu,
gat Ki aA brak alzh'or, Si garA.
Ki enskirA Sur ujz'at enzer
ba kh' nikati Si tyganet baki,
gat ujz'u Si jz'ar wath'et Kur aet h'nia.
He stops and just stares at me, waiting.

"It-it was lovely, M'Lord," I say.

"You don't speak Astaniko, do you?" he asks, shifting the spoon to his left hand. I shake my head. "Ah, a shame. It's a love song, an old one — nearly sixty years, I think. The last three lines say it all, in my opinion. *'You satisfy my every need with a kindness I cannot forget, but all I can give you is love.'*"

I nod, slowly, not sure what to say, and turn back to washing the shelf. Minutes pass, and then I hear him sing again, softly, "*Ujz'u Si jz'ar wath'et Kur aet h'nia.*"

Chapter 7

"C'mon, Khas," I say softly, holding a thin slice of apple between the slats of the crate. "Try a little nibble, you'll like it." He burrows deeper into the straw and ignores me. That's all he's done in the two days since I found him, that and sleep. He won't eat, he won't drink, he just hides in the straw and waves his little paws at me when I get too close. I sigh and step out of the back room.

Schaff is dozing on the counter, but cracks an eye as I rest my elbows on the smooth wood next to him. "No luck, huh?" he asks.

"Are you *sure* you don't know what they eat?"

He swishes his bushy red and white tail in annoyance. "You've asked me that three times *today*. If I knew, I would tell you, just to get you to shut up." He stands and stretches, then yawns, his pointed muzzle full of sharp white teeth. "It's a kholdra — it lives in the mountains. For all I know, it eats rocks." He turns his back on me and settles back down to finish his nap. I step out from behind the counter and head for the front door. "And where do you think you're going?"

"Nowhere," I say, opening the door and stepping outside. The afternoon sun beams down, warming the stone walls of the castle. Sheltered from the icy wind that never stops blowing down off the mountain, I close my eyes and lean back against the castle, letting the heat soak into my body. It's late spring, and this winter has seemed the longest one I can remember. With a contented sigh, I open my eyes and squat down, gathering up a handful of pebbles. Who knows, maybe they do eat rocks. As I straighten up, a flash of color against the gray hillside catches my eye.

A slender woman in a white and pale green print dress is climbing the mountain path, a large basket hanging over one arm and a squirming bundle in a pink blanket in the other. I slip the rocks into my pocket and go down to meet them. Her shoulder-length black hair is held back by a gauzy scarf that matches the green in her dress, and, I notice as I draw near, complements her dark green eyes. I hadn't noticed how pretty she was the first time we met; she was sort of hysterical, and I was a bit distracted by her dying baby girl. She sees me coming and smiles.

"Good afternoon," she says.

I smile back. "It certainly is now," I say, and feel myself flush as I realize how that must have sounded. "I mean, I've been wondering how your little girl is doing." She draws back the blanket and I lean over to peer inside. A pair of bright, gray-green eyes meet mine. Her face is a healthy pink, with round cheeks and a pert little nose, and a head of fine black hair, just like her mother. "She's beautiful."

"Thank you. We were just coming up to see you." She shifts the basket from her arm to her hand. "I made these for you, to thank you for helping us."

"You didn't have—"

"Yes, I did." She hands the basket to me. It's heavy. "I hope you didn't suffer too much because of me. Was your master very angry?"

"No, he—"

"I was just so panicked, I couldn't think," she continues, smoothing the blanket around her daughter's face. "I never would have come here, but I didn't know where else to go. I mean, the doctor wouldn't see her, he said she was under a black curse, and-and I knew of the Traxen Mage's reputation for heartlessness and cruelty, but it's been years since anyone heard screams from the castle, and I—"

"Wait, screams?"

She looks up at me, and I see pity in her eyes. "Yes, late at night, sometimes the wind would bring the most terrible screams down from the mountain. I was just a girl, but I can still remember that sound: a man...screaming..."

I swallow hard and look past her, up at the high tower. Lord Sactaren is standing at the window, watching us, his long black hair dancing in the wind, the streaks of silver and turquoise bright in the sunlight. In a moment, he's gone.

"I listened, last night and the night before, and I didn't hear anything, but...you don't strike me as a man who would scream easily." Her eyes travel over my face, to the scars at my throat, and then she glances away, her cheeks reddening. She shifts the baby to the other arm and digs into her dress pocket. "Here, the money I owe." She presses a handful of coins into my hand.

"This is too much," I say, quickly counting the coins. I've been practicing. I almost don't need Schaff's help anymore.

"The rest is for the Jesren's cow, and something for helping Taler. We didn't know how much the tonic cost, so if it's not enough—"

"You didn't..."

She reaches out and grabs my arm, giving it a firm squeeze. "Yes, Lark, we did. Taler goes to school with my son; his mother and I have been friends for years. They were going to sell their cow to settle the bill, but she's all they have, so some of the other families and I chipped in a few laenes, and—"

"That was very generous, but really, you didn't have to. I gave Taler the tonic, and Lord Sactaren is making me pay for it." I see the pity in her eyes again, and while I appreciate her concern, I don't like to be pitied. I square my shoulders. "It was my choice," I tell her.

"I know, and that's why we can't have you suffering needlessly at the hands of that heartless mage. Thadyn was...a good man, but...he did as he was told, and if you didn't have the money, he wouldn't help. My cousin was bitten by a rotmouth a few years ago. She was brought here, but they were a few laenes short, so Thadyn turned them away. The doctor cut off her arm to keep the rot from spreading. She lived, but...no man will have her now. Can you imagine, being twenty and knowing that you will always be alone?" Yes, I can imagine. "Anyway, I just want you to know that we appreciate what you've done, and we'll do what we can to keep you safe from that horrible mage."

"Well..." I want to tell her that he's not all that bad, but it sounds like I'm the one who doesn't know what they're talking about. "Thank you, Mrs. ... " I realize I don't know her name.

"Raddis. But you can call me Calae." She smiles at me, her green eyes lingering on my face a little longer than I find comfortable. I shift my weight from one foot to the other and she looks away, down at her daughter. "And this is Iana."

"Iana," I whisper, leaning in to look down at her. "Like the goddess of the moon and stars, and protector of unicorns. I had a sister named for *her* sister, goddess of the wild places and the great beasts." Little Iana pushes back the blanket and reaches for me with one tiny hand, and without thinking, I reach up and let her grab my finger. She's strong; I can feel her grip even through my rows of calluses. I realize I shouldn't be touching that soft, perfect hand and I carefully pull my rough, gnarled finger away. "Well, I should probably—"

"Yes, I would hate to get you into any more trouble." She turns and casts a dark look up at the tower. "You know, if he didn't stay up there all the time, I don't think anyone would come to this shop. I know I wouldn't. But until he came down to buy you, it had been...ten years, maybe, since anyone I know had seen him." She lowers her voice and leans toward me. "He's old and ugly, right?"

"Uh, no," I say, the image of my master springing to mind, naked: his golden skin glistening, his body softly sculpted, his delicate features offset by large, exotic blue eyes... I feel myself flush. "He...uh...he uses magic, to-to make himself look...young." I don't have any idea how old he is, I realize with a start. I couldn't even begin to guess how old he *looks*. He's...ageless.

"I'm not surprised," she says with a sniff. "As if there isn't anything better he could be doing with his powers." Her eyes dart to me, then she turns and looks out over the valley. "A lot of people have been sick lately — weak, dizzy, can't keep food down..."

"I noticed," I say. Nearly half of our customers over the last few days complained of those very ailments. Schaff had me sell them marigold and field holly tea.

"I think the village might be cursed. Maybe you could mention that to the mage, if you think it won't get you into trouble."

"I'll see what I can do," I tell her. "Thank you again, for everything. I really have to get back before Schaff tells Lord Sactaren I've run off." I chuckle, but she doesn't seem to get that I'm kidding.

"Yes, yes, hurry," she says, taking several steps down the path. "Oh, I didn't mean to keep you so long. I'm sorry."

"It's all right," I call after her. "I was just... To see your daughter's smiling face was worth whatever he might do to me." I don't know why I say it. She's married with children, I'm a slave, but when she turns and smiles at me, I know I don't regret saying it.

With the basket over my arm, I slip the handful of coins into my pocket and I watch her disappear around the bend in the path. As I turn to head back into the shop, I glance up at the tower window. He's standing there again, leaning against the edge of the window, gazing northward, toward the dark forest they call the Rynnawood. I glance toward the forest and a dark speck catches my eye as it wings swiftly over the tops of the trees.

A raven, one of the big ones with the beaks that can crack a skull and wings like a midsummer thunderhead, climbs into the sky and soars over my head, croaking harshly as it back-wings to land on Lord Sactaren's outstretched arm. They disappear into the tower and I hurry back to the shop.

"Where have you been?" Schaff asks, sitting stiffly on top of the ledger, the white tip of his tail twitching as he narrows his gold eyes at me. "What have you got there?"

"Calae — I mean, Mrs. Raddis — the woman with the baby girl, she was coming up the path when I stepped outside." I set the basket on the counter. "She gave me this." I pull the checkered cloth off the top and the delicious aroma of new-baked bread wafts up, along with the tangy scent of ripe fruit. There's a loaf of bread, the crust glazed with honey, and muffins full of red berries, two different jars of jam, one apple and one blackberry, and a deep peach pie, the golden crust still warm to the touch.

"Well, well, looks like you made a friend," Schaff says, sticking his quivering nose deeper into the basket. "Dibs on the pie."

"Hang on a second," I say, grabbing him by the scruff. He growls and bares his teeth, but until I let go, there's not much he can do. "I thought saving that baby was all *my* doing."

"I helped," he points out.

"That is true," I say, taking the pie out of the basket. I set it on the counter in front of him. "But then you promptly slunk out of here and left me to take the heat all by myself, so it only makes sense that I enjoy this pie all by myself." His eyes follow the pie as I slide it away from him.

"Grrrr, get off me," he barks, swiping at me with claws out. He misses. "I knew Naeven would never do anything to you, you're—" He stops suddenly, his huge ears flicking up and down.

"I'm what?" I press, giving him a little shake.

Snarling, he rolls over, catching me by surprise. All four sets of claws latch into my arm and shred my sleeve, even drawing blood before I manage to let go and pull back. He stands up and shakes himself, his coat all fluffed out and angry looking.

"You're exactly what he wants," he says, jumping up onto the high shelf behind the counter. "Mmm, better than pie," he sneers, licking my blood out of his fur. "What else did she give you?"

"Oh." I almost forgot about the money. I dig the coins out of my pocket. "Not only did she pay what she owed, she gave me enough to cover the sick boy and the cow."

Schaff snorts as I open the ledger. "Peasants. Doesn't it ever occur to them *why* they're poor? You don't see Naeven giving stuff away; that's why he's the richest man on this planet."

"Really?" I ask. The castle's nice, especially the glimpse I've gotten of Lady Sactaren's half, but it's hardly the palace I'd expect of a truly wealthy man.

"Oh, yes, that's why he's in such desperate need of an heir. Should he die without one — and come on, it's a miracle he hasn't died already — all his wealth will become property of the government. Like the government needs any more of our money."

"So that's why he — what's the name of that tonic I gave the boy? — that's why he puts up with that — I mean, that's why he's married to Her Ladyship."

"Neverwort tonic. And whatever you were going to say can't be as bad as she is. And it's not a real marriage, it's a marriage contract, but yes, that's the *only* reason he's with her, if you get my drift."

"The only... Oh. Oh, you mean—"

"Like I said, you're exactly what he wants." Schaff smirks down at me, but I just shake my head and turn back to the books. Tell me something I don't know. "You don't believe me? Just wait, and then I'll say I told you so."

"Mrs. Raddis overpaid," I say, changing the subject. It's not that I don't believe him, it's that I don't want to find out that he's right. I'm not that fond of pain. "The tonic was only seven laenes, what should I do with these extra four?"

"Sounds like you got a tip," Schaff says. "Here's another one — put them in your pocket and shut up. I guess that's two tips, isn't it?"

"I can't take this money," I say. I wrap the coins in the checkered cloth and place it in the corner of the basket. "I'll give it back when I return her things to her."

"Oh yes, do that the next time Naeven allows you out to wander the village."

"Well, maybe she'll come back up here."

"Yeah, and maybe I'll suddenly sprout wings and fly north for the summer. Just keep it—"

"Schaff, come here." We both turn as Lord Sactaren's voice echoes down the stairway.

"Yes, M'Lord," Schaff barks, then growls under his breath, "I wonder what he wants now?"

"Maybe it has something to do with that bird," I say, closing the ledger with a smile. The shop is finally back in the black. Good, I was getting sick of the red ink. It looked like blood.

"What bird?" Schaff asks, leaping onto my shoulder and then to the counter.

"The one I saw fly to the tower window, a big old raven, I think... Hey, what is it?"

He hits the floor running and streaks up the stairs in a red blur, leaving me alone and confused, a condition I'm beginning to get used to in this place. I shrug and glance at the clock; still another hour until I can close shop, not that anyone *ever* comes up the mountain after three. I lean against the shelves behind the counter and shove my hands into my pockets, finding the pebbles I had stepped outside to get in the first place.

I slip into the back room and peek through the slats into Khas's crate. His eyes are closed and he's curled up in a ball, looking so much like a tan head of cabbage. I drop the handful of rocks into the straw beside him and turn back to the shop. I really wish I could find out what he eats—

"Ow!" Something bounces off the back of my head, hard enough to sting. I spin, and dodge to the left as a pebble flies past my ear. Khas has his face pressed between two slats, his bright black eyes fixed on me and a pebble in his paw. I step toward him and he reaches through the slats, throwing the rock at me. I deflect it with one hand. "I guess you don't eat rocks, then," I say.

He waves his paws at me. I snort and make a rude gesture in return. He blinks, then copies me. I make another, and he does the same. Curious, I squat down, bringing the crate to eye level. Khas peers at me, then makes a fist with one paw, holds the other out flat, touches his fist to his palm, and then opens his fist and slides his paws across each other. Raising one eyebrow, I mimic the gesture. He narrows his wide black eyes, grabs another pebble, and flings it at me, hitting me on the chin. I pick it up off the stone floor.

"So, you taught him to play fetch." Schaff bounds down the last few steps and into the room. "But, shouldn't *you* throw it and *he* go get it?"

"What did Lord Sactaren want?" I ask, ignoring his smart remarks.

Schaff trots past me and out into the shop. "Come with me. You need to lock up now and pack a bag. You and Naeven are going on a trip." I stand up, the rock slipping from my fingers and bouncing off the toe of my shoe.

"Just...the two of us?" I swallow, my mouth suddenly dry. I'm not afraid of him, not in the way that I have feared so many men, not any more, but in a different way, he is the most terrifying person I have ever known. I'm not afraid of what he will do to me; I'm afraid of what I might let him do, what I want him to do.

"You agreed to it," he reminds me unnecessarily. "Now move it." I lock the door to the shop and follow him down the hall to my room. "There's a knapsack in the bottom of the wardrobe. I'd take a change of clothes and a heavy cloak. Naeven says this won't take long, but you should be prepared to spend the night in the woods, just in case."

"The woods? Where are we going?" I ask as I dig the knapsack out from under several pairs of shoes and boots. It's not very big, but it's the only one in there.

"The north edge of the Rynnawood," Schaff says. "The Green Mage, Besteth, has a little problem, and needs Naeven's help."

"What sort of problem?"

Schaff shrugs his tail. "Naeven will explain; it's a complicated...thing."

I cram a pair of socks and a heavy tunic into the bag, surprised when I have room for a pair of pants. It should be full now, but it's not. Curious, I grab a black cloak out of the wardrobe and begin to feed it into the knapsack. It fits easily. I grab a jacket and stuff that in there too.

"Yes, yes, it's a magic bag, okay?" Schaff barks. "Can we get moving, please? Knowing you, you'll want to grab some food for the trip, and knowing him, he's already waiting in the courtyard."

Throwing the bag over my shoulder, I start for the kitchens, then turn and run back to the shop, grabbing the honey bread and several muffins out of the basket. I stare longingly at the pie for a moment, but I don't imagine pie travels very well, so I leave it on the counter. I glance in at Khas, curled up in the corner of the crate, and sigh. I wish I knew what do about him.

"Don't worry," Schaff says from the doorway, "I'll take good care of everything while you're gone." Right, like I can trust *that* face.

"You better not eat anything of mine," I warn him, hitching the strap of the bag higher onto my shoulder.

"Or you'll do what?" he sneers. I open my mouth, then close it again. "That's what I thought. Now get out of here. Naeven's waiting." I grab the pie and hurry into the back room, placing it on the top shelf of an empty cupboard and shutting the door. "Like that's going to stop me," I hear him mutter. Scowling, I step over him and head down the hall. Schaff may be my only friend, but that doesn't mean that I wouldn't love to kick him square in the tail sometimes.

I shove open the courtyard door and step through, squinting against the suddenly blinding noonday sun. The smell of grass and pine surrounds me, and I hear birdsong and the whisper of wind through trees. This is *not* the bare stone courtyard I was expecting. I'm standing in the middle of a field of wildflowers, several of which I recognize from the various potions and salves my master has had me prepare the last two evenings. To my right, about an hour's walk distant, stands a shadowy forest, the trees massively tall and straight, not like anything I've seen before. Across the meadow and several days journey away, rise a line of mountains, one beside the next, like jagged teeth rising out of the earth.

"Hey! Did you get lost?" I turn to see Schaff standing in the doorway behind me. No wall, just a doorway, standing in the middle of the field. Even for a mage's castle, this is pretty strange.

"What-what is this?" I ask.

Schaff steps off the flagstone floor of the castle and into the grass, stretching and tearing at the ground with his claws. "You've never seen a world gate before?"

"Well...yeah, but — I thought gates were grouped in complexes. I didn't know somebody could have one in the middle of a castle."

"Well now you do. He's got several, in fact. Now c'mon, Naeven's—"

"Where are we?" I ask. "What world?" I've never seen a sky this blue before.

"Daron, okay? Now get your stupid ass back to *our* world before Naeven comes looking for you."

"Too late."

My heart skips a beat at the sound of that silky, seductive voice. Lord Sactaren steps into the doorway, his golden skin radiant in the sunlight, the silver in his hair glowing like starshine. He's right, you can see the scar.

"I'm sorry, M'Lord," I say, dropping my eyes not so much out of fear as out of habit. And because if I look at him too long, my imagination gets my body into trouble. "I stepped through the wrong door."

"I would have brought you here eventually," he says, "so there's no harm done. But come, we must get going; time is of the essence."

I hurry after him as he sweeps down the hall, his hair fanning out behind him like a silken cloak. "M'Lord," I say, "what is so urgent? Schaff said it was only a little problem."

"And what have I told you about Schaff?"

I smile ruefully. "I can only believe half of what he says, half of the time."

We enter the true courtyard, full of bitterly cold mountain air and late afternoon shadows, and not much else. As we cross the cracked flagstones, Qito, the...*thing*...that looks after the animals leans through the only doorway in the north wall, two sets of reins in one of his many hands.

"*Dikoti, Qito,*" Sactaren says, taking the reins from him. Qito makes a chattering sound and disappears back into the blackness beyond the open doorway.

I can't imagine keeping an animal in such dismal conditions, inside, in the dark, but the two bull elk that Sactaren leads into the courtyard look none the worse for it. The rattle of their hooves echoes off the bleak walls and one of them looks at me and snorts, tossing his head and slashing the air with his antlers. I've never seen an elk saddled and bridled before, but I can't be that surprised. After all, he's also got a unicorn in there somewhere.

The larger of the two elk stands still and proud, his gleaming antlers spreading over his back, seven sharp spikes on each side. I can barely see over his back, and his shoulders and rump are silvered. The other has only four points on each side, and our shoulders are just about even. His coat is a dark gray, each hair tipped with gold, and his rump is the color of old ivory.

"Can you ride?" Sactaren asks, handing me the reins of the smaller beast.

"I've never been offered the chance, M'Lord," I admit, standing at the end of the leather reins to keep out of reach of those wicked antlers. "I'm willing to learn, though."

"Well, you'll have to get closer than that," my master says with a hint of a smile. "That is Goar, the son of Bari." He pats the larger elk on the shoulder and Bari leans down to nibble at Sactaren's neck. Goar flicks an ear back and gives me a look that clearly says, "Touch me and I'll kill you." Great.

"I-I don't think he likes me, M'Lord," I say.

Sactaren walks over and grabs the reins close to Goar's head. "Goar doesn't like anybody, but he'll follow his sire into the bowels of Silrath. Now come on, mount up."

Even with his help, I nearly end up sprawled on the flagstones under the elk's hooves. Still, once I'm astride, with a thousand pounds of lean muscle and solid bone beneath me, I understand why noblemen ride. I feel powerful, looking down on my master, if only for a moment. He swings effortlessly onto the back of the larger bull and turns Bari's head toward the open gate. Goar follows without a single command from me, much to my relief. I can sit back in the saddle, relax, and enjoy the scenery.

What do I know? As soon as we're out of the courtyard, Sactaren urges Bari into a quick trot, which, unlike their easy, rolling walk, bounces me all over the place. My teeth rattle in my head as we pass the far corner of the castle and head north down a steep, rocky slope. I don't think even a unicorn could pick its way down this dizzying stretch of near vertical mountainside. If I could relax my death-grip on the saddle horn long enough to stretch out my arm, I would be able to touch the face of the slope with my hand; that is how steep it is. I stare at the back of Goar's head, at the fur between his antlers, and mutter solemn prayers under my breath.

We make it to the valley floor in one piece, although the backs of my thighs and my ass are already aching from this nightmare of a ride. I'm wondering how it could get worse — because in my experience, nothing is ever bad enough that it can't get worse — when Sactaren again urges Bari to go faster, this time bounding across the open fields of heather and mint and clover. Goar flicks his ears and leaps after them. My head snaps backward, then I'm nearly thrown between the spreading antlers. I fall across his shoulders, one arm wrapping around his neck. I hang on for dear life, but quickly realize that the rocking motion is less if I sit closer to his shoulders. It's hardly comfortable, but it beats walking, I suppose. We cover ground faster than I could ever run, and before I even realize it, we're approaching the western edge of the Rynnawood.

Sactaren reins in Bari and Goar skids to a stop beside him, just beyond the shadow of the great forest. I've never been inside this great Wood, but I've heard plenty of tales about it. Some say the first tree was planted by Maele at the dawn of the world, some say the heart of the forest is older than any other living creature, some say the trees can speak, some say they bleed, some say that no one who enters the wood intent upon harming it ever returns. I suppose I don't really believe any of the stories, but I hope we don't mean the wood any harm, just in case.

"Lark," Sactaren says, staring at the wood, "do you know what makes this forest so special?"

I think about the stories, and then shake my head. "No, M'Lord."

"You see these little trees all along the edge here?" He nudges Bari over beside one of the saplings. The tree is barely taller than me, mounted as I am on the elk. Sactaren reaches out and touches a single, strange limb with no branches or leaves or kinks whatsoever, arching out of the tree's center and back into the forest. "This is this tree's lifeline," he tells me. "It connects it to that larger one back there." I look and see what he's talking about. The twenty foot tree has several of these "lifelines" reaching out to the saplings. "Have you ever seen a strawberry plant, Lark?"

"Yes, M'Lord, lots of them." I spent nearly a whole summer picking strawberries on a plantation down south. Even so, I love the smell of that sweet red fruit, though to this day, I have never tasted one. I had been beaten enough by then, that when they told us anyone caught eating the strawberries would be punished, and then showed us the broken, rotting corpse of the last slave who did, I had no desire to tempt Fate.

"Then you know that strawberry plants will send out runners along the ground, which root and produce new plants. These trees reproduce in a similar fashion. However, while you can cut the strawberry free and it will continue to live, severing one of these lifelines will kill the tree. I discovered that several years ago." He turns Bari and heads into the shadowy woods, Goar following close behind.

"So," I say, looking up at the thick, leafless branches arching above my head, "that means each of these trees is connected to another. It *is* one giant living thing."

"Correct. It's the largest life form I've ever come across. About three million acres, I think."

That's a lot. But if each tree grew from another tree... "Where did the first tree come from?"

"No one knows," Sactaren says, glancing back at me. "It's the stuff of myth and legend. This forest was here long before man came to this land and, Maele willing, it'll be here long after we're gone. I've estimated the heart tree is close to two and a half million years old. It's four thousand feet tall, with probably another hundred feet lost to lightning strikes, and would take you twenty minutes to walk around the trunk."

"Wow," I whisper. The forest rises far over my head now, the dense leaves and branches blocking out nearly all light from above. It's a gloomy sort of twilight, like the hour before dawn or after sunset. "Are we going to see this tree, M'Lord?"

"No. Fortunately, the trouble lies at the edge of the wood, not its heart."

"If I may ask, Lord Sactaren, what *is* the trouble?"

"A salamander," he says, and my hands tighten on the saddle horn, my mouth suddenly dry. "It wandered in from the lava flats this morning. Besteth tried to turn it back toward the wastes, but he's a Green Mage, trained in the ways of plants and flowers and trees. He's no match for the fire of a salamander."

"And we are?" I ask in a small voice.

He laughs, that soft, slippery sound that creeps over my skin and reminds me that there are greater threats than salamanders. "I am," he tells me, "and with me, so too are you. Don't worry, I know what I'm doing."

I do not doubt that. Whether he's mixing potions or reaching around me for some ingredient, nothing he does is ever by accident.

We ride in silence for a moment, just the muted sound of Bari and Goar's footsteps, the low rumble of their breathing, the whisper of wind through the trees. "It's about another hour's ride," Sactaren says at last. "If there's something you want to ask me, now would be a good time."

An hour is not nearly enough time to answer all the questions I have, but it's a start.

"Please, M'Lord, *how* do you plan on killing a salamander?"

"I don't." I raise my eyebrows. "Salamanders are too rare to kill needlessly. No, I plan on capturing it and returning it to the lava flats, where it will cause no further trouble."

"But-but the fire burns though everything it touches; it melts solid steel, even stone. How—"

"There is one thing it will not burn." He turns in the saddle to regard me. I try to think, but I've never heard of anything that will withstand the incredible heat of salamander fire. I shake my head. "Its own skin, perhaps?" I open my mouth, and close it again. "Years ago, and hundreds of miles from here, a salamander burned across a vast grassland, into fields of crops, through a village, and was headed toward a great city. I could not turn it, and every attempt to catch it failed. As the fires licked at the city walls, I was forced to kill the creature, but I made sure that I would never be forced to do the same again. I crafted a net from strips of the salamander's skin, and that should work to contain and transport it."

"Should? You haven't tested it?"

"I haven't had the chance. Like I said, salamanders are rare creatures."

"Forgive me, M'Lord, but even if your net works, we'll be burnt to ash before we even get close enough to see it."

"Relax, Lark," he says with a chuckle, "I have it all worked out."

He doesn't elaborate and I decide not to press. If we're going to walk through the fires of Hell, I would rather not have him irritated at me.

"Why do you have a doorway to another planet in your castle?" I ask after a moment.

"I think you'll find I have doorways to a lot of places," he says quietly. "To answer your question — I like Traxen, I like living by the sea, I like living on the mountain, but the valley is a poor place to grow anything. The soil is old and worn from a hundred years of farming. You saw Daron — that soil is rich and fertile. I harvest herbs, flowers, roots; just about everything I need comes from off-world. And what I don't use personally, the other mages pay handsomely for."

"Schaff said you were rich," I say without thinking. I grimace and hope I haven't offended him. He laughs, but that may not mean anything.

"Schaff would," he says. "Yes, I am rich, which is why it was no hardship to pay what I did for you. And so far, you've been worth every laene."

His tone makes the short hairs on the back of my neck prickle. Most of the time, I can make myself believe that he doesn't have some wicked plan for me, that he's not just biding his time, waiting for the spell to do its work and drive me into his bed. Most of the time. And then there are the times when I'll glance at him across the worktable, or standing before the fire, or walking across the room, and I feel the magic coursing through my blood, exciting my body in ways that leave me embarrassed and uncomfortable. Those times, I know that everything about him, his clothes, his choice of words, his tone of voice, the very way he breathes, it's all meant to seduce me, and by Cheyn's dark hand, it's working.

"Something troubling you?" my master asks. "You've been very quiet."

I draw a heavy breath. "No, M'Lord, I was just thinking about the salamander."

"No, you weren't." I cringe. I know better than to try and lie to him. "It makes no difference, Lark, a man has a right to his own thoughts. I'll leave you to them, if you like, but if you need a bit of distraction as much as I do, I could continue telling you about the Wild Kings."

The previous evening, Sactaren had started telling me tales of the lords of the animal realm — first Iaaeh, King of the Great Eagles, a noble and fierce warrior who lives at the top of a lonely mountain; then Arin, King of the Wolves, a silent hunter and soulful singer dwelling deep in a wild wood; and finally Chaelea, King of the Unicorns, a gentle and wise guardian of a misty valley in a land beyond the sea. I don't know why he's telling me, but I expect the knowledge will come in handy at some point, and the stories are interesting.

"Please, M'Lord, do continue. My thoughts aren't important." The words have barely left my lips when he reins Bari in hard, stopping the big elk dead in his tracks. Goar nearly walks into his sire's rump, and shuffles sideways, snorting in annoyance. Lord Sactaren turns in the saddle, his eyes glittering pale gray in the failing light.

"Your thoughts are part of who you are," he tells me, his voice tight with that impossible restraint, holding back that great storm that I know will one day break free. I just hope I'm long dead before that day comes. "They are the one thing that no man can take from you, no man can control, no matter how hard they might try. Think what you like, Lark; no one but you will ever know what lies inside your head, but I can guarantee that it *is* important, if only to you, and that is enough."

"Yes, M'Lord," I say, nodding my head once. If only he knew.

He sighs and faces forward again, slapping the reins lightly against the sides of Bari's neck. We have barely begun to move again when he pulls the elk to a stop, his head tilted slightly to one side, listening. I hear it, faintly above the trees, the harsh call of a raven. After a moment, he turns Bari's head to the left and spurs him forward.

"The salamander has changed direction," he calls back to me as Goar breaks into a trot to catch up. I groan as my battered backside bounces up and down on the hard saddle. "It's headed this way. We should intercept it in less than twenty minutes."

"The raven told you that?" I ask, relieved when Goar slows back to a walk, his head even with his sire's flank.

"Yes. Years ago I earned the gift of tongues from Carrak, the King of Ravens, a fearless and brazen bird, more than twice the size of his largest subjects. He's so old, the feathers at his throat and around his eyes have silvered..."

I listen, but my thoughts are wandering. We ride toward the fire of a salamander when every other creature on the planet would run the other way, and all I can think about is the soft touch of my master's hands, and running my own hands over his flawless body, exploring his hidden scars. Perhaps dying in the fire would be best.

Chapter 8

I can smell smoke, faintly at first, but it grows stronger, that thick scent of wet wood, full of sap. It makes my chest tight and I fight not to cough. The trees around us have been growing smaller for some time; we're nearing the northern edge of the wood. I think that's where the Green Mage is waiting for us. I don't see anyone as we ride out into the bronze light of evening, the sun hidden behind a thick cloud of smoke hanging low over the scorched grassland. This far from the sea, there's no wind to blow it away. Farther north, I can see the dark, jagged lava flats, the natural home of the salamander, and where we'll have to go, assuming we live that long.

"That's far enough," booms a deep, rolling voice that surrounds us like a peal of thunder. A week ago, I would have been terrified, but now I know a voice trick when I hear one. "Who are you and what is your business in the realm of the Green Mage?"

Goar snorts and stamps a front hoof as Lord Sactaren turns Bari back toward the forest.

"Besteth," he calls into the trees, "you know me and you know why I'm here. Stop wasting time and show yourself."

Goar suddenly leaps sideways, and I grab at one bony antler to keep from being thrown to the ground. He doesn't like that. Kicking out with his back feet, he shakes his head from side to side, and I fly over his shoulder and land on *my* shoulder in the soft prairie dirt.

"Goar, stop!" Sactaren orders, and I look back at the young bull, a white ring showing around his large brown eyes, his head lowered and antlers slashing the air. My master rides Bari in between the angry elk and me, trying to catch hold of the reins. "Lark, are you okay?" he calls over his shoulder.

"Fine, M'Lord," I answer, pushing myself up into a sitting position. My nice green shirt is smeared with mud. At least the grass stains don't show. I try to stand, but my legs are stiff and sore.

Suddenly, a hand is in front of my face, pale and slender, like a woman's. Offering the hand is a lithe young man — young like Sactaren, as in, I couldn't begin to guess his age — clothed in nothing but thin green vines bearing dark green, spade-shaped leaves and blue, violet, and silver trumpet-shaped flowers. Very small leaves and flowers. Meaning he is practically naked. His skin is as pale as milk, but looks fresh, luminous, not sickly or pallid. I've never seen eyes as green as his, green like new grass, like budding leaves, the color that makes you think of spring, and his hair — not as long or as thick as my master's — is silver-green, like spun moonlight. His features are not remarkable, and I find him neither handsome, nor beautiful, though with Sactaren always on my mind, I doubt any man will ever strike me as he has.

"Lord Sactaren?" I call, hesitant to take the offered hand. Maele only knows what a mage can do to you with just a touch. Behind the Green Mage, I see my master bring Bari's head around.

"Do not touch him," Sactaren says in a low voice, walking the elk into Besteth and forcing the pale man to step back. "You beg for my help and I leave my affairs to ride to your aid, and then you would dare to lay your hand upon my assistant without my permission? I should leave your Wood to burn."

"Relax, Traxen Mage," Besteth says, his tone just shy of mocking as he addresses my master. "I meant him no harm. Had I known you were so possessive of this one... Who is he?"

I climb stiffly to my feet and brush the grass and moist earth from my clothes. Sactaren backs Bari up until I am standing at his knee.

"Lark is my new assistant. Lark, this is Lord Jan Besteth, the Green Mage, master of the Rynnawood."

I nod respectfully. Besteth regards me with one eyebrow raised. "What happened to Thadyn? He wasn't killed, was he?"

"I grew tired of him," Sactaren says shortly. "Where is *your* assistant?"

"You know how your reputation precedes you, Sactaren. She stayed at my castle so you couldn't steal her away to bear you an heir." He smirks, and I don't like him. I glance toward the forest, where a column of thick, gray smoke rises up from less than a mile in. I don't know why we're just standing here, trading veiled insults while the Wood burns. "How is the little wife, anyway?"

"Spirited. How is your son?" Besteth's face darkens. "Oh, have you not been able to lift the curse? I apologize for my thoughtlessness. Now, shall we get on with this?" He swings down from the saddle and hands me Bari's reins before walking within arm's length of the Green Mage. The big elk looks at me for a moment, then lowers his head to the grass and begins to graze. Goar, reins trailing on the ground between his feet, makes a wide circle around the two mages and stops at his sire's side, pawing the ground restlessly.

"Are you sure you can handle this, Traxen Mage?" There it is again, that mocking tone.

"Watch yourself," Sactaren says quietly, his eyes hard as chips of stone. "I *will* leave you to burn. I already have your favor once, and I have yet to need your help; I cannot imagine calling on you twice in my lifetime, but I do enjoy having you in my debt. You remember what that feels like, right, Besteth?"

"Let's get on with this," Besteth says between his teeth.

I watch as Sactaren rolls up his right sleeve, baring his arm to the elbow, and then offers his hand to Besteth. The Green Mage places his hand in Sactaren's, palm up. The two mages stare at each other, eyes locked together, and I feel a stillness settle over the grassland, like the calm before a storm. The air is thick, heavy, and my skin itches. Sactaren reaches behind his back with his free hand, up under the edge of his loose tunic, and pulls out a long, slim, silver dagger. Besteth moves slightly, widening his stance, but his green eyes never leave Sactaren's blue ones.

I jump as my master drives the dagger through Besteth's palm, and then on through his own. Neither makes a sound, but their lips are pressed thin and white, their eyes tight with lines of pain. I'm breathing as sharp and shallow as they are; the air presses in around me, making my heart pound. Blood, thick and dark, begins to drip slowly from the dagger point onto the grass.

"By Mage's blood, this pact is made," they chant together, "help freely given, shall be freely repaid."

There's a sound, like rushing water, and a gust of wind crashes into me from behind, nearly knocking me off my feet. The wind whirls around the two mages, lifting dry grass into the air, and there's a flash of light as Besteth takes hold of the dagger and pulls it out of their hands. The wind dies, leaving the grassland silent and still in the last light of evening.

"It was a pleasure seeing you again, Besteth, as always," Sactaren says, taking back his blade and slipping it into the sheath at the back of his belt.

"The pleasure was all mine, I'm sure," Besteth replies.

The Green Mage flexes his hand, and I can see no blood or wound or scar upon him. I take another look at him, moonlight pale and barely clothed in vines, and I wonder what sort of scars *he's* hiding. I'll probably never know. They turn away from each other, Sactaren walking toward Goar, Besteth heading for the forest.

"All right, Lark," he says briskly, grabbing up Goar's reins, "tell me what just happened."

"Well, M'Lord," I say as he begins running his hands up and down Goar's foreleg, "it looked like you and Lord Besteth made a blood oath."

I watch as his long, thin fingers explore the elk's ankle, sliding up the back of his leg, fanning out at his shoulder. I tear my eyes away before my body starts getting any funny ideas, glancing around for the Green Mage, but he's gone.

"That's what it looked like," he says, moving to the hind leg. "What did it *feel* like?"

"It-it felt like...magic." A memory of that heavy, prickling feeling passes over my skin and I shudder, because it should have been an unpleasant feeling, and it wasn't. As a mage's assistant, I should be glad I like the feeling of the otherworldly power racing over me, filling my lungs with every breath I take, coursing through my blood with every beat of my pounding heart, and perhaps in time I will be, but for now, I shudder.

"It was an old kind of magic, one that is rarely used, except between mages over matters of some importance. Aha, there you are." He straightens up, what looks like a small stone held in the palm of his hand. Bari is still grazing, and I lean across the back of his neck to see what Sactaren has. It's a cocklebur. "This is what made Goar throw you — this and that vindictive mage, the Master of the Green Magic." Now *his* tone is mocking. I'm beginning to think these two men don't like each other very much.

"M'Lord, how could a—"

"Besteth has mastery over all life which grows in the soil and feeds from the sun. It's no difficult trick to make a cocklebur bite hard enough to upset a hot-tempered beast." He flicks it out into the grass. "And now that the pleasantries have been observed, we can get to work. Mount up, Lark." I groan inwardly at the thought of subjecting my body to any more punishment, but clamber awkwardly into the saddle without a sound. "It's just a short ride," Sactaren assures me with a secret smile. I'm going to have to work harder at keeping my thoughts off my face. One of these days, they're really going to get me into trouble.

Smoke drifts between the trees like a swarm of wraiths, and I pull the collar of my shirt up over my mouth and nose, but that doesn't help the stinging in my eyes. Flashes of heat roll over me as the wind shifts, bringing with it the muted roar of a great fire. I'm trembling inside, deep in the pit of my stomach, and my sweaty hands clutch at the saddle horn. Goar keeps close to his sire, and both of them seem nervous, their ears flicking back and forth, steps hesitant. Sactaren finally reins in the elk and we sit as the heat licks across our skin constantly now, that roar filling my ears. Bits of soot and ash settle on my clothes and on the short coats of the elk, and ahead of us, between the trees, I can see a faint, dull red glow.

Sactaren swings down from Bari's back and begins taking the gear off the elk. Never having deliberately dismounted an elk before, I try to mimic Sactaren's motions, and somehow wind up on my ass in the dirt. I climb to my feet and brush the old leaves from my clothes.

"Would you take Goar's saddle and bridle off, please?" Sactaren asks.

"Of course, M'Lord." When the gear is piled at the foot of a spreading tree, Sactaren rubs each animal on the nose, speaking softly to Bari, then whacks the big bull on the rump. Both elk take off, bounding out of sight toward the edge of the forest. "E-excuse me, Lord Sactaren, but...how are we going to get home?"

"There's no guarantee we *will* be going home," he says, and my stomach tightens into a knot. "Should we fail, I don't want them burdened with saddle and bridle. Life is hard enough." *No kidding*, I think to myself. "Don't worry, I don't intend to fail." I force a faint smile. I don't think he's convinced. That's okay, neither am I.

He turns to the pile of gear and drops to one knee, opening a battered knapsack about the same size as mine, strapped to the back of his saddle. I hadn't even noticed it before this. Shows how distracted I've been.

From the knapsack he pulls a crystal lantern, which he lights and hangs from a branch overhead, casting dancing shadows across the ground. Next, he removes a thick cloak, which he spreads on the forest floor beside him. Upon this, he lays out two small leather pouches, a silver bowl, a wooden spoon, a large earthen jar almost as big as my head, a net made from strips of dull, scaly orange skin, and two pairs of thick goggles, the straps made from more of that orange skin and the lenses from an amber-gray glass.

"All right, Lark, time to remove our clothes," he says, rising to his feet. He pulls his tunic off over his head and drops it on the cloak. His belt joins it, then both shoes. I watch, fascinated and terrified. What is going on? How is this going to stop that salamander? "Do you need assistance?" he asks, glancing at me as he slips his trousers down.

I drop my eyes to the ground. "No, M'Lord, I-I don't..." I swallow noisily and begin to unbutton my shirt. "Why do we..."

"Need to be naked?"

My fingers fumble with the buttons as his voice caresses me, touches me, teases me, and my face burns as my body reacts. Damn him and his magic tricks. He can use his power to excite me all he wants, but we both know that it's just the spell. It's not real. I say to hell with the buttons and pull the shirt off over my head, throwing it down onto the cloak at my feet. When he speaks again, his voice is normal.

"I have in this jar a salve that will protect us from the flames." Out of the corner of my eye, I see him kneel on the cloak and remove the skin from the mouth of the jar. The cool scent of mint fills the air. "Unfortunately, the magic only works on skin. Anything else will catch fire or melt."

I pull off my shoes and glance at him. He's scooping a pale green salve into the silver bowl. Taking a bracing breath, I drop my pants and kick them into the pile with the rest of my things. Thank Maele, I'm not as erect as I had feared, but he will definitely notice, if he looks. He doesn't even glance at me, instead opening one of the leather pouches and shaking a small amount of bright red powder into the salve in the bowl.

"What is that?" I ask, clenching my teeth as I draw his attention to me. His cool eyes start at my feet and move to my head, slowly, lingering on every inch of my body. Finally, he nods and turns back to the salve, using the handle of the spoon to mix the powder in.

"This is powdered root of koetran. It causes the salve to dry quickly and not rub off." He sticks the spoon end back in the big jar and stands up, the bowl in his hand. "Turn around, please."

I do as I'm told, looking out into the black forest, slivers of orange showing more brightly between the trees. I hear him approach, and start to tremble. *He won't hurt me*, I tell myself again and again, but I've been lied to often enough that I can't trust anyone, not even myself. I tense as something cold and moist touches my back, then I feel his fingers, sliding across my skin, over my scars. It takes a moment for me to realize that he's rubbing the salve on my back, where I would have a hard time putting it.

He reaches around my arm and offers me the bowl. "Hold this, please." I take it, and he dips both hands back into the minty smelling salve. His hands are firm, but gentle, moving swiftly over my shoulders and up the back of my neck. I try to hate it, hate him, for what he's doing, for what his spell is making me feel, but I had no idea that another's touch could feel so good, magic or not.

"Go ahead and start rubbing it on yourself," Sactaren says, reaching around me to scoop more salve from the bowl. His fingers, where the salve has already dried, are a chalky white. "Unless you *want* me to do it all."

My breath catches in my throat as his hands slide down my spine, stopping just below my waist and then working their way back up, spreading the salve across my back. I try to swallow, but my mouth is dry and tastes of smoke and ash. My skin is hot to the touch as I start applying the salve to my chest, my hands shaking. My heart is pounding, blood surging through my veins, and I am swiftly aware that my slight arousal has not gone away. In fact, it's getting worse.

"There," Sactaren says suddenly, making me jump, "I think you can get the rest yourself." He steps in front of me and takes the silver bowl, dipping his fingers in and beginning to spread it across his own chest. I want to cover myself, I want to run away, but I can't move, the thought of what he might do to me rooting me to the spot. Without looking, he holds the bowl out toward me, but I just stare at it. "Come on, Lark, it's getting dry, I..." He glances at me, then his eyes travel down my body and I see a hint of rose color his golden skin. "Enjoying yourself?" he asks with a smirk.

"No, no, M'Lord, I-I'm not—"

"No," he says, his smirk fading into a slight frown, "you're not." I flinch as he reaches for me, his fingertips touching my cheek, drawing forth the strangest sensation; it's like a thick liquid, both hot and cold, moving underneath my skin. I gasp and pull away. "Damn it," he mutters, "not again." My heart pounds in my throat, strangling my words as I try to speak.

"Wha-what is going on?" I ask. He reaches for my arm now, and I jerk away without thinking.

"Lark," he says softly, "please give me your hand and I will explain." I hesitate, then hold out my hand. He takes it and steps closer to me. "Sometimes, some people react to magic this way. It happens to me occasionally. The magical property of the salve causes this..." he touches my arm with his right hand, and that hot/cold liquid sensation follows the path of his fingertips, only now I can see the blue light glowing beneath my skin, "...to build up in your system. Mages call it salyr a'havon — literally 'the price we pay'. It's not dangerous — there's a little of it in everyone, all the time, but when it becomes concentrated, this can happen."

"But...*why*? Why..." I glance down at myself, "why this?"

"I'm not sure," he says, letting go of my hand and turning away. The salve in the bowl has dried and he bangs it out against a tree root, then fills the bowl again from the jar. "When this first happened to me, I was told that it was the gods' way of keeping us humble, of reminding us that for all our power, they have the last laugh. That may be, but some of us now believe that the salyr a'havon somehow mimics the same chemicals that make us feel lust, fear, rage, despair — any of the primal emotions. Why it usually manifests as lust is still a mystery, but it's better than being consumed by a mindless, numbing terror that steals your sanity, don't you think?"

"If you say so, M'Lord," I say softly.

He sighs and walks back over to me, a fresh bowl of salve in his hand. "I'm sorry, Lark," he says, and I can tell he means it. "If I could do this myself, I would send you out to wait with the elk, but I can't. I need you." He holds out the silver bowl.

More salve, more magic, more lust. I guess it's not that bad, once I get past the embarrassment of it. That's the worst. But if it saves the Wood, I guess it's worth a little embarrassment. If that's the price I have to pay, I can live with that. I dip my hand into the bowl and get started covering my arms.

We work in silence for several minutes. I have done both arms, both legs and am starting on my face when Sactaren hands me the bowl. "Keep it away from your eyes," he tells me, "or it may blind you. That's what the goggles are for." He wipes his hands on his hips, trying to remove the excess salve. "And make sure you work it into your scalp. I'm afraid your hair cannot be saved; the salve only works on skin."

I run my fingers through the stubble on my head, then his words hit me and I look at him in horror. His hair will burn, too. That beautiful, thick black hair, with its silver and turquoise, the charms and feathers, all will be reduced to ash. I'm tempted to reach out and touch it, run my fingers through it, just once before it's gone. Sactaren catches me looking and smirks.

"Don't fret, Lark. I haven't been able to grow a head of hair since before you were born, and it never looked this nice, believe me." He reaches up and twines his fingers into the hair at his temples, wincing as he jerks it loose from his skull. My eyes widen as he peels his scalp off, leaving his head red and raw, and glistening wetly in the light of the lantern. He turns away and gently lays his hair across his pile of clothes, his hands gliding the length of it before he stands and walks back to me.

Much of his fluid grace is gone without the rippling cloak of raven hair trailing down his back, but even with his raw skull leaking thin trails of blood down his cheek and the side of his neck, I have never seen a more beautiful man in my life. Standing before me, he dips his hands in the salve and rubs it over his head, smearing thick lumps of clotted blood and thin, amber colored liquid across his forehead and neck. I reach up and wipe it away and he glances at me. I just scoop up more salve and begin putting it on his back, as he did for me. I run my rough hands over his hidden scars, shocked by the size of some of them. He has a crater in the meaty part of his back, just below his left shoulder blade, that I could fit my entire fist into. I can only imagine how much that must have hurt.

"How are you doing?" he asks after a moment.

"Almost finished, M'Lord," I say.

He chuckles. "I meant, how are you doing, with the salyr a'havon?"

Oh. I feel my face flush. "It-it's awkward," I say. I'm tempted to slip behind a tree and let my hand grant me a little relief, but the thought of doing so with my master just a few feet away — so close, close enough that it needn't be my rough fingers stroking my flesh, it could be his, soft and smooth, those long fingers that always know exactly what they're doing... The forest spins around me and I clutch at his shoulders to keep from falling.

"Are you okay?" he asks, looking over his shoulder.

"I'm sorry, M'Lord," I say, letting go and staggering back. "I just got dizzy all of a sudden."

"I'm not surprised," he says, sounding faintly amused. He takes my arm and walks me to the cloak. "Sit."

"I'm fine, M'Lord, really," I say, but he gives me a gentle push toward the ground.

"Sit. The salve needs to be applied to your feet anyway." He takes a seat beside me and brushes dirt and leaves from the bottom of his foot before coating it with a thick layer of the salve. He stares out into the Wood as he waits for it to dry. My feet are so tough from a lifetime barefoot, I doubt even salamander fire will hurt them, but I slather the salve on good and thick none the less. "Once we're into the fire," he says suddenly, "it's imperative you only breathe through your mouth. The heat will be so intense, it will sear your lungs in an instant and leave you to suffocate if you don't. It may be hard to see. My goggles aren't perfect, but they'll keep the jelly in your eyes from boiling. Don't take them off. My salve will protect you from the fire, but *don't* touch the creature itself. My magic is no match for its deadly skin."

"So, how do you plan on catching it, exactly?" I ask after we switch feet.

"We find it, we throw the net over it, we carry it back to the lava flats."

"Oh." I guess I had been expecting something a bit more magical.

"I find that the simpler a plan is, the less there is that can go wrong. Of course, a lot can still go wrong." He draws a slow breath and lets it out between his teeth, softly hissing. "All right, let's get this done." We stand and he looks me over from head to toe. "Unless you want it burnt off..." he says, looking pointedly at my engorged flesh, "you better get some salve on that."

I know. I'm just afraid touching myself is going to get messy. I think if Sactaren *looks* hard at me, I might spill my seed on the forest floor. He holds the bowl out to me and nods his head toward a tree just lit by the pale lantern light. "You might want to do it over there." I feel my face burn, but dab my fingers in the salve and head for the dark side of the tree.

I grit my teeth and rub the salve on my flesh and down between my legs, making sure to cover my sack and work it through the stiff hair at my groin. The touch of my own hand makes my knees feel like rubber. I lean against the trunk of the tree, each short breath burning in my throat. I finally have my skin covered in salve, and I groan as I wrap my hand around myself and give my flesh a few short strokes. That's all it takes and my head snaps back as my seed splatters on the trunk of the tree, glowing a soft, ghostly blue as it drips toward the ground. I stare at it, my breath ragged in my chest, and then slowly back away.

"It glows," I say as I stumble back into the lantern light. Sactaren looks up from a bowl of fresh salve, one eyebrow raised. I point back toward tree. "I-I... M'Lord, it glows *blue*."

He nods and finishes stirring the salve. "Found a little relief, did you? It's only temporary, I'm afraid. Until we can wash the salve off, the magic will just build up in your system again." He rises and turns toward me. "As for your glowing ejaculate, salyr a'havon must be expelled through bodily fluids: blood, sweat, saliva, bile, tears...or semen. Blood is painful, and the others are practically useless. Semen is over quickly and doesn't have to be unpleasant. I'll leave the decision up to you, though. If you want me to bleed you, I will."

"No, no blood, please," I say quickly. I've bled enough for two lifetimes.

"All right, then. Now come over here, into the light more. I'm going to inspect every inch of your body, Lark, and then I want you to do the same for me. This is very important, do you understand?" I nod. He reaches out and touches the slick burn scar on my jaw. "Did that hurt to get?"

"Very much, M'Lord."

"Salamander fire doesn't hurt, you know. It's so hot, it kills the nerves before they can register the pain." He takes my hand and lifts my arm out away from my body, inspecting it and dabbing salve on here and there. "Even a tiny spot like this," he shows me a bit of skin, not even as big as the tip of my little finger, "this will let the fire in, and once it turns your skin to ash, and the ash blows away, the fire burns into your muscle underneath, and then the bone, until all that is left is a shell of salve and skin, with everything inside burnt to ash." I swallow hard.

He finishes with my right arm and moves across my shoulders to the left, looking between my fingers, under my arm, front, back, then he works his way across my chest. He checks both my legs, finding several places I missed between my toes and high on the backs of my thighs. I drop to one knee and let him check my head, my ears, my face; his eyes dark and intense as he studies me. "All right," he says, motioning for me to stand, "just a couple last places to check." He gives me a pointed look and I shiver.

I need something to lean against, my head swimming as he takes a knee before me, one hand reaching up to dab salve on my flesh, his touch fleeting, teasing. I grind my teeth as he taps the back of his hand against the inside of my thigh, but I spread my legs, letting him rub salve behind my balls. I feel my insides clench and I ball my hands into fists, refusing to lose control of myself now.

"You okay?" he asks. I nod; that's about all I can do. Speaking requires too much of my concentration, and right now, I'm a little busy. He stands and steps behind me and I close my eyes, biting back the whimper of fear that rises in my throat. I know what he's going to do, but that doesn't stop me flinching when I feel his fingers touch the skin behind my sack. I have too many memories of men touching me there, memories that end in pain. He drags his hand upward, his fingers sliding between my cheeks, coating the inside curves of my ass. I stifle a gasp as I feel my insides go molten again, just from his touch. I don't know how much more of this I can stand. "All finished," he says, stepping away from me. I'm shaking again. "Okay, my turn."

He's a lot better at applying salve than I am, so I find few bare spots, even though I make damn sure to check thoroughly. The last thing I want is to be stranded out here with this magic racing through my blood, filling my body with perverse urges. I especially take my time on his face, perhaps unnecessarily touching up a thin spot or two, just so that I can touch his cheek, his lips. I know it's just the magic, either the salyr a'havon or the enchantment he placed on me, but the combination of the two makes me not give a damn.

I still hesitate to touch his flaccid member, though I need to look at the underneath side if I am to be thorough. Sactaren saves me the trouble by lifting it for me, and I let out a quiet sigh of relief. He's got it covered. I don't need to touch him. He spreads his legs and I do as he did, feeling the velvet skin of his sack tighten as I rub on the salve. I move behind him and scrape the last of the salve out of the bowl before tossing the empty vessel over onto the cloak. Swallowing loudly, I place my fingertips behind his sack and drag my hand up his ass. I finish and turn away.

I've had to do some of the most horrible, disgusting, degrading things in my life, things that make me sick to think about, things that this would never begin to compare to, but nothing has ever made me this ashamed of myself. I *liked* touching him. If I have the chance to do it again, I will, and more, if he'll let me. I've never felt like this before and I don't know what to do, except feel shame. Spell or not, salyr a'havon or not, I should be able to control myself better.

"All right," Lord Sactaren says, grabbing up the second leather pouch and shaking the contents into his hand. He hands me four pellets of that scaly orange skin and a hard lump of sky blue resin. "The plugs fit in your ears and nose. This," he holds up the resin, "is secreted by ice drakes. It's what allows them to breathe frost. When we get to the fire, hold it between your tongue and the roof of your mouth and breathe across it, but not until we're at the flames, or it'll freeze your lungs. We won't be able to speak or hear, so always keep me in sight, okay?" I nod. We're both going to die, I just know it. I hope Schaff has the decency to turn Khas loose after we don't return. I couldn't stand the thought of him starving to death in that crate. "Any questions?"

"What do kholdras eat?"

He blinks at me, and I realize how stupid and random that sounded. After a moment, he smiles. "Golden Goat Shoes," he tells me. "It's a kind of lichen, grows on the shady side of rocks."

"Thanks." Sactaren hands me a pair of goggles and gathers up the net. "Won't the glass melt?" I ask, tapping at the smoky lenses.

"That's isinglass — thin sheets of a mineral called mica. It's flame resistant...to a point."

I look out toward the eerie orange glow flickering between the trees. Sactaren reaches up and takes down the lantern, then blows out the flame, plunging the clearing into blackness, but not for long. I glance over at my master, his skin copper in the sinister firelight, and he places his hand on my arm.

"Stick close to me, Lark. I won't let anything happen to you."

He draws a deep breath, then slips the goggles over his head. I do the same, wincing as I force the dry, scaly plugs into my ears and nose. The roar and crackle of the flames is replaced by the rushing of blood through my ears, and I feel my heart beat against the back of my tongue. Sactaren shakes out the net, then gathers it back up and motions for me to follow him as he sets off toward the glow of the fire. I glance behind me, toward the edge of the forest, then sigh and hurry after my master.

Chapter 9

The heat is suffocating, the smoke thick and choking when we step out of the trees and into the inferno. Sactaren taps me on the arm and places the lump of ice drake secretions in his mouth. I do the same and take a shallow breath. My throat burns — the air colder than deepest winter — and I want to spit it out, but he motions toward the fire and we hurry into the flames.

I can feel them licking at my skin, a slight, ghostly touch, and I shudder. Visibility through the goggles is less than perfect. There's a slight distortion, like I'm looking through dirty water, but I see well enough to follow Sactaren through the firestorm. Even with the ice drake resin, it's hard to breathe. The fire is burning up the air. After about twenty feet, the fire dies down; there's nothing left to burn and we're standing in the blackened ruin of the Wood, smoke rising up from black mounds that used to be forty-foot trees.

Sactaren points to the south and we tramp through the hot ash, sometimes sinking up to our knees, each step sending up plumes of the gritty dust. I brush it away and feel the hair on my arms crunch and crumble. I touch my scalp, and my golden stubble is hard and brittle, and breaks off under my fingers. I guess I won't need another haircut for a while.

We reach the inside edge of the fire-line and follow it to the head of the burn. That's where the salamander will be. Like an arrow cutting through the air, the salamander crawls through an area and the fire spreads back and away from it, never ahead of it. If we find the point of the arrow, we find the creature. Sounds easy enough, right? Try it sometime.

The fire is hotter here, feeding not just on wood, but on the oil secreted by the salamander's skin. We have to tread carefully and avoid anything that burns white hot. That's the oil. It'll burn right through the salve. It gets harder to walk the closer we get. I think the heat is fracturing the layers of isinglass; I can't see much more than red and gold light dancing around me, and a road of brilliant white points leading us forward. There's very little smoke down here, it all rises so fast on the heat, but there's also very little air. I'm gasping like I've just run for miles. I can't catch my breath.

Sactaren grabs my arm and points ahead of us, his body little more than a vague silhouette against the flames. I look and, barely fifty feet beyond, the fires burn an intense blue-white. It's the salamander. Sactaren hands me one side of the net and motions for us to walk toward it, surround it, and drop the net on it. I nod, but I'm not sure it'll work.

I pick my way across the burning ground, my fingers wound tightly in the strips of scaly skin, holding on for my very life because I cannot see my master anymore. The flames leap up between us, the heat beginning to crack the isinglass in my goggles. If I lose hold of the net, I'm not sure I could find it, or him, again. As long as I hold the net taut between us, as long as I can feel him tug at the other end, I can hold back the fear of being lost in this firestorm forever.

The net goes slack and brushes against my leg. I stop, heart pounding against the insides of my ears, and gather it up into my hands. I look out into the fire, but dancing flame and smoke surround me. I start to step toward him, but the oil is thick here, almost a complete smear that I can find no safe place to step across. So I just stand here, staring into the fire where he should have been. Why did he let go of the net? Did it just slip out of his hand, or did something horrible happen? I'm terrified that he stepped into the oil and the salve was breached, and all I will find of him, if anything at all, will be a beautiful, burnt out husk.

I shake my head and turn with a jerk, my fists clenched in the net. He's not dead. He can't be. Mages don't just die. I turn back toward the light of the salamander, glowing like a fallen star. That's where he will have gone. Whatever happened, he still has to catch that creature. I hurry forward. If he gets there first, he might try something desperate if he thinks the net is lost. As I draw within ten feet of the salamander, the outermost layer of isinglass splinters and begins to melt. I don't know how many more layers there are, but I bet it's not going to be enough if I don't hurry.

I shake out the net, debating between creeping up on the creature and just making a mad dash for it. The decision is made for me as another layer of isinglass shatters. No time to creep. I pick out my steps and bolt forward. I can't actually see the salamander, but I know it has to be in the center of the blue-white flame — nothing else I know of burns that hot. It must have been milling around this area for a while; the oil is thick all around it, leaving me nowhere to step. Now I'm wishing I had spent some time on a fishing boat. Holding tight to one corner of the net, I fling it out over the heart of the fire.

It falls short, but startles the salamander. The blinding ball of flame scuttles forward. Cursing under my breath, I pull the net back, but it flares golden-white. It's not burning, but the oil it picked up off the ground is. I hold it away from me and race after the salamander, dragging it through the flames and ash just beyond the oil slick to try and wipe off the white fire. The damn thing's no good to me if I can't touch it.

One good thing about sending the salamander running — the oil is scattered much thinner as it dashes out into woodland not yet touched by its fiery presence. I chase it between spreading trees, watching in horror as it stops and rubs against each trunk, instantly setting them ablaze. Dead leaves explode into the air as it passes by, raining down as fine black ash. My breath is burning in my lungs again, bitter winter cold, and I spit the lump into my hand, choking on smoke, but not heat.

The blue-white fire keeps ahead of me for a dozen feet or more, but then it slows, madly dashing this way and that, touching fallen sticks, rotting limbs, and broken branches littering the ground. It's like it can't pass by without setting something on fire. I skid to a stop and drop the net on top of it as it pauses to set a branch ablaze. It scuttles toward the edge of the net and I stomp my foot on the ground in front of it, scaring it back the other way. It crawls onto the branch and I quickly lift it, gathering the corners of the net in one hand. The salamander thrashes around, the branch crumbling to ash and falling to the ground.

Gasping for air, my heart beating so hard I can feel it in my eyes, I hold the net at arm's length and walk out of the fire. I stop at the first tree I come to and lean my back against it, trying to catch my breath as I watch the blue-white fire begin to die. With nothing to burn and no heat to feed on, the salamander grows quiet and I begin to see its reptilian form emerge from the cooling fire. It's about as long as my arm, with a fat, stumpy tail, a flat, wide head, and stiff spikes running along its spine in between. Its legs are short and powerful, but it has no claws to speak of. I guess when you have no natural enemies, you don't really need to protect yourself.

Pulling off the goggles, I blink hard, my eyes watering as a cooling breeze whispers around me. I remove the nose and ear plugs, the stink of burnt hair instantly assaulting me, and the roar of the inferno suddenly much too close. I lean my head back against the tree and cough, my lungs feeling heavy and thick. I guess breathing smoke will do that to you. The net gives a weak jerk and I turn my attention back to my captive.

Surrounded by a thin veil of orange flame, the salamander looks up at me with huge black eyes, its skin glowing like molten metal — yellow, orange, and a deep, dark red rippling along its body like fire dancing over a bed of dying coals. It's beautiful, not at all like the rust orange lizard I'd been expecting.

"Definitely worth every laene."

I jump and turn. Sactaren is walking toward me, his body ghostly white with salve and streaked with smears of black ash. He looks like the lower half of an Inurian centaur.

"M'Lord," I whisper, my voice harsh and raspy, "thank Maele you're alive."

He reaches up and pushes his goggles up onto his forehead, then gives me a tired smile.

"I don't know what happened," he says, his voice just as rough. "It just slipped from my fingers. I went back and crossed over to find you, but you were gone."

"I'm sorry, M'Lord, I—"

"Don't apologize. By the gods, don't apologize. You caught it, Lark, all by yourself. You saved the Rynnawood. How's that for making a difference?"

I blink hard and look back at the glimmering creature in the net, my knees suddenly weak. I fall back against the tree and press my hand to my forehead.

"I-I didn't even think," I whisper as he comes over and takes the net from me. "I just...I just...chased it, and..." I close my eyes, suddenly lightheaded.

"Come on," Sactaren says with a slight chuckle, "let's get this fellow home, so *we* can go home."

"Please." I shove myself away from the tree and follow him through the Wood, keeping the fire line on our left as we head for the northern edge. "What about the fire?" I ask after a while.

"What about it?" He sounds exhausted.

"Isn't there something we can do to put it out? It's still burning."

He shakes his head. "The heat has driven all the moisture out of the air; I couldn't make it rain if I wanted to. Which I don't. Besteth asked me to catch the salamander, not put out the fire. My part of the pact is fulfilled."

"But, M'Lord, the Wood...the trees..."

He kicks a raised root and stumbles, cursing under his breath. "Damn it, Lark, that's not our problem! I did what I agreed to do, now let it alone, will you?"

I shut my mouth and follow in silence, trying to keep a frown from creeping onto my face. *I* did what he agreed to do, *I* caught the salamander, but I'm not about to say so. As his slave, I am but an extension of him. Anything I do, he receives the credit, he receives the pay, he receives the glory. I know that. He just makes it easy to forget, sometimes, that I am a slave.

We have to cross the fire line again to reach our things, but it's just regular fire, a wall of red-orange flames that we don't even need the goggles to cross. The salamander flares in the heat, kicking at the net as the life returns to it, but it quiets down once we exit the other side. When we reach our pile of stuff, Sactaren hands me the net without a word. I don't want him angry at me, but I'm not sure apologizing will help. He doesn't always react to apologies like I think he will.

He wipes his hands on the cloak, then sticks the tips of two fingers in his mouth and whistles. Grimacing, he turns and spits on the ground, then lights the lantern and places it back in the tree. While he slips into his trousers and tunic, I just stand and hold the salamander. I expect him to put his hair back on, but he leaves it spread upon the cloak. "Get dressed," he tells me, taking the net from my hands. "Bari and Goar are on their way."

I'm slipping into my shirt when I hear the rumbling beat of elk hooves and I groan to myself. Yeah, this going to be a fun ride home. I can already feel the magic starting to affect me again, and I can't look at my master without wishing I could feel the touch of his hands on my body again. I take the salamander again as Sactaren silently saddles each of the beasts, his brow furrowed in more than concentration, I suspect. Once the elk are ready, he finishes gathering his things into his knapsack, until only his cloak and hair, and my shoes, remain.

I grab up my shoes, but I can't bear the thought of forcing my feet into all that hot, tight leather. They dangle from one hand by the laces as I watch him carefully roll his hair up inside the cloak and then feed it into the bottomless knapsack. Maybe he can't put it back on until the salve is washed off. In one fluid motion, he swings up onto Bari's back and holds out his hand for the net. "Will you carry the lantern?" he asks as I hand the creature to him.

"Of course, M'Lord," I say as I open my knapsack to stuff my shoes inside, and the scent of fresh, honeyed bread hits me like a fist in the gut. I'm *starving*. My mouth begins to water as I rip off the butt of the loaf and take a bite, the crust crisp and the inside soft and light. I don't think I've ever tasted anything so delicious. I take out the bread and the muffins, and stuff my shoes down into the bottom of the bag. Nothing in the world would make me happier than to sink my teeth into one of those moist, fruit laden muffins, but I place them, and the bread, back in the bag. Now is not the time. Maybe once the salamander has been released, Lord

Sactaren will accept one by way of apology. I'd even give him both, if it meant he would start speaking to me again.

I sling my bag over my shoulder and scramble onto Goar's back, almost falling off again as I stretch out and pull the lantern out of the tree. Sactaren slaps the reins against the sides of Bari's neck and the big elk moves out. We make our way silently out of the forest and across the wide grassland. I watch the stars of Isurus, the Shark God, lift above the horizon as the night sky turns overhead, forever chasing, never catching, the three dolphin lords — the Dreamer, the Singer, and the Watcher. I glance behind us, where the Great Dragon is all but obscured by the smoke. Only the brightest two stars, the Eye and the Heart, wink faintly between billows.

The thin, pale green crescent of Id Erith has risen from behind Traxen Peak by the time the grass thins and disappears altogether, the elk's feet clattering as they step out onto the lava flats. Sactaren pulls Bari to a stop and dismounts, handing me the reins.

"Wait here," he tells me, his expression troubled as he turns away, but no more so than mine. He didn't even glance at me.

I watch him walk out into the volcanic wasteland, far out, until the glow of the salamander is almost lost to sight. It flares, then vanishes, and I can only wait with the elk for our master to return. It is a long, lonely vigil. A slight breeze picks up, keening across the open waste of the lava flats, and I gather my collar about my neck. The elk snort and stomp their feet as a wolf howls, miles away. I hope.

I'm starting to wonder just how long I'm supposed to wait when I hear the *crunch* of footsteps approaching from the lava flats and I raise the lantern high, trying to catch sight of him. He appears out of the darkness, like a phantom, his eyes hollow and shadowed as he looks down at the ground.

"Is it done, M'Lord?" I ask stupidly. Of course it's done — he's back, isn't he? He just nods and takes the lantern from my hand, his fingers brushing harmlessly over mine, and I jump. It's the first time he's ever done something that seemed...careless. I stare at him, wishing I knew what to do, what to say, until he blows the lantern out and is swallowed by darkness.

As my eyes adjust to the dim, green glow of Id Erith, I feel him take Bari's reins, too, and I can make out his pale form standing beside the large bull elk. He grunts as he hoists himself into the saddle, his motions not nearly as smooth and refined. Perhaps he is just tired. Perhaps he's hungry.

"M'Lord?" I say as he turns Bari's head toward the mountain.

"Yes, Lark?" He sounds more than tired, he sounds troubled, almost sad. I turn in the saddle and reach into my knapsack, wincing as my pants pull tight across my slight arousal.

"You-you must be hungry, M'Lord," I say, offering him the muffins. He doesn't speak, but nudges Bari up beside me and takes one from my hand, his long fingers trailing over the back of my hand, and I almost smile, because he did it on purpose. By the wan green light, I watch him take a bite, and my mouth waters.

"This is very good," he says after he swallows. "I didn't know you could bake."

"I can't," I say. "Calae — I mean, Mrs. Raddis — the young woman with the baby, she brought them to me, to thank me for saving her daughter's life. She also brought the rest of the money she owed, and enough to cover the Jesrens' cow and son, so the books are right again."

I'm so glad he's speaking to me again, I don't realize that *I'm* doing all the talking until he holds the bitten muffin back out to me. "Is-is something wrong, M'Lord?" I ask, taking it and bringing it to my nose to see if it smells sour or burnt. I take a hesitant nibble; it melts in my mouth, sweet and buttery, like something out of a dream.

"There's nothing wrong," he says quietly. "Those were given to you for your trouble. You should enjoy them."

"I don't mind—"

"She gave them to you," he interrupts, not so quiet now. "I don't think she would have wanted you to share them...with me." He sounds so bitter. "Come on, let's just get home and get this over with."

He spurs Bari forward, the big elk bounding away over the grassland, and Goar leaps after his sire. I grab at the saddle horn, the muffins falling from my hands. I don't look back, though in the tall grass, in the weak moonlight, I wouldn't be able to see them, but...I don't look back.

I want to ask my master, beg him, to slow, but I can't. I don't understand what I did to make him so angry, so full of darkness. I just wish I knew what he was hurrying home to do, to get "over with". I hope it doesn't have anything to do with me, but knowing my luck...I'll probably end up wishing I had died in the forest.

Chapter 10

The elk scramble up the last steep hillside, their breath pluming out before them in the chill mountain air as they make for the castle gate. I silently thank Maele as we cross under the thick archway, smoky torches guttering around the inner wall, casting dancing shadows across the bare flagstones. Sactaren dismounts wearily and I slide off, landing hard on my bare feet. My whole body aches, and not just from the hard ride. The salyr a'havon has caught up with me again.

Breathing hard, I stand and wait while my master leads his elk to the dark doorway in the north wall. He says nothing to Qito that I can hear as the many armed creature emerges and takes the reins, and when Sactaren turns, his brow is furrowed, his eyes heavily shadowed as he walks toward me. I want to touch him: his face, his chest, his... I feel my face burn and pray that he can't see.

"Follow me," is all he says. He leads me down a hall, one I recognize, vaguely, but haven't been down since my first night at the castle. When he stops, I swallow hard, because we're standing outside his private bath. He pushes open the door, allowing a choking cloud of steam to escape, and gestures for me to enter. I step inside, standing next to the wall as he follows me in and begins to undress. "Take off your clothes," he tells me, without even a glance in my direction. I'm tempted to say, "No, not until you tell me what is going on," but I'm so tired, and I ache so much. I just want this — whatever it is — to be over so I can go to bed and forget about it.

I shrug out of my shirt and pants and stand, painfully aware of my erection, while he moves about the room, seemingly oblivious to it. He has two bars of dark blue soap in his hands when he steps to the center of the room and slides into the water, stepping into the middle of the bath. The water comes up over his navel, the steam beading up on his chalk white skin. I watch him work the bars of soap in his hands, forming a thick, heavy blue lather. He begins to wash himself — his chest, his arms, his head — and I stand riveted against the wall, unable to tear my eyes from him as his warm, golden skin is slowly revealed. I fight to catch my breath, my hands twitching as I struggle to keep them off my aching flesh, a groan rising up in my throat as I watch his soapy hands slide down his flat stomach and disappear beneath the water.

"Lark," he says, his voice toneless, but tight, restrained. I don't answer, I can't; I'm choking on sounds I don't want to make. "Lark?" He glances over at me and his expression softens, but remains troubled. "Lark, come here. I need your help; I need your hands."

His voice pulls me like a silken rope, but he's not using any tricks. It's just his voice, it's just him. Anything he asks of me, I will do. He holds out one of the dark blue bricks of soap as I flounder into the hot bathwater, my knees seeming to want to bend in all the wrong directions. I take the soap with trembling hands and he turns his back to me, inviting my touch. I step closer, into the deeper water, the nearly scalding heat sliding up over my hips, and I gasp, a pained and strangled sound. I grit my teeth and begin to wash his back.

"I'm sorry," Sactaren says after a moment, as my sudsy hands slide across his shoulders. "Lark, I am so sorry."

A cold knot forms in the pit of my stomach because I can't think of what he's done that he would be sorry for, so it must be something he's about to do. I had a master who would do that — apologize and then beat the crap out of me. I didn't like it then, and I don't like it now.

"S-sorry for what, M'Lord?" I ask, trying to keep the tremor out of my voice and failing.

"I can still bleed you," he says, not answering my question. "It would be more painful, but not...not—"

"No, please, M'Lord, please, not blood," I whimper.

He looks at me, a long look filled with lust and regret. "If there was another way," he says, and then he closes his eyes and turns away, and I am shocked by the pain and sorrow that is in his voice, that rides between his hunched shoulders. He can't...he can't be this upset about...me, can he? What am I to him?

"M'Lord," I say, barely louder than a whisper, "this-this isn't your fault."

"Yes, it is," he replies with a bitter bark of laughter that makes me jump. "I could have — I *should* have checked to see whether you were susceptible to the salyr a'havon, and I didn't. Just a moment, that's all it would have taken, and I could have spared you this, but I didn't want to know; I wanted you...to..." He stops, shakes his head, and sighs. "Never mind. It's too late now. It's over." He just stands there, a froth of blue soap drying and dying across his shoulders, slowly trailing down his spine toward the chalk white salve coating his lower back and disappearing beneath the water.

Hesitant, I step toward him, trembling inside, but my hands have stopped shaking as I reach up and begin to wash him again. His shoulders tense and he glances back at me, but I keep my eyes downcast, concentrating on scrubbing the salve from his skin. After a moment, he looks away and his muscles slowly relax.

I lick my dry lips and taste the mint of the salve, the acrid bite of the ash, and my own sweat. His skin glides under my hands, slick, warm, rough, flawed, and I wonder what he would feel like pressed against me, my chest to his back, or his to mine. My breath catches in my throat and I feel a wave of dizziness wash over me, but just for a moment. I have to try not to think things like that.

I run the hand with the soap in it down his flank and then up the back of his thigh, my hand sliding over the curve of his ass. He tenses again, but does and says nothing as I continue to wash the salve off. I know I shouldn't be doing this, even as I bend down to run my hand up the inside of his thigh, but my thoughts don't seem to be controlling what my body does. He hastily steps out of my reach as my hand slides between his thighs, brushing the velvet skin of his sack.

"I think that's enough, thank you," he says, sounding slightly out of breath. His eyes linger on me as he steps toward the edge of the bath and places his bar of soap on the wet flagstone floor. With clean hands, he splashes water onto his face and over his head, then sinks to his knees, letting the steaming water swirl over his back and rinse the blue foam away.

When he stands again, I watch the water cascade down his glistening golden body, and I take a step toward him before I realize what I'm doing. I stop, the blue brick of soap slipping from my fingers. I can't take my eyes off him. He's so beautiful, so perfect. I lurch forward, my breath thick and heavy in my throat, and he turns, his whole body stiffening at the sight of me.

"All right," he says, reaching for the soap floating between us, but never taking his eyes from me, "now we just have to…"

I reach for him…

He grabs my wrist and pulls me toward him, jerking me off balance, then spins me around and twists my arm up behind my back. Pain shoots through my shoulder and I cry out. He stops pulling, but grabs my other wrist as well, pinning it beside the first. I feel him trace a figure on each wrist, then I feel the cool touch of his breath as he blows across my hands. He lets go of me and I stumble away from him, tripping over the terraced bottom of the bath and falling hard onto the floor, stunned as I lie half in and half out of the water. I tried to catch myself, but my hands remained behind my back as surely as if he had tied them there. I'm gasping for breath as I lay with my chest against the cold, wet flagstones, my stiff member pressed against the side of the bath, the air raising gooseflesh up my back. I struggle, water splashing onto the floor as I kick my legs, crying wordlessly into the flagstones, but I can't get free; he's bound me with magic.

"Lark, I need you to calm down."

His voice sends a thrill of fear through me and my body goes rigid. I can't move as he steps closer, right behind me, and I close my eyes, choking on a scream as I wait for his hands to find me, hold me down, spread me open. His hand closes on my arm and he pulls me to my feet. My knees won't hold me and I fall into him, my cheek resting against his shoulder as I fight to stand.

Sactaren grabs me, his hands firm and strong on my arms. "It's all right," he says, pushing me up, holding me up, catching my eyes with his. I don't know if it's magic, but looking into his eyes, so large and pale blue, I feel the fear start to bleed away. "You're not in your right mind," he explains. "That's why I bound your hands back — and that is the *only* reason. Now please, trust me."

I try to think of a single reason why I should, but it's hard to say why you should trust someone. It's much easier to find reasons *not* to trust them, though at the moment, I can't think of any. I reluctantly force myself to stand before him, hands bound behind my back, heart pounding in my throat, body aching for his touch. After a moment, he reaches out and catches the bar of soap I dropped as it slowly floats past him, just under the surface of the water. Though it takes every bit of control I have left, I don't move as he raises his hands toward me.

He washes the salve and ash from my body — nothing more — but every inch of me tingles under his fingertips, aches as he moves methodically down my body, starting at my scalp and working down my neck, across my shoulders, along my spine. His hands are firm, and damnably thorough, bringing heat into my face as I choke on dark moans of painful longing.

"Please," I whisper before I can stop myself, "please."

"Not yet," he says, and I close my eyes as hot tears roll down my face, tears of shame and frustration. I grit my teeth until my jaw aches as he finishes washing all but my most personal of areas. Finally, he steps back and sets the bar of soap beside the first. "Catch your breath," he tells me, turning away. Why does he look so upset? Surely, he's been dreaming of having me at his mercy since he laid eyes on me. "I'm going to do this quickly, and you may find it hard to breathe at times."

I already feel like someone's standing on my chest. I open my mouth to gulp air, and words come out instead.

"You don't seem to be enjoying this, M'Lord," I say, shocked to hear myself speaking, and appalled by what I'm saying. I try to shut myself up, but he's right; the magic has done something to me. I've gone insane. "Isn't this how you wanted me?"

Lord Sactaren stares at me for a moment, eyes shadowed by heavy brows. I want to apologize, I want to fall to my knees and beg his forgiveness, but I can't move; I can't make a sound.

"No," he says finally, slowly shaking his head. "I never wanted this. I never wanted you bound and unwilling, afraid and in pain."

He falls silent, but the air echoes with things unsaid. He does want me; maybe not like this, but I can feel it when he looks at me, I can see the longing in his eyes. Again, I want to apologize, but my body is not mine to control.

"Touch me," I whisper, my voice hoarse and strained. He swallows hard enough for me to hear. "Please, Lord Sactaren, touch me."

He takes a step toward me and I can see the tightness in his movements, the restraint. He's fighting against himself, fighting against what he wants to do to me. I want to back away from him but lean forward instead as he raises his hands to my face, his soft fingertips gliding along my jaw line. His eyes are intense as his fingers rise to hover over my mouth, and my breath catches in my throat as the tip of his tongue slides along his lower lip. Fear strikes deep and cold through the center of my body as his hands begin to tremble. His steely control is slipping. A gasp escapes my lips as he raises his eyes to mine, thin streaks of dark crimson bleeding into the winter-sky blue. I don't know what he sees in my face, in my eyes, but his trembling hands ball into fists as he lowers them.

"When we're alone," he says, his voice a silken murmur, "you can call me Naeven, if you like. I'm not so enamored of my title that I need to hear it all the time." He closes his eyes and takes a slow breath. When he opens them again, the bleak winter sky has returned, chill and almost colorless. "Are you ready?" he asks.

I struggle and fight against myself. Being imprisoned in my body is worse than anything he might do to me...at least, worst than anything *I* can imagine. "Yes," I manage to gasp.

He nods once, sharply, and then reaches up and places his hands on my head, his palms warm against my bare scalp. His eyes go unfocused and he stares over my shoulder, his lips slightly parted. I draw a sharp breath as I feel the hot and cold fluid begin to move under my skin.

"If I knew you better," he says after a moment, "this would be easier. I could call it to your center with a single touch. As it is, I must draw it to the surface and then coax it where it belongs."

His hands slide down the sides of my head, down my neck, the strange sensation following his touch. He drags his palms down my chest, stopping just below my navel, the salyr a'havon settling like liquid lead low in my groin. Sactaren raises his hands to my face and repeats the motions. As he places the magic in my belly for a third time, I suddenly realize what he meant about pain and pleasure. I feel it gathering, hot, cold, heavy, molten, like I'm pleasuring myself and I've come too far to stop, where I have to finish, no matter what, only I can't finish. I can't touch myself. I seal my lips against the whimpers that rise up in my throat. It's becoming easier to make my body obey, but it's still not me who struggles against the spell binding my wrists.

Sactaren presses his hands harder into my chest, forcing me back a step. "Don't make me bind you further," he says. The fear that his words stir within me makes it possible for me to still my body.

He quickly works his way down my chest, then moves behind me, drawing the salyr a'havon down my back. My breath hisses between my teeth as I fight against the ache growing in my loins. I want to feel something, anything against my flesh, I don't care what. He touches my hands, cleansing my arms one at a time.

"By the blood of Cheyn, I can't take much more of this," I curse, my voice thick and strangled.

"I'm almost done," Sactaren says, his breath sliding across my wet shoulder and making me groan. His hands close about my upper arms. "Step back — mind the edge — I need to reach your feet." He walks me backward, up the terraced floor to the very edge of the bath, and sits me down on the cold, wet stone floor, my stiff flesh standing against my stomach as I watch him kneel before me, the water swirling up around his shoulders. His hands find my feet and he pulls the magic to the surface far easier than before. Apparently, he knows me better now. Under the water, the salyr a'havon glows a bright, forget-me-not blue, pulsing with the rapid beat of my heart as he works his way up my left leg, my mouth going dry as he caresses my thigh before depositing the light in my already heavy groin.

"Please," I whisper, closing my eyes and turning my face to the ceiling, "please...Master, please..." I can't keep quiet as he draws the magic up my right leg; I cry out, in pain and desperate for release. "Please! Please stop this, please."

"I'm trying."

His touch seems to linger and burn as he shifts the last of the salyr a'havon to my loins, and I sob in relief — that's it, he's cleansed my whole body, he can finish me now. Only he doesn't. He places his palm in the center of my chest, his other hand resting lightly on the back of my neck, and I feel the magic answer him, burning like ice, cold as flame under my skin.

"W-what is...going on?" I gasp. He doesn't look at me — or can't — staring over my shoulder as he speaks.

"The salyr a'havon runs deep into your body. What I've been shifting is only what lies just under your skin. Now that I have felt the magic inside you, now that I know it, this will not take long. I promise."

I can only whimper as he closes his eyes and presses his lips into a thin line. A shadow forms across his brow and I gasp, my body jerking as the muscles in my neck and back tighten as one. I stare blindly ahead of me as white light eats at the edge of my vision. I can feel him drawing the magic out, out of my blood and bone, out of my heart and lungs and gut, out of my muscle and tissue and soul, ice and fire, liquid flame, freezing, burning. I can't see, I can't speak, I can't breathe, but I can *feel*.

I feel him lower the salyr a'havon to my groin and I want to scream, but I can't make a sound. He speaks, but his words are just noise to me; I can't understand. I feel his hand leave my neck, touch my wrists, and my hands are free again but I can't move. His hand touches my jaw, turns my head, and I can't resist. I can't do anything. Except die. The sound of his voice, the touch of his hand, even the indescribable pain and pleasure throbbing through my body — it all starts to slip away, like a dream upon waking, and a terrible, cold calm settles over me. I'm dying and I don't even care.

The calm is shattered as I gasp, the hot, wet air thick and heavy in my lungs, and then I scream, so loud my bones rattle and my voice tears. He's touching me. *Stop. More.* His hands slide along my length. *Don't. Please.* He strokes me. *Yes. No. Please.* I feel like I'm being ripped apart. I shudder and scream again as the salyr a'havon leaves my body.

The scream fades into a sob as I lean forward, crushing my face against his shoulder, my hands gripping his upper arms so tight my fingers hurt. My head swims. I'm not entirely sure what just happened. The pain quickly leaves me, even the memory of it is like smoke on the wind, thinning until nothing is left. I draw a shaking breath, suddenly feeling foolish for my hysterics, and realize that I am naked in my master's arms.

I draw back, his hands grabbing my arms as I sway on my feet. I can't face him, I can't meet his eyes, my neck burning with shame as the memory of his hands, so soft and firm on my aching, throbbing flesh, sends a shudder of pleasure through me. My eyes fall upon his stomach, and I go cold inside as I watch my semen slowly run down his skin, glowing a vibrant blue. I spilled myself onto him. I feel sick.

Lord Sactaren lets me go and I glance up at him, but he's looking down at himself. I want to die. He trails the tips of his fingers through the thick liquid, dragging it back up his stomach. His brow is furrowed, but he doesn't look angry or disgusted. He watches it shimmer on the tips of his fingers, then raises his fingers to his mouth. I jump back, floundering in the water as he licks my seed from his fingertips. He regards me for a moment, his face dark and unreadable, then he turns away and washes my semen from his body. I stand, stomach trying to heave itself up my throat against the far wall of the bath, the water slapping against my thighs as he finishes rinsing himself off and silently climbs out of the water.

He crosses the room and grabs a towel off the rack, and I begin to shake, deep inside. He is aroused. I feel my face burn as my eyes linger on the smooth, golden length of him. I want to touch him. My knees are shaking as I climb out of the bath and onto the wet flagstone floor. I want to feel him against my palm, hot and hard, his skin like velvet. After what he did for me, I owe him this. I owe him my life. He turns as I approach, the towel crushed to his chest as he wipes away the damp clinging to his skin. I want to lick away those glistening beads of moisture from his collar bone, from his neck, from his jaw line. His eyes are guarded as he looks at me.

"It's late," he says, and his voice is heavy, weary. "Can we discuss this tomorrow?"

I don't answer; there's nothing I want to talk about, now or tomorrow. I wet my rough lips and reach for him. I think he starts to step back — he shifts his weight from one foot to the other, the muscles in his legs and his grip on the towel tightening. I brush the damp cloth aside and drag my knuckles down his smooth, flat stomach. He draws a sharp breath, but doesn't try to stop me as my fingers meet the base of his member. He's even hotter than I'd imagined, hard and burning. I can feel his heartbeat fluttering just under the skin as I close my hand around him. I'm mesmerized, hardly able to breathe as I begin to slowly draw my hand up his flesh.

"Lark, stop." He grabs my wrist and I jerk back.

"I'm sorry, M'Lord," I say, though I'm not sure what I'm sorry for. I must be doing something wrong for him to stop me so suddenly. Perhaps I was holding him too tight, or my hands were too cold, or too rough. I dig my fingernails into the rows of calluses lining my palms. I have hands like broken rock.

"Lark." I reluctantly raise my eyes to meet his. "Don't be sorry. While there is little in this world that I would rather have you do, I cannot in good conscience allow this. You have been through a terrible ordeal that has left you weakened and vulnerable, and I will not take advantage of that. Perhaps another time, when you are not so tired and confused." He looks at me a moment longer, and I can see in his eyes that he has little hope of that happening.

We towel off in silence. I steal glances at him, but he's someplace else, far away with his dark thoughts. I don't understand why he stopped me. Even as he was speaking, I could see the longing in his eyes. He should have jumped at the chance. A single word from him and I would have fallen to my hands and knees and let him take me. As I realize I still would, I feel cold inside.

I glance up as he leaves without a word, the towel wrapped tight around his waist. I do the same, gathering up my dirty clothes before heading to my room. The lamp glows warm and golden, but the shadows it casts are deep and cold. I drop my shirt and pants on the floor beside the door and stagger to the bed, the damp towel falling to the flagstones. I'll pick it up in the morning. I slide into bed, feeling the cool caress of the clean sheets on my naked body, and I shudder as the memory of Sactaren's touch sweeps over me. I press my face into the pillow and squeeze my eyes shut. Why did he stop me? Did he not realize what I was willing to do for him? No, there has to be something else. I hold out my hands and stare at them, dark with dirt that will never wash out of my skin, nails chipped and cracked, palms thicker and rougher than the soles of most men's feet.

He wanted me, until he actually felt my touch, felt my work roughened hands upon him. I clench my fists and blow out the lamp, plunging the room into darkness as my eyes begin to sting, burning with hot tears of shame and anger. What is *wrong* with me? I am not like this, I do not do these things. I have never touched anyone in such a way before, and now I have touched my master. If he were anyone else, he would have killed me. The fact that he didn't makes me afraid. If he's willing to let such a mistake go unpunished, what *does* he want from me?

I raise my head from the pillow, my heart pattering in my throat as I stare through the darkness toward the door. Did I hear something? I don't know.

A thin line of guttering torchlight glows through the crack beneath the door, and my breath catches as something passes in front of the light. It lingers a moment, then moves off in the direction it came from. I sit up, grabbing at the covers to throw them off and chase after him, but freeze as I realize that it might not be Sactaren in the hall, and wouldn't Schaff have a laugh at the sight of me, naked and shaking, calling after my master in the dead of night.

With a sigh, I lay back down and draw the blankets up to my chin, staring out into the darkness as I wait for sleep to claim me, or dawn to find me, whichever comes first.

Chapter 11

I wake with a start, thin silver light filtering in through the high, narrow window. Lying on my back, I stare up at the ceiling, breathing deep and fast as my pounding heart quickly returns to a normal rhythm. Swallowing hard, I let the dream fade away — I don't even try to remember the details — but I can't forget what it was about. My sheets are damp and smell of sweat, and I can still feel his hands gliding across my body.

I throw back the covers, the chill morning air raising gooseflesh on my arms and back as I sit up, rubbing my face with both hands. If only last night had been a dream, too. But it was more like a nightmare. I groan and dig my fingers into my bare scalp as the memories flash through me. How can I ever face him after what I did, after what I almost did, after what I tried to do...

"Great Maele, I touched him," I whisper, my voice rough and raspy. I try to clear my throat and begin to cough, thick and painful, like my lungs are being shredded. I breathed too much smoke. When I catch my breath, I wipe the back of my hand across my mouth, expecting to wipe away blood, but it's just flecks of spit. I imagine Sactaren has some powder or crystal that will fix me, but were I on death's door, I wouldn't go to him now, not after...

My stomach knots up, making me wince. I'm *still* starving. It's a familiar feeling, and I could ignore it for most of the coming day before it became too much to bear, but with the kitchens and larder full of food, I really don't see the point in going hungry. And this early, I could make my way to the shop and retrieve my pie from the cupboard without Schaff around to bother me. I allow myself a small smirk as I imagine his frustration at not being able to get into the cupboard. Serves him right, after all the crap he's flicked at me, after all the help he *hasn't* been. I don't believe for a moment that he didn't know kholdras ate Golden Goat Shoes—

"Khas!" That starts me coughing again, and I wrap my arms around my ribs as I stumble over to the wardrobe. How could I be so thoughtless? I grab a pair of black trousers and a loose, pale blue tunic, my bare feet slapping against the stone floor as I run down the hall to the shop. I pause in the doorway of the back room to shrug into the shirt, and cast a fearful glance at the foot of the tower stairs. Is he up there somewhere, alone? I can't imagine that he'd be with his wife. Since the night I arrived, he's only mentioned her a few times, in passing, and I've not seen her again.

Pushing those thoughts aside, I walk to the counter where Khas's crate sits. The rosy light of the rising sun glows in the front windows, but is weak and faint in the back room. I peer through the slats, but I can't see him amidst the straw. I hope I'm not too late. Grabbing the crate, I carry it to the door, setting it briefly on the floor as I undo the main lock. The straw rustles as I pick it back up and I sigh in relief. He's not dead.

Sunrise paints the sky behind the mountain — beautiful, but useless to chase away the chill of night. I wish I'd grabbed a cloak. The wind cuts right through me as I head along the eastern side of the castle, toward the rocky lower slopes of Traxen Peak. Golden Goat Shoes grow on the shady side of rocks. I climb up among the boulders, carrying Khas in his crate, and peering all around the rocks for anything that resembled a golden goat shoe. There're all kinds of dry moss and scaly fungus looking plants clinging to the rocks, even some grass and a stumpy, twisted tree or two, but nothing that jumps out as what I'm looking for. My fingers are cold and stiff from gripping the narrow slats of the crate, and I finally have to set it down on a flat slab of stone and rub my hands together. Khas peers out at me and mimics the gesture.

"You seem like a smart little critter," I say, breathing warm air onto my fingers. "Why is it nobody's ever taught one of you to talk?" He tilts his head to one side. I shake my head and go back to my search. "This would be a lot easier if you could tell me what I'm looking for," I grumble, picking at a white patch of lichen with a frilly edge. Not likely, I decide, holding it up in the sunlight. I glance over at Khas. "What do you think?" He stretches one arm out through the slats, reaching toward me. I raise my eyebrows. Maybe this is the right stuff after all.

I walk closer and hand it to him. He grabs it and throws it back at me. Maybe not. He sticks his paw out again and I look to see what he's pointing at, but he's just pointing out over the valley, out toward the sea. "I don't get it, Khas," I say with a shrug, turning back to the rocks. I scrape up three more likely lichens: a crusty rust brown one, a spongy yellow one, and a feathery orange one. "All right, you picky little pest, which one?" I mutter.

I hold up the first, the brown one, and he sticks his paw out again, like he did with the white lichen. Instead of giving it to him, I hold up the second, the yellow one. He turns his paw over, palm up, if it were a hand. I hold up the last, the orange one. His paw turns back over. We regard each other for a moment, my heart thumping a little quicker as I realize that I may be on to something here. I hold up the yellow lichen again. Khas turns his paw palm up again and presses closer to the slats, his middle pair of versatile paws grabbing on to the rough wood as he strains toward me. I hand him the yellow lichen and he snatches it from my fingers, pulling it into the crate and tearing at it with sharp, chisel-like teeth. I step back and glance down at the two lichen in my hand, the two that he didn't want.

I toss them aside and hunt around for several more of the spongy yellow lichen, the Golden Goat Shoes, and then I grab his crate and head back to the castle. As I round the eastern corner, I raise my eyes to the tower window, and stop short at the sight of Schaff seated on the window ledge, his bushy red and white tail flicking back and forth as it hangs over the edge. I can't tell if he sees me, but I hurry back into the shop. I really shouldn't be out of the castle unsupervised. If Schaff gets it into his head to tell Sactaren he saw me trying to run away...

I return Khas's crate to the counter in the back room, my heart thundering in my ears as I cast nervous glances at the tower stairs. Several minutes pass and I begin to relax. If Schaff wanted to cause trouble, he wouldn't waste any time about it. Something touches my hand and I jump, but it's just Khas, reaching through the slats again. I hold up another lichen, a thrill of excitement running through me as he holds out his paw again, palm up.

"Finally figured out what to feed him, eh?" I jump again, dropping the lichen as I spin around. Schaff yipps in amusement as he slinks down the last few steps and pads across the room toward me. "A bit jumpy this morning, aren't we?"

"Schaff, have you ever heard Khas make a noise?" I ask, ignoring the insinuation in his voice. "A bark, squeak, chirp, whistle, anything?" His ears swivel up and down as he looks from me to the crate and back again. I pick up the Golden Goat Shoe and hand it to Khas.

"Not that I've been paying *any* attention to your pet rat, but no, kholdras don't make noise."

"That's right," I say, bending down to look in at Khas. He looks up from his lichen and makes that one gesture again, fist against palm, then open and slide across. "They *can't* make noise, so they talk with their hands."

"Naeven said last night was rough on you," Schaff says after a moment, "but he didn't say you'd completely lost your mind. Kholdras arc just dumb animals; they can't talk at all."

"He showed me his words for yes and no, I think," I say, holding out my hand palm down — no — then palm up — yes.

"Whatever," Schaff says, walking past me and leaping up onto the front counter in the shop. "You got a minute, Dr. Doolittle? Naeven wants me to go over a few things with you before it's time to open shop."

I close my eyes and let my head drop forward. "What does he want?" I ask quietly.

"Come out here so we can talk without waking him," Schaff tells me, the white tip of his tail flicking from side to side as I head out into the shop. His wide golden eyes follow me as I walk. "So, that was you screaming last night. You've got quite a set of lungs. I bet they heard it all the way down in the village." My face burning, I turn away from him and pretend to organize the bottles of healing bath salts on their shelf. When he speaks again, his tone is almost civil. "The salyr a'havon can be quite nasty. You're lucky you were in Naeven's hands." Now I can hear the smirk in his voice. "...so to speak. There aren't many mages like him. Or men, for that matter." He falls silent and I glance back at him. He's staring through a beam of golden sunlight, watching the dust motes dance lazily in the air, his eyes hooded and sleepy. After a moment, he blinks and begins to wash a paw.

"When...when he found out the salyr a'havon was in me, he said 'Damn it, not again.' What did he mean?"

"You're not the first to have that happen, you know," he says, looking at me like I'm stupid or something. "Years ago, Naeven had another assistant who was so sensitive to magic, it would take him if he was even the same room with an active spell. He had to be cleansed every time a spell was completed, and, unlike you, he was not the type of guy Naeven wanted to bed, and since being bled is almost unbearable, Naeven got a new assistant, and that solved all his problems."

"And what happened to the guy who — the one like me?"

"Naeven told him he wouldn't be needed to help out in the evenings."

I'm silent as that sinks in. "I can't help him anymore?"

"You can run the shop, but he doesn't want you in the tower ever again. If you're going to sprout an erection every time he uses you to augment a spell, you're more trouble than you're worth."

I'm not sure why this news makes me feel like a large stone has been dropped onto my stomach, but it does. I've been dreading seeing him, dreading the long climb up his twisting stairs, dreading working at his side, but now that I don't have to, I feel cold, empty inside.

"Hey, it's not like it's your fault," Schaff says. "You should be glad; you get more time off, and you don't have to worry about the salyr a'havon again. Unless you liked getting all naked and soapy with him?"

"You're horrible," I say, turning away from him. "Is there anything else he wanted?"

"You, I imagine," Schaff says with a snicker. I stalk toward the door, but he calls after me and I stop with my hand on the latch. "He wants to know if he hurt you."

I slowly shake my head. There was pain, but I can't remember feeling it, all I remember is the glorious touch of his hands, the heat of his skin... I close my eyes, resting my forehead against the door as a hollow ache fills my chest. Never again, I realize, and though I should be glad, I'm not. "He didn't hurt me," I say at last.

"You sure about that?" Schaff asks. "Not all pain is physical, you know."

I grip the door latch, torn between the desire to run away before I say something stupid, and the need for guidance, reassurance. Schaff is the last person I would trust with my thoughts and feelings, but he's also the only person I have to talk to. He's been here long enough, maybe he knows something, anything I could do.

"What is *wrong* with me?" I groan, banging my fist against the heavy wooden door. "I don't — I don't want to feel like this."

"Like what?" He doesn't *sound* like he's laughing at me.

"Like — *I don't know*... Like I've never felt before, like I *want* him to-to do things to me. I shouldn't want that. He's my master. My only desire should be to please him, but I-I..." I want him to please me, I want him to touch me, to use his hands to make me feel good. That's not right. "I don't understand the emptiness..." I pound my fist against my chest, "...in here when you told me he didn't want my help anymore. It was like I-I... Would he cast a spell on me, to make me feel like this?"

Schaff is silent for a long time, but I can't gather the courage to look back at him. If he's laughing at me...

"If he thought he had something to gain by doing so, yeah, Lark, he would. He can be terribly selfish."

So that's it then, I *am* bewitched. Anger flares inside me, but also a cold sort of comfort. It's not *my* fault I feel this way. "What am I going to do?" I ask quietly.

"Well...you could just wait for it to wear off. Most spells do, in time. Or you could confront him. Maybe he would lift it, though it wouldn't be without a price. Or you could accept it. I mean, he wouldn't bespell you without a reason, right? So go on," he snickers, "run upstairs and ask him to take you. I bet you'll even like having his cock in your ass."

I cringe and jerk the door open, tripping over the uneven ground as I run away from Schaff's cruel laughter. I *hate* that word. I scramble over the rocks, not knowing or caring where I'm going. My feet slide out from under me as I hit a patch of loose pebbles, and I crash against a large boulder, a thin cry escaping my lips as my shoulder and hip hit the rock. I lay on the cold stone, hot tears stinging my eyes and wetting my cheeks. After a moment, I sit up and lean back against the face of the boulder, knees drawn up to my chest, out of the wind and out of sight of the castle.

I *hate* that word. The most evil of all my masters, Lord Machavar, used to make me say that word. When I wasn't crawling around his manor like a dog, I was on my knees with him inside me, one way or another. He would make me say things, things that still make me nauseous to hear, things that will never again pass my lips for as long as I live, things like "Let me suck your cock, Master," and "I want your cock in my ass, Master," and my personal favorite, "Please, Master, fuck me harder." Of all the men I have ever belonged to, he is the only one that I would hunt down and kill, were I a free man.

I cross my arms on my knees and bury my face in them, weeping like a child. I hate him, I hate Schaff, I hate Sactaren, I hate this place, I hate feeling like this, I hate, I hate, *I hate*! And I hate being so full of hate. I just... I want to break something, hurt someone, and that isn't me, any more than lusting after my master is me. I never thought I would long for a pick or a plow, but I do. I wish I were working the fields, or the mines, somewhere simple, anywhere but here.

"You okay, son?" I jump, scrambling to my feet as I try to wipe away the tears with the back of my hand. The man takes a step back, looking surprised. "Hey, easy there, lad, I ain't gonna hurt you." I put the boulder between us before I give him another look. He's strong and healthy for a man past his prime, tanned and wiry from plow and scythe, dressed in farmer's clothes, but with his good straw hat upon his head.

"Who are you? Sir," I add quickly. I'm in enough trouble without being rude.

"Are you the mage's boy?" he asks. I nod. "Great Maele, you're even younger than she said. Sorry, I'm Darimi. Calae is my daughter; she said you saved Iana's life." I nod again. He glances in the direction of the castle, licking his lips nervously before speaking again. "She, uh, she wanted me to check on you. She heard...uh, last night she heard..."

I feel my face color. She heard me screaming. "I'm fine," I say, studying the rocks between his shoes. "Her concern is touching. Please thank her for me." He nods, once, then turns and starts back down the mountain. "Wait, sir, did you need something from the shop? I can open early if—"

"No, son, but thanks."

"You-you came all the way up here just-just..." Just to check on me.

"My daughter has a kind heart," he says, adjusting his hat to better shade his eyes from the sun. "When she sees someone suffering, she has to help, and if she can't, it tears her up inside. I can't stand to see my little girl cry, so yes, I came up here just to look in on you."

He glances back at me and I clench my fists. His eyes are filled with pity. Pity is what people give you when they don't have the power to give anything else. I would just as well they keep it.

"Thank you both, then," I say, trying to keep my voice even and not let my irritation show. "Please assure your daughter that I am well, and that last night...it wasn't what she thinks happened." I would probably be more convincing if I didn't drop my eyes to the ground but I can't help it, any more than I can help the heat creeping up my neck.

"I see why she's taken to you," Darimi says after a moment. "If you ever need anything, any farm in the valley will take you in, after what you did for the Jesrens, and for my granddaughter. Take care, son." I watch him until he disappears around the first bend in the trail. *Any* farm would take me? A runaway slave? Anyone caught harboring a fugitive slave becomes the property of the slave's owner. I truly doubt anyone, let alone everyone, would risk becoming Sactaren's property, just for me. It's a nice thought, though.

I glance back at the sun rising higher above the southern edge of the mountain. I better get back to the castle. I still have time to grab a bite before the shop opens. Maybe I can get back at Schaff by not sharing my pie with him. It feels stupid and petty even as I think it, but after what he said to me, I don't care. I *hate* that word.

Chapter 12

Schaff is lazing on the counter in a pool of sunlight as I shove the door open and stalk inside. He flicks an ear, but otherwise doesn't acknowledge my return. That's fine; if I never have to talk to him again, it will be too soon. I walk around the counter and into the back room, both relieved and disappointed to find the stairway dark and empty. Khas has curled up in his straw, a half eaten Golden Goat Shoe clutched tight in his forepaws. I take a moment to look at the wounds on his back and head. They seem to be healing right up, though it's hard to tell through all that thick, sandy fur.

My stomach knots up, reminding me unnecessarily that I still haven't eaten. I open the cupboard and lift down the heavy peach pie. The moment the earthenware dish leaves the shelf, I know something is wrong. I know it was heavier than this when I put it up there. I set it on the counter with a thump, making Khas jump in his sleep.

"Schaff, what in the unholy name of Cheyn did you do to my pie?" I hiss, turning toward him.

He swishes his tail and rolls onto his back, his paws sticking up in the air. "I *told* you a cupboard wouldn't stop me." He stretches lazily and cracks one eye at me. "What are you so pissed about? I left you a slice." Yes, a nice, neat wedge, one of about six, it looks like. "H-how did you... Who cut this for you?"

"Nobody. I did it all myself."

"But...but you're..."

His ears flatten against his skull. "I'm what — an animal? I'm a machiran, slave, and more of a man than you'll ever be." He rolls to his feet and leaps down from the counter, heading back into the castle. "Besides," I hear him call back to me, "you don't live in a mage's castle for twenty-three years without learning a trick or two. Just look at what Naeven's already taught *you*."

I look down at the pie and my mouth suddenly tastes of ash, which of course reminds me of last night, which makes my face color. I push the dish away.

I can feel his hands moving over my body, so soft, so perfect, and I shiver. I rub my own hands together and hear my rough palms scratch against each other. There has to be...there has to be something... I scan the shelves. Maybe a hand cream? I hear the shop door open and grimace. I'd forgotten to lock it. Oh well, it must be about time to open anyway. I take a moment to straighten my shirt and brush the dust off my sleeve before I step out into the sun-lit shop.

"Hello?" I say, glancing from one side of the room to the other. I could have sworn I heard the door, but there's nobody here. I even lean over the counter in case there's a child or a goblin or something.

"You are not Thadyn." The voice is slick and whispery, dark, a voice from nightmares; and it's far too close for my liking, especially since I still can't find its owner.

"No, I-I'm Lark," I say. "I'm Lord Sactaren's new assistant. Forgive me, sir or-or madam, but I can't see you." Something large and gray drops down in front of my face and I jerk back with a yell, pressing myself against the shelves behind me.

"Is this better?" It's a spider, huge, each of its eight, many jointed legs as long as my arm and covered with short, stiff hairs. Its body is narrow and angular, charcoal gray with faint golden stripes and dark red spots, and it has more eyes than I can count — three large and black in the front of its head, and many more, smaller and an opaque amber color, on the sides. It regards me, its shiny black mouthparts twitching restlessly, looking like it could easily take a chunk out of my flesh. I wonder if it's poisonous. I try to swallow, but my mouth is dry.

"How-how may I-I help you?" I ask, though my first instinct is to grab a broom and swat it. I'm not generally afraid of spiders, but I've also never seen one the size of a sheep before. It drops down a little farther on a nearly invisible silken thread, and I flinch.

"Relax, young Lark, I will not eat you," it says with a grating chuckle. "I am Aracha, the Spidersmith. It is a pleasure to meet you. Is Lord Sactaren about?"

"He's...ah, he's asleep right now. I-I could wake him, I suppose, if you want." I pray that he will say no; I would rather stay here and be eaten than venture up those stairs.

"No, that is quite all right." I let out a relieved breath. The longer it is before I have to face my master again, the better. Like maybe sometime next year. "Just tell him that I brought his package, as promised."

Three of his long, hairy legs reach over his shoulders and I hear the sound of something sticky being torn from his back. He holds out this something, and I hesitantly reach out and take it. It's about a foot in length and almost cylindrical, wrapped completely in silver spider silk. I expect the silk to be sticky, but it's cold and smooth.

"I'll tell him," I say, stepping into the back room and placing it on the counter next to Khas. "Do I-do I need to pay you? Sir?"

"Do not bother with the formality, young Lark," he says with another rasping chuckle. "And no, I have already been paid. You *can* tell your master that the blade's core is the purest silver I could find, and that I hope it serves him well." I stiffen as he stretches out one long, gray leg and drags the furry tip over my scalp. "You are still a slave?" he asks.

"Y-yes," I say with a slight nod.

He drops down on his thread until his back four legs are resting on the counter top. The front four beckon to me. "Let me see your hand, then — the right one."

I hold out my hand and he takes it between the tips of his front legs, turning it this way and that, bringing it much too close to his shiny, sharp mandibles for my liking, and peering at it with his eerie black eyes. Finally, he unwraps a thick strand of silk from around his body and wraps it around the base of the middle finger of my right hand, making chattering, clicking sounds as he does. Without another word, he winds the thread back around his body and nimbly hauls himself up his thread and to the ceiling. He scuttles along the underside of the rough timbers as easily as I walk upon a well-worn path, crawling down the wall and opening the door.

"I hope to see you again soon, young Lark," he says, then slips through the doorway and shuts the door behind him. I lean back against the shelves with a sigh. Can't I have just one normal day?

"Were you talking to the six-legged rat again?" Schaff asks, sauntering into the shop with his bushy tail in the air.

"No," I say, giving him a dirty look. "The Spidersmith was just here."

Schaff stops dead, his sharp golden eyes narrowing. "You mean the blacksmith?"

"No, *Spider*smith, Aracha, I think. He brought a package for Lord Sactaren."

"And you didn't call me?" Schaff hisses, leaping up onto the counter and taking a swipe at my forearm. I jerk back just in time. "I've been waiting for that big bug for more than a month."

"Well, maybe you shouldn't have run off," I tell him, scowling. "How was I supposed to know you wanted to talk to him?"

Schaff fluffs his tail and the hair stands up along his back, but he just glares at me, that's all. I don't care. Let him glare, let him be pissed; it's not my job to keep him informed. He's supposed to be helping *me*, not slinking off whenever he feels like it, leaving me alone to deal with Maele only knew what—

"You're right," he growls after a moment, much to my surprise. He shakes his fur back into place and begins to wash his face. I guess that's all the apology I'm going to get.

I take a breath to say, "Of course I'm right," but I start to cough again, that thick, chest-rattling cough that feels like my lungs are tearing loose.

"Breathed a bit of smoke, did we?" Schaff asks with a smirk. He jumps down off the counter and beckons me into the back room with a flirt of his tail. "Let's see; where is it?" he mutters, scanning the shelves. "Ah, that brown glass jar next to the basket of snakes' skin, open it and take a big whiff."

Not entirely sure that he's not trying to kill me, I open the jar and take a deep breath. It's full of dry, faded geranium flowers, cedar branches, and rowan berries. It doesn't smell particularly strong, just a faint scent of cedar, and I raise an eyebrow at Schaff.

He grins, showing pearly, needle-like teeth. "You may want to grab a bucket."

I barely have time to set the jar down and run to the corner before the coughing seizes me, clawing through my lungs until I fall to my knees over a tin bucket and hack up slimy brown phlegm and darker, thicker things. I have tears running down my cheeks when I finally collapse back against the cupboards, each gasping breath burning like white fire in my chest. I wearily wipe them away and glance over at Schaff.

"Thanks," I say, climbing to my feet. I push the bucket toward the far corner with one foot and head back out into the shop. Schaff takes his customary place atop the ledger and begins to wash his face again. "Okay," I say after a moment, "so, what is a spidersmith?"

He smoothes back his whiskers and flicks an ear at me. "A spider...who is a smith. Spider. Smith. What part of this are you not grasping?"

"I meant," I say between my teeth, "what does a spidersmith do?"

"Smith's stuff." The tip of his tail is twitching and I realize he's toying with me. Verbal cat and mouse games, just what I'm in the mood for. I open my mouth to ask what kind of stuff, but he doesn't wait for me. "Aracha makes the greatest blades. Any kind of knife, dagger, sword, ax, he's the one you ask when you want the best. He makes beautiful jewelry, too. The Lady Sactaren wears one of his rings as her wedding band. If you're lucky," he says with a smirk, "maybe Naeven will get one for you, too."

"I doubt it, if he doesn't even want my help anymore," I say, casting a dark glance toward the back room. "Not-not that I want a ring from him, or anything else," I add quickly. Schaff chuckles and I want to backhand him off the counter. He'll scratch me, I'm sure, but it will shut him up, at least for a moment. Before I can decide if the pain would be worth it, the shop door opens.

"Oh, great," Schaff mutters, pasting a wooden smile onto his pointed muzzle.

It's Lord Drumar, dressed to impress in a white, long sleeved silk shirt, dark burgundy vest, black suede jacket, black trousers, his knee high black boots embellished with silver stitching, and his burgundy cloak edged with silver fur. He leaves the door open, letting in a chill breeze that blows feathers and dried flowers off of shelves.

"You're still here," he says, looking down his narrow, pinched nose at me. I don't bother trying to smile; it will only come out as a pained grimace. The best I can do is polite disinterest. I hope.

"How can we help you, Lord Drumar?" Schaff asks, and I'm glad I didn't get around to swatting him. He's so much better at this than I am.

Drumar eyes me for another moment, then turns and begins flipping through Sactaren's catalogue of spells. "The annual North Kadrian Hound Competition is in a few days," he says, speaking to the book, I guess, because he doesn't look at Schaff or me. "Lord Gahnet of Sechamira has won Best in Show for the last eight years running. His hounds are blessed by the gods, or something. What I need is a spell, nothing fancy, just enough to take a little meat off those beasts, maybe a bit of mange — no, a lot of mange, and fleas, or worms, just something to take them out of the competition—"

"I'm sorry, Lord Drumar," I say, cutting him off, "I'm afraid Lord Sactaren is booked up until the end of next week."

Schaff gives me a look, but I ignore him. I will not be party to such blatant cheating, or to mistreating animals. Drumar closes the catalogue with a snap and straightens up to his full height, a full hand taller than me, but across the counter, he's not so intimidating.

"I am willing to pay extra if he can work me into his schedule."

"Sorry, that's just not possible."

He huffs indignantly and glances around the shop. "Well, there must be something in here, a powder, or a charm—"

"No, there isn't," I say coldly. "Thank you for coming; please shut the door on your way out."

He glares at me, but there's nothing he can do, except stalk out into the wan morning sunshine and slam the door behind him.

"Well," Schaff says after a moment, "I didn't see that coming."

"Sorry," I mutter, walking around the counter to gather up the merchandise that litters the floor, "but I just couldn't stand the thought—"

"Me neither, but...I didn't have the balls to tell him to take a flying leap off the mountain and have a nice day." He chuckles. "The look on his face... I really didn't think you had it in you, kid. So, when are you going to talk to Naeven about this whole assistant thing?" I groan and begin gathering up the leaves, flowers, feathers and what-all scattered about in front of and under the shelves. "Don't tell me you're not gonna?"

"I'm not; I can't," I say, accidentally crushing a delicate sprig of faerie's cloak between my rough, clumsy fingers. "I would rather face ten Lord Drumars, than see Sactaren again. You...you don't know what it was like, what I tried to do—"

"He said you tried to jerk him off." I feel my face burn. "He wanted to let you, but—"

"My hands were too rough," I finish, looking down at my palms.

Schaff is silent a moment, then clears his throat. "You know..." he says slowly, "your hands would be easy to fix." I throw a suspicious glance his direction. "Well, maybe not *fix,* precisely, but we could soften up a lot of those calluses in just a few days. Of course, if we did, the question then becomes, how do we get you into Naeven's bed? Er, you do want another shot at him, don't you?"

"I don't know — I mean, no, of course not, I-I..."

He cocks his head to one side. "Then why do you need girly hands if you're not going to put them to good use?"

I throw the jumbled handful of crap into an empty basket and drop it onto the counter beside Schaff. "I never said I wanted 'girly hands'," I hiss at him between my teeth. "I never asked if there was something that would soften my calluses, okay?" Never mind that I was thinking it, I never said it.

"Okay," he says with a shrug of his tail. "But I don't think it would hurt, do you? Fortune favors the prepared, right?"

"I thought fortune favored the bold," I say.

He winks at me. "Not if they're unprepared. Come on, I'll fix you up." I follow him into the back room. "Now, let's see...first,

soak your hands in a bowl of warm water and a few drops of that."
He gestures with one paw toward a small, crystal bottle full of an
iridescent pink liquid.

I open the bottle and take a whiff. It smells flowery. "What is
it?"

"Rhododendron flower, mermaid's tears, aloe, and purple
something. Hibiscus, maybe?"

"Hang on, mermaid's tears? I thought mermaids couldn't cry."

"It's filtered sea water, you idiot, now shut up and pay
attention. After soaking, dry with a soft cloth and then rub your
calluses with one of these pumice stones." He nudges a basket of
rough, round rocks with his nose.

I pick one up hesitantly. "These aren't going to-to make me..."
I glance down at my crotch.

Schaff makes a disgusted sound in his throat. "It's not a magic
rock; it just scrapes off the thick skin. Although..." He eyes me for
a moment, then shakes his head. "Maybe later," he mutters. "Okay,
after the stone, rub in some lavender hand cream and you're all
set. Do it this evening, since you seem to have a bit of time on your
hands." He snickers and I roll my eyes. "Use the cream a couple
times a day, and do the whole process again in three days."

"I don't know," I say, "it seems like a lot of work for—"

"Hey, some things are worth a little work. Some things are
worth a lot a work."

He's as somber and thoughtful as I've ever seen him, and it
worries me. "Why are you doing this?" I ask. "Why are you helping
me?"

He looks shocked. "*Why*? You even have to ask?" He falls over
on his side and throws one paw across his face melodramatically.
"Oh, Lark, you wound me. I help you because I care, because I want
you to be happy. Is that so hard to believe?"

"Well...yeah. Since I arrived, you've not missed a chance to
torture me—"

"Okay, so I play a bit rough," he admits, rolling to his feet.
"But deep down under all this fur, I am a good guy. Remember
that."

He leaps down off the counter and heads out into the shop,
leaving me decidedly uneasy. I hate that feeling, like he's already
done something he knows I won't like, but I haven't found out yet.
I can't imagine what it might be, but I pray it doesn't involve
Sactaren.

I hear the shop door open and hope it's human this time.
Lucky me, two men shuffle into the shop, barefoot, in tattered

canvas trousers, one bare-chested, the other with his faded red vest hanging open. The one with the vest is sporting a relatively new black eye and a shiny gold hoop in his left ear. Both have sun-bleached blond locks, matted and pulled back in loose black ribbons, weathered bronze skin, and fearsome tribal tattoos covering their lean bodies.

"Morning, gentlemen," I say with a smile, though they look more like pirates than gentlemen to me. "How can I help you?"

They both wince, the one with the black eye pressing the heel of his hand to his temple.

"Could'ja shut up?" he hisses, his words slurred by more than his accent. "Screechin' like a fuckin' gull."

"We need some juice, quick like," the other says, laying a handful of grubby laenes on the counter.

I glance at Schaff. "They're hungover," he mutters. "Look in the second cupboard to the right of the hand creams; grab the large bottle of green liquid and two glasses."

I find the bottle easily enough, right between a bottle of blue liquid for heartburn and an orange liquid for sinus congestion. I grab the glasses and start to head back into the shop, but something in the tower stairwell catches my eye. Slender and shimmering, pale silver and dark gold, my heart skips a beat at the sight of this vision, draped in a shining white robe, hair like spun starlight flowing over its shoulders, almost colorless eyes held in deep shadow. It looks like Sactaren, and at the same time, it doesn't, it can't be. It regards me with those cold eyes and I shudder.

"C'mon, man, hurry up, would'ja? We're dyin' out here."

I glance toward the shop, just for a second, and when I look back, the specter is gone, if it was ever there to begin with. I take a step toward the stairs. "Hey, slave-boy, I've seen barnacles move faster." With one last glance toward the stairs, I hurry out into the shop.

"Sorry," I mutter, quickly pouring two glasses of the green stuff, which smells like a cross between vomit and wet dog. They gulp it down in one swallow, and, from the faces they make, it tastes at least as bad as it smells, probably worse.

"Thanks, kid," says the one with the black eye, setting his empty glass down with a thump. He nudges his companion in the ribs. "Doncha just love this town?" They laugh like...well, like drunken sailors as they leave, letting the door slam behind them.

The remainder of the day is uneventful. After lunch, old Mrs. Magroven drops in and buys a location charm to find her glasses, which she's misplaced three times since I started working. Near closing, the Roughlet family comes in to buy more marigold and field holly tea. They're sick again, which reminds me that I forgot to mention the sickness plaguing the town to Sactaren. I feel horrible as I watch them leave, the children weak and pale, because there's nothing on Maele's green earth that is going to send me up those tower stairs now. Maybe when Sactaren comes down to restock the supply room. Maybe.

As soon as the shop door is locked up for the evening, I want to slip out and hide in my room. If I don't see him, I won't have the chance to say something stupid, but I have to give him the package from Aracha, and if I can work up the courage, tell him about the sickness. I tidy up the back room and mix more packets of tea blends, waiting, but he doesn't appear. The longer I wait, the more time I have to think about everything he's done to me: bewitching me, seducing me, torturing me, and then tossing me aside because I wasn't good enough. I never pretended to be anything but a rough, worn out slave, but it was like he expected me to shed my battered exterior and emerge like some gaudy butterfly. I'm not a butterfly, damn it. I am just what I am — good, bad, whatever, this is me.

I feel like a fool. Sactaren has given me so much. He's treated me like I'm worth something, he's made me feel more like a human being than any man who's ever owned me and I was stupid enough to believe...I don't know, that he cared about me, that he liked me? I am a slave; I am dirt to him. Just because he doesn't beat or rape me doesn't mean I am anything more than dirt. It just means he is a better man than any I've known. I'm sitting on the short, wooden stool, watching Khas sleep, when Schaff comes in and rubs up against my leg.

"C'mon, let's get something to eat," he says. I glance toward the dark and silent tower steps. "Unless...you want to go up there and tell him how you really feel?"

"I'd rather dance with Cheyn," I mutter, rising to my feet. I'm through with waiting, I'm through with him and his charm and his spells and his fickleness. "If he doesn't want my help, that's fine. It's his loss." I start to leave, then turn back and grab Khas's crate. "Better take you with me," I tell him as he peers out at me with sleepy eyes, "before Sactaren gets it into his head to make you into a hat or something."

"Hang on," Schaff calls after me, "what about the stuff for your hands?"

"I like my hands the way they are," I tell him as I stalk out of the shop. "They suit me." Hard, rough, and unwanted. Yeah, they suit me.

Chapter 13

It's late and I'm hungry — late enough that I'm willing to bet that Schaff's asleep, and hungry enough to risk running into him if he's not. Wearing just a nightshirt and robe, I slip out of my room and creep down the corridor, the floor like ice under my bare feet. It would have been nice if whoever had laid the carpet in Lady Sactaren's half of the castle would have bothered to finish the job, instead of hacking it off in the middle of the hallway. I pause at the kitchen door and glance toward Her Ladyship's domain — midnight blue carpet on the floor, tapestries and silks hanging from the walls, oil lamps with globes of amber glass instead of smoky, guttering torches — the difference of night from day from this half of the castle. But why?

If Sactaren is half as rich as he and Schaff say he is, then why is his area of the castle so bare, so empty? Only the tower feels lived in. But surely, he must come downstairs to sleep; there's no room up there. Mages still have to sleep, right? I shake my head and ease the kitchen door open. No one's waiting for me, so I cut myself a slice of bread and dig through the ice box, finally deciding on a leg from a roast chicken. I sit at the scarred kitchen table, my eyes wandering around the room as I make short work of the food.

Everything in here is old, used. Someone cooked in here, once. But the oven is always cold, the fire just a bed of coals, the knives and pans and everything else always put away in their places. Thadyn said there was no cook, so where does the bread come from, where does the roast chicken, and pheasant, and venison come from? Is this just another facet of the mage's castle? I toss the chicken bones into the waste bucket and wipe my hands on the front of my robe before I notice a towel lying on the counter. I glance down at myself and grimace. I've left greasy smears on the russet cloth. I need to remember that I'm not just a slave anymore. Sactaren's words send a shiver through me, and it's like I can feel his hands gliding across my skin again, so soft and cool, and gentle. He never hurt me. The magic hurt, but his hands never did. Shaking my head, I take a steadying breath and head out of the kitchen.

"Oh." I jump and whirl about, my heart hammering as I look down the hall, toward Lady Sactaren's part of the castle. "I didn't know anyone else was awake." Her Ladyship is standing in the hall, a good ten feet beyond the edge of her territory, her hands clasped in front of her, looking startled. Not nearly as startled as I am to see her.

"Please don't tell my husband I was here," she says, biting the edge of her lip. She's wearing a pale pink nightdress, a sheer white silk robe doing little to hide her state of undress.

"I-I — no, of course not," I say, lowering my eyes to the floor. I hear her move, and to my surprise, she walks closer.

"Who are... Wait...you're the new slave: Alarik."

"Lark, M'Lady."

She's silent for a moment. "Was I right, Lark?"

"I beg your pardon, M'Lady?" I ask.

"Did he hurt you? Was that you I heard screaming last night?" Heat races to my face and neck, and I turn my head away. "I'm sorry. I should have done more to save you from him."

"M'Lady, it wasn't—"

"I know, but...I knew what he was going to do to you. I should have...warned you better, something. I was just so angry at Thadyn..." I glance up at her and she wrings her hands. "But that shouldn't have stopped me from trying to help you. You didn't deserve to be subjected to his sadistic perversions."

"M'Lady," I say again, "that wasn't what happened." She blinks at me, looking surprised. "I-I helped him with some magic yesterday, and the magic...got into me, or something, and he...got it out. I don't quite understand it, but he didn't hurt me."

"Is that right?" she says quietly. "Well, then, you're very lucky. You still have time to save yourself."

"M'Lady, are-are you telling me to run away?"

She looks horrified. "No, no — you can't do that. I've seen what my husband does to runaway slaves. There's no escaping him, but...he prides himself on his seduction, so he won't force himself on you. He'll just...give you no other choice, if you let him. That is his game, to feed his ego and coax you into his bed, but once he has you there..." She covers her mouth with one hand and turns her face away. "What he will do does not bear thinking about."

I swallow hard. "What-what can I do?" I ask in a whisper.

She steps toward me suddenly and takes my hand in both of hers. I have to fight not to pull away. "Remember," she says, "remember that it's just a game to him. No matter what he says or does, all he wants is to possess you, to win. Don't let him." I give a slight nod and she lets go of me, absently wiping her hands on her robe as she turns away.

"Th-thank you, M'Lady," I say, keeping my voice low. She glances back and smiles, and then returns to her part of the castle.

I glance around and swallow hard, then hurry back to my room. Not until the door is closed do I dare breathe. I was right — I am just a toy to him, a pawn, something to amuse himself with. But if that's true, why doesn't he want me helping him? Does he really think himself so irresistible that I will surrender even if he's cold to me? I'm stronger than that. I will never give in to him.

Over on the table, Khas rustles in the straw of his crate. His large, black eyes gleam with lamplight from between the slats, watching me as I cross the room to stand beside the table. He steps up against the slats, sticking his foremost pair of limbs out toward me. He gestures rapidly as I pull out the chair and sit down.

"I wish I knew what you were saying," I murmur. He stops, his round ears twitching at the sound of my voice. "I know you're smart; it's not your fault you don't have a voice. If you did, I know I could teach you to speak." After the day I've had, I would certainly appreciate the distraction.

We regard each other for a moment, then he turns away. I start to get up but he comes back to the slats, a short piece of straw held in one paw. He points at it, then makes a slashing motion through the air, his thumb and two lower fingers tucked against his palm, and the first two fingers extended. I copy him, sort of, and he shows me again, slower. When I have it right, he points at the straw again and makes the gesture. I raise my eyebrows, a slight gasp escaping my lips. He's teaching me!

After straw, he finds a rock in the bottom of the crate, one of the ones I tried to feed him, and punches his fist into the air. Rock. Easy enough. Then he holds out a piece of a Golden Goat Shoe. That's a bit more complicated. He starts by making a loose fist, his thumb stuck out and pointing to the side, then he rotates his wrist, bringing his thumb to point upward. After this, he tucks his thumb against his palm and extends his first two fingers again, then brings his fingertips toward his face. I swear, it takes me ten minutes to get the motions right. When I do finally get it, Khas claps his paws together and bounces around the crate. I have to admit, I'm pretty happy, too.

He's out of things to show me, straw, rocks, and goat shoes being the extent of the contents of the crate. Well, not quite. I point at him and he cocks his head at me. I point at the straw and make the gesture for straw. Same with the rock. Then I point at him again. He seems to get what I mean, because he shows me a new gesture. Using both hands, he places the fingertips of his right hand against the palm of the left, then slides the right along the fingers of the left. I point at myself and he regards me for a minute, then places his right fist against his left palm and slides his closed fist along his fingers. I mimic the gestures and absently bite at the inside of my lower lip. They're so similar, these two words. I'm thinking they must be kholdra, for him, and human, for me, rather than names. I wonder if kholdra even have names. I yawn suddenly, so I guess it's too late to find out tonight.

"Sorry, Khas," I say, standing up and pushing in the chair, "I gotta sleep now." I point at my bed. He holds out one hand, palm down, but parallel with his chest, and then lays the other hand onto top of the first. Bed, sleep? Whatever, that's where I'm headed. I hear him burrow down into the straw as I walk away and a faint smile lifts the corners of my mouth. I'm learning to speak kholdra. Who ever would have thought? With a sigh, I slip out of my robe and toss it on the foot of the bed before sliding under the quilt and turning out the lamp. After the last few days, I can't wait to see what tomorrow brings.

Chapter 14

A crate of new merchandise is waiting for me when I enter the shop in the morning. The package from Aracha is gone, too. I try not to feel disappointed as I put the bottles and charms away, but I can't help it. I dreamed of him. Kinda made it hard to wake up angry.

The crate is empty and I sigh. Not even a note of apology, explanation, nothing. I glance at the dark stairwell, fighting the urge to slip up those twisting steps and seek comfort in his light, gentle touch. I clench my fists and turn away, stalking out to lean on the front counter, scowling at the front door. Sactaren's touch be damned. I keep forgetting — he's making me feel this way with his charms and his magic. It's just a game; it's not real. I just have to keep fighting until it wears off, that's all I can do.

I guess I'm lucky he's avoiding me. I can't imagine how hard it would be to resist him, were he here, whispering in my ear; his touch so deliberately casual, the musky, smoky scent of him surrounding me— I jump as Schaff leaps up onto the counter in front of me.

"So," he says cheerily, "are we feeling brave this morning?" My scowl deepens. He either doesn't notice or doesn't care. "If you are, I could be persuaded to keep an eye on the shop while you tip-toe up—"

"Forget it," I snap, slamming my hand flat on the counter. "I would rather die than go to him, after what he's done to me."

"And what did he do?" Schaff asks, sounding genuinely perplexed.

"I've been used and abused and thrown away by every man I've ever known," I say, leaning down into his face. "I didn't care, because I hated them, because they made it clear that it was my place to do and be whatever they wanted, that I meant nothing to them. But he...he..." I don't even know how to explain it.

"So, you're not mad because he doesn't want you," Schaff says after a moment. "You're mad because you wanted him to want you."

I turn away. "Yes — no. He bespelled me," I say. I can't forget, or forgive, that. "He *made* me want him. He made me do things, feel things I would never do, never feel. I know better than to lust after my master."

Schaff makes a noncommittal grunt and settles down for his nap. I shuffle around the shop all morning, rearranging the displays when I am not helping customers. Thadyn left the place in a decidedly organized mess. Everything *looks* neat and tidy, but it is in no order whatsoever. The lavender wands are stuck in beside the blessing seeds; the dream sachets are stacked with the fever stones; yucca root and lilac blossom are in the same basket, for love of Maele! After that is finished, Schaff teaches me a game; simple at first glance, but I can't seem to beat him. He assures me that I'll get better. Apparently Thadyn did.

On the back inside cover of the ledger, a nine square grid is drawn. We take turns placing stones in this grid, his black, mine white, in order to make a row of three, either vertically, horizontally, or diagonally. He calls it Kit-cat's Toe, which just sounds stupid to me. Maybe it's because I never win.

He's just beaten me for the eleventh time in a row when he sits up suddenly, the smug grin vanishing from his face. "Lord Sactaren," he says, quickly hiding the game with his bushy tail, "what a surprise."

I turn slowly, trying desperately to think of something to say before I face him, because I know the ability to form a complete sentence will leave me once I lay eyes on him. I'm right.

He's dressed plainly today: barefoot as usual, soft looking, gray trousers, and a flowing white shirt tucked in but left unbuttoned, and his hair — not the sleek curtain of black, but a more feathery, shimmery mass of palest gold, almost white, though clearly not, as it lays against his shirt. Glittery crystals hang from the ends of several thin braids, locks of burgundy and black twisted about the pale gold. It still falls nearly to his waist but it's wilder, a mane of unkempt morning sunlight. Several locks hang in front of his eyes, and I want to reach up and brush them aside. Eyes as crystal blue as his should never be covered.

"What's the matter, Lark? You look like you've seen a ghost," he says, and his voice reaches right through me. I'd forgotten how much he can do with just his voice.

"I-I..." I lower my eyes. "Your hair."

"Yes, well, I'd grown tired of the black."

I say nothing else; I can't think of anything else, and he's silent so long I'm beginning to think he's waiting for something. Do I owe him an apology? Suddenly, I can't remember.

"Schaff," he says finally, stepping forward and reaching around me to drop a small bag onto the counter. The contents clink like money. "It seems I'm in need of a new assistant." His words hollow me out, like everything inside me has died. "Please try and choose one without any unwelcome surprises this time." He turns and disappears into the back room without a single glance at me.

Unwelcome surprises? Is that what I am, an unwelcome surprise? I look back at Schaff as he clears the pieces from the game board with a swipe of his paw.

"I won, so you go first," he says, hunkering down to study the empty squares.

"Shouldn't you head down and choose another assistant now?" I ask bitterly.

"Me? Do I look like I'm wearing my shopping shoes?" He rolls his eyes. "I don't leave the castle, okay? I'd tell you who to look for, just like I told Thadyn."

"You-you told him to get *me*? Why?"

He shrugs his tail. "I had a feeling about you. Still do, actually."

He's making no sense, but I let it go. I don't really care. "So, are you going to tell me?" I ask.

"Nah, it'd be a wasted trip. Are you going to make a move?"

"How do you know?" I ask, dropping a white stone in the center square.

He shrugs his tail. "I just do."

I roll my eyes. Lazy pest. Well, it is getting on into the afternoon. Good slaves tend to go early. I guess he's right. "So you'll tell me tomorrow, then?"

Schaff grins as he beats me again. "Maybe. Are you in a big hurry to be replaced, or something?"

I close my eyes and I can see Sactaren, staring right through me, turning away as if I don't even exist. "Yes," I say, "I am. The sooner, the better."

We both jump as something clatters to the floor in the back room. Several black banishing stones come bouncing through the doorway and spin to a stop at my feet. Schaff leaps down and I'm right behind him, but the back room is empty. The little basket has been knocked from its shelf and round black stones are scattered across the flagstone floor. I raise my eyes to the dark, empty stairwell.

"Er, Lark, don't mention this to Naeven, okay?" Schaff says suddenly. "It's my job to keep the castle free of rats, and..."

"Yeah, okay," I say, righting the basket and beginning to gather the stones back up. Rats. Of course. The great Lord Sactaren wouldn't waste his precious time eavesdropping on us. What was I thinking?

Chapter 15

Schaff does not send me to the slave market the next morning, claiming that it was going to rain, which, to his credit, it did. But he does not say anything the next morning, either, though the skies are clear and the breeze coming off the ocean is almost warm. I do not bother to ask why. The odds that I will get a straight answer are not in my favor. This morning, as I make my way into the shop, Schaff is already sprawled out in a puddle of sunshine on the counter, his red-gold coat glowing like a bed of coals.

"So, how's the weather this morning?" I ask as I slip behind the counter and into the back room. Another crate is waiting for me. I stifle a sigh and begin to put the bottles on the shelves. "Is it a good day for a walk?"

"Will you quit asking me that?" Schaff growls, though it's the first mention I've made in two days. "There's nothing down there that's better than what's up here. Quit being such a dipshit and talk to him."

"We have nothing to say to each other," I mutter. Some things don't need to be said.

Schaff stretches, nearly rolling off of the ledger and peers sleepily in my direction.

"Lark? Er..." He jumps awake, his ears flicking up and down nervously. "I-I thought you were — erm, how's your pet rat this morning?"

I narrow my eyes at him. "He's fine. Why?"

"Just curious," he says and starts washing his tail. "You teach him to talk yet?"

"No, but he's teaching me..." Schaff is obviously not paying attention, so I don't even bother finishing the sentence. "That reminds me, I need to get him more food. Holler if anybody comes in, okay?"

"No problem."

I slip outside and lean against the sun-warmed face of the castle. Asking about Khas, agreeing to watch the shop so quickly...Schaff is hiding something. What had he said? *I thought you were...* Who, Sactaren? Not even Schaff would call Lord Sactaren a dipshit — would he? I head out into the shadow of the castle, climbing among the piles of broken rock. Golden Goat Shoes aren't that hard to find, now that I know what I'm looking for.

And so what if Schaff had thought he was talking to Sactaren? It wasn't like he said anything important. *There's nothing down there that's better than what's up here. Quit being such a dipshit and talk to him.* Schaff wants Sactaren to talk to me? Or maybe he doesn't. Maybe he knew it was me all along. Maybe he's just fucking with me. I wouldn't put it past him.

With my hands full of lichen, I carefully pick my way through the rocks, heading back to the castle. I try to keep my eyes on the ground ahead of me, but I can't help it — I glance up at the tower window. He's watching me. I know it even before I see him, seated on the sill, his back against the window frame, pale hair spilling over his shoulder and dancing in the wind. I pause, just for a moment, just a hesitation between steps, and then I tear my eyes away and hurry into the castle.

Why does he torment me so? He has to know what the sight of him does to me, and yet he's always there, so beautiful, as if to say, "See what you're missing? See what you will never have?" To make someone long for your touch, and then deny it to them — it's torture of the soul, that's what it is. Does he want to break me, does he want me to come crawling to him, begging him? I would like to say that I won't, that I'm stronger than that, but I've never been in a situation like this. All I can say is that I won't do it today, not unless he does something more than sit in a window and look pretty.

I'm half expecting him to be waiting in the shop when I return, but there's no one but Schaff, asleep on the ledger once again. I step into the back room, not sure if I'm relieved or disappointed to see that he's not standing in the stairwell, and put the goat shoes into an empty basket. I've walked to the stairwell doorway before I realize it, but once I do, I just stand there with one hand on the wall and look up into the darkness. He's up there somewhere, perhaps still in the window. I could go up there. It wouldn't take but five minutes to tell him... What? That I hate him, or that he doesn't need to find a replacement? I'm not sure either is true right now. I hear the shop door open and I turn from the stairwell with a sigh.

"Good morning, Lord Drumar," Schaff says, and I groan inwardly. What the hell does he want now?

"Has your master gotten rid of that worthless... Never mind," Drumar says, his upper lip curling as I step out of the back room. He's dressed in white and midnight blue today. He drops two shiny coins on the counter. "I would like five tablets out of the black box. Now."

"You mean Rapture?" Schaff asks with a predatory grin. "Planning a special night with the missus?"

"Hardly," Drumar snorts. "It would take more than five to get her knees apart."

"So, who's the lucky lady?" Drumar glances at me. "Beat it, slave," Schaff snaps at me. "Go make yourself useful." I want to backhand him off the counter, but head into the back room instead, pretending not to listen as I search through the cupboards for a black box.

"My wife has a new lady-in-waiting," Drumar says, his voice smug. "Just this sixteen-year-old slip of a girl, but she's got these tits like you wouldn't believe." He and Schaff chuckle and I feel nauseous. "She's a little...nervous, you know."

"She turned you down, eh?"

"Slapped me in the face, actually. But that's what you're here for, right?"

"Absolutely. Hang on while I go see what's taking him so long. I swear, he can't find his ass with both hands and a map." Drumar laughs uproariously.

I lean against a shelf, out of sight, and wait for Schaff. He trots in and shudders from whiskers to tail. "What was that all about?" I ask, teeth clenched and lips barely moving.

Schaff shakes his head. "Rapture is an aphrodisiac," he tells me, like I care. "Couples take it to loosen up; it makes sex a lot more enjoyable, from what I've heard. It can also be slipped into someone's drink, making them a lot more open to unwanted advances."

I glance toward the doorway. "You mean, he's going to drug that girl and rape her?"

"I've heard that he's done it before. Thadyn never questioned anyone's motives. Too bad for Drumar that he's... Uh, Lark, what are you doing?" I step over him, my fists clenched at my sides, and stalk out into the shop.

"It's about time," Drumar says with a sneer.

Without a word, I walk around the end of the counter and slam my fist into his face. I'm not really a fighter; the few scraps I've been in all ended badly for me, but I catch him by surprise and he stumbles backward across the shop. I grab his coins off the counter and follow him, hands shaking, not even sure what I'm going to do when I get to him. I must have the fury of five Hells written across my face, for Lord Drumar scrambles to the door and jerks it open, stumbling out into the bright sunlight, a dark smear of blood gleaming red across his chin. He grabs his horse and clambers up into the saddle. I throw the coins at him as he rides away, finally finding my voice.

"And don't you *ever* come back!" I shout, stooping down to grab rocks and fling them after him as well. "Go on, run, you filthy, raping coward, before my master turns you into a toad, you bastard!"

My voice echoes from the mountainside, and all down the valley I see men and women in their fields straighten up and turn my way. I look from them to the cloud of dust thrown up by Drumar's horse, and then up at the tower window, where Sactaren is standing, watching me. "Great Maele, what have I done?" I whisper, suddenly feeling like I want to vomit. I stagger back into the shop, finding Schaff seated atop the ledger, his wide gold eyes following my every move.

"Will wonders never cease?" he asks finally. "You punched him in the face."

"I...did," I say, looking down at my knuckles. They're red and already starting to swell. I flex my fingers, wincing slightly as something pops back into place. "Oh, shit, I did."

"Yeah," Schaff says slowly, "you probably shouldn't have done that."

I lean back against the closed door and sink to the floor, wrapping my arms around my knees. "He's going to kill me, isn't he?"

"Naeven? Nah, I don't think so," Schaff says, jumping down and padding over to sit at my feet. "I just meant...I have a feeling that this is going to cause you pain in the future. But it's just a small feeling, so it could be months before it comes to pass, or not at all. I can be wrong. I have been. Well, not lately."

"Schaff, what the hell are you talking about?" I ask.

He looks up, like he didn't realize he'd been rambling on. "I get feelings," he says after a moment. "I know things, like when it's going to rain, or when there's going to be an earthquake, or when Naeven needs to be somewhere."

"And you have the feeling that there's pain in my future?" I let out a short bark of laughter. "You don't have to be psychic to know that. I'm a slave."

He harrumphs and walks away with his nose and tail in the air. "Fine, don't believe me," he says, "but don't say I didn't warn you. And you might want to get up. A customer is coming." He curls up in the corner, facing the wall so he can better ignore me.

I sit a moment, waiting for someone to push against the door, and when no one does, I snort and stand up, brushing the dust off the seat of my pants. "A customer, huh? Now, is this a big feeling, or a little feel—"

I jump back as the door swings inward, banging into my elbow and sending bolts of tingling pain shooting to my fingertips. I grit my teeth and dance backward, rubbing furiously at my aching elbow while Schaff rolls around in the corner, laughing himself silly.

"I'm sorry, is...this a bad time?" A young man I've never seen before hesitates in the doorway, glancing back and forth from me to Schaff.

"No, c'mon in," I say, shaking out my arm and aiming a kick in Schaff's direction as I slip behind the counter. "How can I help you, sir?" He's a farmer type: faded overalls, dirty handkerchief, battered straw hat, but I'm betting the hat is older than he is. If he's my age, I'd be surprised.

"Well, I — you know, I'm not even sure I'm in the right place." He steps inside, rubbing his dirty hands together and shying away from the shelves of various animal bones, pelts, and skulls. "See, I moved my family up here from Ovash, and I bought this farm on the other side of the headlands, but—"

"All you can get to grow is weeds, right?"

He jumps as Schaff leaps up onto the counter. "Er, right."

I'm guessing he's never seen a machiran before. He starts to reach out, like he's going to try and pet him, but I catch his wrist. "He really hates that," I say with a laugh. He looks at my hand, at the tracery of scars disappearing up under my sleeve, and his face pales.

"Thanks," he says. "I-I'm not sure what you can do, but everyone I've talked to said to come here."

"Well, they were right. First of all, how big a farm are we talking?" Schaff asks.

"Eighty acres."

"Okay, so too big to just spread some cow shit and unicorn milk and call it done. This is going to take a spell." He taps a paw on the cover of Sactaren's spell catalogue and I flip it open. "Now, how much money do you have?"

"How much is it going to cost?"

Schaff gives him a crooked smile. "Depends on how much you've got."

I swear, if Schaff worked on his people skills half as much as his caustic humor...

"We don't have much," the young farmer says stiffly, "but you can have it all if you can make that barren land give a decent crop this year."

"What's your name?" I ask before Schaff can completely alienate the young farmer. He gives me a funny look. "I'm Lark," I add with a friendly smile.

"Jaek," he says. "Jaek Chorel."

"Nice to meet you," I say, then turn to the catalog. "Now, Jaek, it looks like a basic enrichment spell is going to run you a quarter laene per acre. That's..." I do the figuring in my head, "one coin for the whole farm, I think." Schaff gives me a slight nod. "Yes. This says a basic spell is good for a few weeks and best for hardier crops. What are you growing?"

"Sweet potatoes, mostly, though I was just about to sow some feed corn for the animals."

"Sounds like you need a spell to last all season, then." I flip through several pages of the book. "A laene an acre...that'd be four coins, total."

"I can do that," Jaek says, a slight frown on his face as he digs into his pocket and places the coins on the counter. "How soon can you get out to my place?"

"Our master is quite busy," Schaff says, jumping back into the conversation. "The night of the new moon is his first opening, I'm afraid."

Jaek worries his lip between his teeth for a moment. "I was hoping to plant this week, but next is good enough, I guess."

He gives us directions to his farm and Schaff fills him in on how to prepare the fields for the spell. I don't know enough about magic for what he says to make sense to me. I excuse myself to the back room and kill time by sorting a bag of mixed semi-precious stones. Luckily, it's just separating colors, because my mind is definitely not on the task. I keep stealing glances toward the tower stairs.

Shoving the piles of stones aside, I rise to my feet, then quickly sit back down. What am I doing? Nothing I can possibly say to that man will make a difference. I jump up, knocking over the little wooden stool, and stride toward the stairs, my hands balled into fists. Maybe it won't make a difference, but I'll feel better for saying it. I return to the table and right the stool. No, I'll only make him more angry with me. I wipe away a single frustrated tear before it has a chance to fall. Maybe I should. Maybe if he's angry enough, he'll just get rid of me. I wish he would.

"I just wish I belonged to anyone else," I mutter, scraping the stones back into their velvet bag. I hear a sound and turn, my heart beating wildly as I stare into the dark, empty stairwell. Damn rats. For a second, I though Sactaren had overheard me. But no, I'm sure he has much better things do, like sitting in his window, waiting for my replacement. Is that why I'm still here, because Schaff keeps stalling? "Damn it, Schaff," I groan, hiding my face in my hands, "just find someone, will you? I hate this."

Chapter 16

Spring is in the air, and everything on the planet with a pulse has gone completely crazy. This morning an entire gaggle of giggling girls invade the shop, decimating the basket of rose quartz, heart-shaped love charms. They want potions to make their breath fresh and their teeth white, creams to cover freckles and soften skin, charms to make their breasts big and their waists small. Girls with straight hair want curls, girls with curly hair want it straight; everyone wants stardust on their cheeks and roses on their lips. I am exhausted by the time they leave.

This afternoon, it is the guys, one or two at a time, a steady parade of aftershave lotions, performance enhancing teas, Rapture tablets, and contraceptive potions. I lock the door behind the last one and lean against the thick oak with a sigh.

"What is it with everybody?" I ask Schaff as he intently stalks a rock cricket across the floor. "It's like, the sun comes out and suddenly they can't keep their hands off each..."

I swallow hard. Lord Sactaren is standing in the doorway of the back room, his winter blue eyes tracking Schaff as he slinks between the shelves. He doesn't look at me, doesn't even acknowledge my presence, and I hold perfectly still, as if afraid to draw his attention, though I know damn well that he misses nothing. Schaff suddenly leaps high in the air, a predatory grin on his pointed face, his front legs held stiff as he lands upon the unfortunate insect, squashing it into a yellow-gray smear.

"No wonder I don't have a new assistant," Sactaren says, causing Schaff to glance up sharply.

Schaff flicks one ear back and slowly forward again, taking a moment to shake bug guts from his paw before speaking. "My Lord, impatience only leads to disappointment. You know that." Sactaren's eyes shift to me and I look down at the floor to keep him from reading my face. Longing, anger, resentment, sadness — I'm not sure which he will see, since I'm not sure which I feel the most. "Perhaps tomorrow."

"If you value your hide, it better be tomorrow," Sactaren says, his voice hard. "I don't care what you bring back, just get me a new slave."

I press my lips into a thin line and stare determinedly at the dusty flagstones. I don't see what right he has to sound so angry. I haven't done anything; Schaff hasn't done anything. I glance at him, and he's watching me.

"You should be pleased to know all your subservient sucking up has paid off," he says, and his words sting. "I received a message just this morning from a local lord, offering quite a sum of money for you. Not quite as much as I paid, but certainly more than you're worth. Congratulations. As soon as I have a new slave, you have a new home."

I meet his eyes, this time hoping he can read me, because I'm *glad* he's selling me.

"As you wish, Master," I say quietly, seeing a flicker of anger spark in his eyes before I bow my head again.

I know he hates being called Master; that's why I did it. If he's going to be angry with me, the least I can do is deserve it. Besides, now that I am to be sold, odds are he won't do anything to me. Most people won't buy broken merchandise. Out of the corner of my eye I see him turn with a jerk and disappear through the supply room doorway. A second later, I hear something glass shatter upon the stones. I glance at Schaff, who gives me a dirty look.

"Cheyn take you, Lark, why do you have to be so fucking stupid?" he hisses, padding toward the back room, his tail slung low.

"Go to hell," I tell him, following. "I've had enough of his crap — hiding away in his tower, watching me from his window, storming around like this is my fault. *He's* the one who didn't want me to help him, *he's* the one who didn't want me to touch him, *he's* the one who let me get taken by magic. He was probably hoping I would, so he'd have an excuse to fondle me. He couldn't just come out and rape me like the rest of them."

We step into the supply room, where a thick, white cream is slowly oozing down the wall next to the stairwell, spatters of cream and shards of glass littering the floor halfway out into the room.

"Wow, you really pissed him off this time," Schaff says.

"I don't care," I say, jaw tight as I scan the shelves, trying to figure out which of the jars was now exploded against the wall, but nothing seems out of place. "I almost believed him, you know. I almost believed that he was different, that he wouldn't hurt me, that he wouldn't use me. But all masters are the same, I guess." I watch the cream drip down the wall for a moment, then glance down at Schaff. "What is that?" I ask.

Schaff leans down and sniffs a fleck of cream, jerking back with a sneeze and shake of his head. "Carnation, willow bark, avocado oil, and...something else — phoenix ash. What was he..."

He glances up at me, and his eyes go wide. "Oh, Naeven, you didn't."

He streaks up the stairs in a blur of red and white. Scowling, I turn away. I don't care. One more day, that's all I have to put up with, and then I'll never have to see either of them again.

I'll never see them again, I realize as I pour water from the bottomless pitcher into a bucket and grab the mop out of the corner. I try to tell myself that this is a good thing, but I can't ignore the empty, hollow ache in my chest. I slop water onto the stones and begin to mop up the mess. Even taking these last few days into account, I've never had a more kind and generous master, but even taking his kindness into account, no one has ever hurt me as he has. I pause, glancing toward the stairs as their voices echo down the narrow stone stairwell. I can't make out words, but both are shouting, both are angry. I strain to hear, and jump as a sharp *bang* makes the jars clink together on their shelves. Sactaren must have slammed a door. I frown. There aren't any doors upstairs. I wait, but I don't hear another sound from above.

Slowly, I clean up the cream and the broken glass. A lord wishes to buy me. I was so shocked by Sactaren's words, I didn't really hear them, until now. I impressed a lord. I've waited on several minor lords these past two weeks, all with small manors and a few hundred acres of land, with servants and other slaves. I can't think of anything specific I might have done to "suck up" as Sactaren so viciously put it. I could be bought by any of them.

Fields again, though. I like working in the magic shop; I don't want to end up hoeing someone's crops all day. And other slaves... I've been at the bottom of the pecking order enough times to know I don't want to be the new guy again. They give you the rockiest part of the field and the dullest hoe; they take your food, spill your water, and shove you to the wettest, draftiest spot in the slave quarters. I stop dead. I'll be made to sleep on the floor again, in slave rags. I grit my teeth. I don't care. I won't let myself be coaxed into his bed just to keep my feather mattress and fancy clothes. I will give up nearly anything to keep that shred of my dignity — knowing that I have never given in to any of them. Some slaves do, becoming nothing more than sex toys and whores, just to save themselves a beating or two. I will always prefer to be beaten.

I glance toward the stairs, wondering when Schaff will come slinking back down. I haven't heard anything since the door slammed. With a sigh, I admit to myself that I will miss *him*, at least. I've never had a friend before. I'll probably never have one again, but I don't care; I *can't* stay here. Every time Sactaren walks into the room, or I hear his voice come whispering through my dreams, I can feel his hands again, and I'm torn between blackest despair and blazing desire. All the friendship in the world isn't worth one more minute of that.

Chapter 17

The lamp is turned low, the slats of the crate casting thin black shadows across Khas's sleeping form. I sit at the table and just watch him, his stumpy little ears and tail twitching now and again in his sleep, his breathing deep and easy. I've been sitting here since I realized...I can't keep Khas, either. Golden Goat Shoes only grow in the mountains, and anyway, slaves aren't allowed to keep pets.

The more I think about it, the more I realize what I'm giving up, and the more I wonder if it's truly worth it. And I'm not just talking about the clothes and the room and the access to the kitchens and Khas. Sactaren's allowed me responsibility, and choices, and feelings, and the one thing he's asked of me, he's never really asked for. I know he wants me — well, wanted me, I'm not so sure now — but he never asked, never ordered, never took. He has given me so much, would it be so horrible to give him something in return if it meant I could stay? Being here is the closest I've felt to free in thirteen years.

I rise quietly and walk to the door, stopping with my hand on the latch. Do I really want to do this, or is it just really late and I'm not thinking clearly? If I go to him, I am destroying that last bit of self-respect I have suffered so long to keep. I take my hand back, then quickly strip off my tunic and toss it onto my bed. I can't imagine why, but he seemed to like seeing me bare-chested. Maybe it will be enough of a gesture, and I won't have to say anything.

Self-respect is fine, but it won't keep you warm, or dry, or fed, and it won't mend broken bones, or erase scars. I reach up and run my fingers over the knife scar on the side of my face, the one Sactaren used his magic to hide. Taking a shaky breath, I pull the door open and slip out into the hall, easing it closed behind me.

"Going somewhere?"

I tense, my heart climbing into my throat as his voice slithers around me, cold as a serpent. I turn, slowly, to face him. He's standing in the deep shadow between two guttering torches, his eyes glinting as he scours me from head to toe, his gaze lingering on my naked skin. I was right, I guess. Yay for me.

"M'Lord, I-I..." I swallow my damn stammering like a bad taste. "I couldn't sleep."

He steps closer, the amber light playing over his hair and making it shimmer between sunlight and starlight, gold and silver.

"What a coincidence," he says, stopping not half an arm's length from me, close enough that I can smell his heavy, wild scent, "neither could I."

He's wearing a robe of white and silver silk, the thin material flowing around him as he moves, and I'm struck by the image of his specter standing in the stairwell, watching me. It wasn't a ghost, it was just him. He closes the distance between us until I can feel the cold silk against my chest, and every muscle in my body tightens, fighting the urge to shrink away from him.

His fine hair tickles my neck as he leans close and speaks in my ear, his voice as cold as the silk whispering around him. "I know what's keeping me awake," he says, "but what could possibly be troubling your sleep? Regretting your decision, perhaps?"

He fills my senses so completely, I fumble through my thoughts, trying to figure out which decision he's talking about. The only thing I was afraid of regretting...was not walking from his tower when I had the chance, not becoming his assistant at all. Did I? No, you can't regret an experience like that, just because one facet of it was painful. Pain is part of life.

"No, M'Lord," I say, my voice trembling only slightly, "I made the right decision."

"Is that so?" His voice is little more than a hiss. "Then why can't you sleep?"

I didn't expect my words to make everything right between us, but the venom that drips from his voice is startling. "M'Lord, I-I..." I don't understand what I said to anger him, unless *he* wishes I'd walked away. "I want to-to..." Words fail me, but not my nerve, not yet, and I raise my hand, my fingers trembling as I touch his arm, just above the elbow. He goes still, like he's not even breathing, and I hesitantly move my hand higher, feeling his firm muscles through the thin silk.

"What are you doing?" he whispers, voice tricks forgotten.

I don't answer, I can't; I just clench my jaw and let my hand slide from his arm to his chest, trying to ignore the way my calluses snag on the silk. I hear his breath catch as my thumb grazes the hard nub of his nipple. I do it again, and a shudder runs through him, his breath heavy and erratic on the side of my neck. I close my eyes, fighting hot tears of shame, as I run my hand across his chest like a whore.

"You...don't know what...you're doing," he groans, like he has to remind me that my hands are clumsy, inexperienced. If he doesn't like it, he can... But no, I have to do this, I have to show him what staying here means to me, what I'm willing to do.

My other hand finds his waist, but I'm not sure what to do with it. This would be so much easier if he would do something, but he just stands there, close enough to share the same breath but separated by a thin layer of silk. I try to keep it that way, try to avoid touching his bare skin with my rough hands, but his robe gaps open down his chest, exposing a golden slice of his flawless skin, and somehow, my wrist brushes across it. The next thing I know, he's pressed his face into the hollow of my neck, raising gooseflesh down my back as he groans into me.

His hands slip between us and I feel him untie the sash holding his robe closed. I swallow hard, drawing my hands back as the silk slips off his shoulders. The last thing I want right now is for him to pull away from my touch. This is hard enough as it is. His palms press against my stomach, rise toward my chest, his touch carrying an air of desperation that sits like a lump of lead in my gut, heavy and cold. He clutches at me, one hand following my ribs back to where they meet my spine, and then he pulls me to him, his chest hot against mine.

"Lark," he whispers, and I close my eyes, choking on a sob. I've never heard my name spoken like that, with such longing, such need. It scares the hell out of me. Like a cat, he rubs his cheek against my jaw, his lips grazing my neck as he fights to speak. "I don't un-understand why-why you're doing this..."

"I don't want to be sold," I say, my voice barely above a whisper. "I'll do anything, whatever you want, M'Lord, just please let me stay."

He goes very still. "You want... That's why..." He pulls away from me as if burned, his face contorted in an ugly mix of anger and disgust. "You could have just asked," he hisses, teeth bared. "You didn't need to whore yourself to me. What do you think I am?" I recoil from him as his eyes bleed from ice blue to sinister crimson, the color nearly swallowing the black as his pupils shrink to pinpoints. "Do you know how easily I could make you mine?" he asks, and my entire body trembles as his voice resonates through me, rattling me clear to the bone. "Do you have any idea the things I could do to you? And you couldn't stop me; you wouldn't want to. You would beg for more."

He takes a step toward me, reaching out with one hand, the silk robe hanging off his arms making a slithery sound. I fall back with a strangled yell, tripping over my own feet and slamming my shoulder into the cold stone wall. Pain shoots down my arm, but I shove myself away from the wall and jerk the door to my room open, dashing inside and pulling it shut behind me.

I stand and stare at the door, a deathly stillness settling over me as I realize what I've done. The door has no bar, no lock, and is the only way in or out of this room. I've trapped myself. All he has to do is pull it open and he has me. I back slowly across the room, watching the thin strip of amber light glowing under the door, and my heart stops beating for a moment when a shadow moves in front of that light. He just stands there for the longest time, so long I realize that I'm holding my breath and have to let it out. I hear him lift the latch and I shrink back against the wall.

He slips into my room, his robe wrapped securely around him and the sash cinched tight. His movements are unhurried, stiff and deliberate, the master of restraint once again, but that does nothing to ease the feeling that I'm trapped and he's going to do something horrible to me. He doesn't look at me, staring instead at the dying lamp on the table, but his eyes are back to being blue.

"It's late," he says, and I flinch, even though his voice is soft. "I'm going to forget tonight ever happened, and I suggest you do the same. As for you wanting to stay — it's probably a moot point now, but even if you did wish to remain, I don't think that it's possible...especially after what has happened. I apologize and bid you good night."

I watch him leave, not daring to move even long after he's gone, not until I realize that I'm shivering, my bare skin as cold as the stone wall I'm leaning against. I sink onto the edge of my bed, feeling like I want to throw up.

"What have I done?" I whisper, wrapping my arms tight around myself. Whore. I am a whore. I hear the rustle of straw and raise my eyes from the floor. Khas is standing at the bars of his crate, waving his paws to get my attention.

You hurt? he asks, using simple gestures I can understand. I don't know the hand motions to explain what I've done. I'm not sure I could find the words right now, either.

I sick heart, I tell him.

He shifts himself to the left, finding a larger gap to talk through. *White owl hurt you? Owl scary.*

Sactaren, the White Owl, silent and deadly in the night. It fits.

No, I say with a sigh, *I did bad. Owl angry.*

Khas scratches his cheek with one of his middle paws, glancing to the closed door and back to me again. *Sleep,* he says. *Light come, owl go nest. Make all bad good.*

He turns away and curls up again. I wish it was that easy, I wish my biggest fear was being torn apart and eaten, but after what I've seen, death is the least of my worries.

Chapter 18

Just after dawn, with Khas's crate in hand and a long cloak fastened about my shoulders, I slip out of the castle, not through the shop but by the main gate. I don't want to risk running into Sactaren or Schaff; I just want to get this over with. After this, I'll have no reason to stay.

Low clouds wreathe the tip of Traxen Peak, glowing rose and gold, while the snow covered slopes of the mountain sit a pale gray and deep purple. I pick my way toward it, through the fields of broken rock and scree, part of me wanting to keep walking right up the mountain and down the other side, but I draw to a stop beside a low table of stone, a sigh escaping in a thin cloud of white as I set the crate on the rock.

What? Khas asks as I lift the cover off the crate and take a step back. He peers at me through the bars for a moment, then nimbly leaps up onto the edge of the wood and then down onto the stone. He scampers around the crate, sniffing the rock, eyeing the sky, his ears twitching this way and that. I stand and watch, knowing that this is the best thing for him, but that doesn't ease the raw ache in my throat when I think about never seeing him again. He turns toward me, huge black eyes squinted against the rising sun.

What? he asks again.

You go home, I tell him, my hands trembling.

He glances at the crate. *No keep me more?*

I swallow hard and gesture no. What right did I have to keep him, anyway? He wasn't just some dumb animal; he had feelings, he had needs and wants. He didn't deserve to be kept for the amusement of another. Oh Maele, I'm just as bad as all the others, for what is a pet but another word for a slave?

He bounces toward me on his lower extremities while gesturing excitedly with his front paws. *Come, come, you see home,* he says, springing down from the rock and zipping off between the boulders. I see him pop up several feet away, sitting atop a pile of scree and gesturing to me again, *Come, come.*

I can't move, can't speak, as I hold out my hand, palm down. He tilts his head, his ears twitching thoughtfully, then he starts scampering back toward me.

No! I violently slash my hand through the air and he backpedals to a stop. *Go home. Now. I no see. I go home.*

He takes a hesitant step toward me. Tears stream freely down my cheeks, stinging in the icy breath of the mountain. *You bad,* I tell him because I don't know words enough to make him understand. *Go now, go!* I kick a small rock and he ducks as it bounces over his head. Ears flat, he scurries up onto the pile of scree again, grabbing a stone and flinging it at me before disappearing down the other side.

I grab the crate and empty the straw out onto the ground, but it slips from my fingers and hits the rock with a splintering *crack.* I stare at it for a moment, then stomp my foot down onto the slats. The thin, dry wood flies apart and I kick at the ruined pile of kindling, a sob shuddering through me. Covering my face with my hands, I fall to my knees and just let myself weep.

How long I kneel there, I'm not sure, but when I raise my tearstained face into the bitter wind, the sun has burned away the clouds around Traxen Peak, leaving its face bleak and inhospitable. I lurch to my feet and stagger back toward the castle, drying my face on the edge of my cloak as I pick my way through the rocks. I don't look back. Whether Khas is standing on some lonely pile of rocks watching me walk away, or he's gone forever, I don't think I could bear it either way.

I enter the castle and head for my room, but stop outside the door. I don't want to go in there, silent and empty without Khas. It's too early to open the shop. After a moment, I shuffle down the dark corridor toward the kitchen. I'm not hungry, and couldn't eat even if I was, but it's the place I have to go. I push against the door.

"Lirrik." The voice draws my attention and I turn as Her Ladyship steps out of a doorway, her long green dress whispering across the stone floor as she walks toward me. "Are you all right?" she asks.

"Not really, M'Lady," I say. "I just lost my...best friend. And last night... You were right, Sactaren is playing with me, and I-I almost gave in to him."

"Almost? What stopped you?"

"Well, he did, M'Lady."

"Really?" She sounds surprised. "This is worse than I thought, then."

"What-what do you mean?"

She steps closer, leaning in to whisper to me. "He never turns down sex, unless he wants something else as well." She reaches out and touches my arm, her fingers warm through the thin fabric of my shirt. "He wants your soul."

I jerk back, suddenly unable to breathe. "My what? He-he can't—"

"He can. He's done it before. He'll imprison your soul in a crystal and use it to power his spells. He'll bleed the life out of it and when he's done, your soul will crumble to dust, like you never even existed."

I swallow hard and glance down the hall toward the shop. My soul. *That's* what he wants from me. I-I have to stop him, I have to get away. I turn back to Lady Sactaren as a thought hits me. "Does that mean he's not really going to sell me?"

Her look of concern slips away as she stares at me. "What?" she asks, her voice suddenly hard.

"Lord Sactaren, he-he asked Schaff to find a replacement. He's going to sell me to another lord—"

"And you couldn't have mentioned this earlier?" she asks, drawing away from me. "I could have been in my garden, instead of down in this tomb with you. What a waste of time." She turns on her heel and stalks down the hall.

"M'Lady," I call after her, "what...what does this mean?"

She stops and turns, her face pinched and twisted into a look of pure loathing. "It means, you stupid slave, that now I have to start all over with your replacement, which is a damn shame, because you were so gullible and trusting, it was almost too easy to turn you against him. You believe anything anyone tells you, don't you?"

"You...lied to me?"

She laughs, cold and bitter. "Did I? I don't know. Honestly, I know less about my husband than you do. For all I know, it could all be true, but technically, yes, I lied. There's a lot of that in this castle. You're lucky you're getting out. Goodbye."

I watch her disappear down the hall, and then I shove open the kitchen door. The room is empty, but suddenly, I don't want to be alone. I turn and head for the shop. It's a good hour yet until time to open, but maybe Schaff will be in there, maybe he can tell me what the hell is going on.

Still clutching the cloak about me, I pause in the inner doorway of the shop, taking what could be one of my last long looks at the charms, potions, and salves I've come to know so well. No sign of Schaff, though. I sigh and step behind the counter, heading for the back room, but stop dead as an agitated voice reaches my ears.

"...not listening to me. He's too much of a temptation. All the time, I hear..." Sactaren's voice grows indistinct. I inch closer, straining to hear, but I can't make out words, only sounds, until, "...risk losing control again."

"Oh, come on, he's just a slave," Schaff replies scornfully. "Go in there, throw him over a table, and get it out of your system. A few days and you'll get tired of him anyway."

I wrap my arms around my body, feeling sick. Schaff, how could you? I thought he was my friend, I thought—

"No." Sactaren's tone is final. "He *has* to go."

"You know you'll regret it if you sell him." Just from the devious undercurrent in his voice, I know his tail is twitching, that brutal cat-with-a-mouse mirth he tries to pass off as playfulness. "Imagine his fine ass being plundered by somebody else, somebody else's cock in his sweet mouth, because that's what'll happen to him, you know that. With those long legs and firm ass, his strong hands and broad shoulders, full lips and big doe eyes, that's all he's good for."

I lean my forehead against the edge of the shelf beside me and close my eyes as my stomach churns. Is that all people see when they look at me, something to fuck?

"Watch it, Schaff, or Maele help me, I *will* put that collar back on you."

Schaff is silent for a long time. "You're far too sensitive," he finally says with a sniff. "If the kid means that much to you, why don't you just tell him, and stop all this bullshit?"

"I can't." His voice is so soft, I can barely make out the words, and if he says more, it's lost to me.

"Well, that sounds like a load of crap to me, but it's your life, I guess," Schaff says after a moment. "I think I'll go wake our little prince and see if he needs help packing his bags. Oh, that's right, he's a slave; he gets tossed out with the rest of the trash."

I slip out of the shop, pausing in the corridor just long enough to jerk my shoes off before I race toward my room, my stocking feet silent against the flagstones. I slide to a stop and grab for the latch of my door, breath coming in short bursts. Yeah, I look like I just got up. Right. I dash down the hall and into the kitchen, throwing myself onto one of the rickety wooden stools at the counter.

Swallowing down the taste of bile, I fight to catch my breath. I wish my head would stop spinning. I wish I could stop feeling like I was going to throw up. I wish I could kill Schaff. My eyes sweep the counter, falling upon an old steel knife lying beside the bread basket, its pitted blade a dull gray, but the edge gleaming a cold silver. I reach out, slowly, and touch the worn wooden handle.

I was eleven when they taught me to kill, barely more than a boy the first time I felt blood gush over my hands, hot, thick, sticky. I belonged to a sheep rancher, and when it came time to slaughter the spring lambs, I was too scrawny and gangly to hold them still, so it fell to me to slit their throats. I had two black eyes and a cracked rib before I let them turn me into a killer, before I gave in and drew that gleaming blade through the snow white fleece, staining it the ghastly red that you only see in fresh blood. Schaff's fur won't turn that color; it's already red.

I jerk my hand back and clench my fist, pressing my knuckles against my lips until I taste blood. I can wish him to burn in the darkest Hell, but I can't send him there. I'm not a killer.

"Hey, you're up early." I stiffen, anger riding between my shoulder blades like a dead weight, and slowly turn as Schaff trots into the kitchen. "What's the matter, your pet rat wake you?" He glances around. "Where is he, anyway? I didn't see him in your room. And what's with the cloak?"

"I turned him loose," I say, barely recognizing my own voice. It sounds flat, dead.

Schaff's ears stand straight up, his restless tail going still. "You what? Why? I thought—"

"Slaves can't have pets," I say.

"But...Naeven said you could keep him." He leaps up onto the table, his eyes darkened by a frown as he looks at me.

I slip off the stool and walk to the counter under the window, staring out over the idyllic farm valley. "Yeah, but I'm not going to be his much longer, am I?" I ask, gripping the edge of the counter until my fingers hurt. "You're going to send me for my replacement today, aren't you?"

"No."

"Why the hell not?" I shout, turning on him. "Why do you keep dragging this out? Why can't you just let me go? Do you think you're doing me a favor? Because you're not, so stop."

He hangs his head a moment, then lies down on his belly, his front legs crossed at the ankle. "Lark, we need to talk."

I head for the hall. "I have nothing to say to you."

"Then just shut up and listen," he calls after me. "I was talking with Naeven, and—"

I stop and stalk back to the table. "I heard you," I hiss, "and I am more than just some fuck-toy."

His eyes widen, dazzlingly golden as they catch the light of the sun. "Oh, shit. Lark..." I turn and walk away. Nothing he can say will excuse what he said. "That'll teach you eavesdrop, now won't it?" he shouts after me.

I stop, I almost go back, but it's what he wants. He wants to see me riled up, but I'm not going to play his games any longer. If he won't go buy a slave, then by Maele, I will.

I storm into the shop and dig the sack of coins out from under the counter. I know that if I stop to think about what I'm doing, I'll talk myself out of it, so I don't stop. I stalk back down the hall and cross the courtyard, hesitating only a moment before I step through the dark doorway into Qito's lair. I guess with all his extra arms, I'm expecting a spider's nest or something, but it's just a stable.

The smell of dry alfalfa and large beasts is unmistakable, as is the soothing rustle of feet shifting in straw and the deep, slow breathing of the animals around me. It's very dark inside, the only light coming from three crystal lanterns hanging from the main support beams and burning with an eerie blue-green light. I step over to the first stall, hoping to see one of the elk, namely Bari, and I stop short at the sight of a massive beast, obviously cousin to the dog and wolf, but not quite either. Its fur is mottled pale gray and sandy gold, with dark, red-brown markings on its face and across its shoulders. It has to be nearly ten feet from the tip of its long, broad muzzle to the end of its shaggy tail, and I bet its back would come even with my chest, though I would have to wake it to be sure and I'm not about to that. I back away, turning instead to the stall across the way.

Not quite what I was looking for, but certainly a lot less deadly than the wolf-thing. An elegant red stallion peers at me over the door to his stall, huge brown eyes watching my every move. He's beautiful, his coat a deep, glossy red, except on his muzzle and from the knees down, which is black as soot. He whickers softly and shakes his head, his ebony mane rippling like a sheet of satin in a soft breeze. He's not very big, his shoulder just even with my chin, but he has to be the most beautifully sculpted and powerfully muscled animal I have ever seen. I've never ridden a horse before, but if I can ride an elk, a horse shouldn't be a problem, right? I swallow loudly and take a step toward him, my hand outstretched. He blows hot breath on my fingertips as he stretches out his neck, trying to nuzzle my hand. That's when I notice the scars.

In the center of his forehead, where you would expect to see a horn on a unicorn, someone has carved the symbol of the sun into his hide, the raised tissue gleaming pink. On his neck, just below the curve of his jaw, is an intricate, and I would guess, magical, symbol I can't identify. My eyes slide across his shoulder, where another, different, symbol has been carved, and there's another in the middle of his chest.

"What has he done to you?" I whisper as my fingertips slide over the velvety soft skin of his nose. I jerk back and turn, suddenly seething with restlessness, resentment, and anger, and underneath it all, an overpowering hunger I can't explain. How could Sactaren do this to a horse, to a gentle, beautiful animal like this? Well, never again. I reach for the door latch.

"*Kio, kio!*"

Something shoves me away from the stallion's stall, and, with a shout of surprise, I fall into a pile of hay. I look up, as something large and black looms over me, something with far too many arms.

"Qito, what the hell?" I ask, sliding on the hay as I struggle to my feet. It's the first decent look I've gotten of him, though in the eerie blue-green light, his skin is blacker than coal and his eyes flash the milky green of a blind dog. He has six arms, three on a side, and walks like an animal, up on his toes. He also has a tail, which I've never noticed before.

"*Nak dhian kio bakraka, Luchiher,*" he chatters at me, gesturing at the horse. "*Kio di abak Chactaren nak di hatiko.*"

I shake my head. "I-I don't understand," I say. "I just want to ride him to the village. I'll bring him back, I promise."

Qito chatters, too fast for me to catch any words, and waves his arms wildly, suddenly lashing out and striking the horse on the nose. I jump as the stallion squeals, kicking the inside of his stall door hard enough to splinter the wood, and snaps at Qito.

"*Luchiher di ek iknakra, naknah. Ek an-hy-er.*"

Qito reaches for the horse again, and I gasp as the stallion bares his fangs. Slim and wicked, they gleam in the eerie light, like the canines of a carnivore, except only in his upper jaw. The lower teeth are all flat grass cutters. The stallion looks at me, and his once innocent brown eyes are filled with a dark intelligence that makes the hair on the back of my neck stand on end.

"He would have ripped my throat out, wouldn't he?" I whisper, slowly raising my hand to my neck. The stallion snorts and turns his back on us. I glance at Qito. "An-hy-er?" I ask. Qito shakes his head and pushes past me, disappearing into one shadowed corner of the stable. An-hy-er. I glance at the horse and shudder at the thought of those fangs. Fangs! "He's a vampire!" The stallion looks past his shoulder at me, his ears back flat against his skull, and I swallow hard. A vampire stallion... Maele save us all.

Hands grab me from behind and a startled shout escapes me. I glance back, not at all relieved to see Qito's dark form standing there. I try to shrug him off, but he damn near lifts me off the ground as he shoves me toward the door, pinning my arms to my sides as I try to break free. "Hey, Qito, damn it, I need a ride!" He dumps me in the courtyard and bars the door as I scramble to my feet. "Fine!" I shout, my voice echoing from the blank walls. "I'll walk!" I storm out of the castle, breaking into a run as soon as I'm clear of the main arch, and soon the castle, even the mage's tower, is lost to sight behind the barren hills.

Of course, I didn't bother putting my shoes back on, so my socks are soon wet and muddy, and I have to stop to take them off. Breathing hard, but not painfully, I lean against a boulder and strip off the socks, tossing them off the trail with a flick of my wrist. It's a good thing I never liked socks, since I likely won't ever wear them again. Pushing away from the boulder, I head down the trail, one hand absently brushing against the lump in my pocket, making sure the money bag is still safe. I don't know how much is in it, but it is by far the most money I've ever carried, enough to buy a slave...or free one.

I imagine reaching the village and just walking on, on to the next town, on to some place far away. This is enough money to buy food, clothes, lodging, a berth on a ship. It's enough to start a new life. Run away, with Sactaren's money? It's tempting, so very tempting, but I am not a thief any more than I am a killer. I'll get him a damn slave, the biggest, meanest, ugliest, dumbest bastard they have, or maybe a woman. If Schaff is to be believed, Sactaren has little interest in women. At least she'd be safe from him in that respect.

As the mountain trail begins to level out and farm houses appear in the distance, I raise the hood of my cloak. The last thing I want is to be recognized. Farmers glance up from their plowing, but a barefoot traveler in a black cloak isn't novel enough to interrupt their work. I pass a redheaded girl in her early teens, wielding a stout staff and guarding a score of sheep as they graze on the hillside. I remember her from yesterday, buying freckle concealer. It worked, her pale face glows like fresh milk, not a single ginger spot in sight.

I grow uneasy as the edge of the village draws near. I can see the slave market, with just a handful of people milling around waiting for the auction to begin, and I remember sharply my own time up on that rickety platform, being inspected like livestock, my worth being measured against a handful of tarnished coins. I pull the cloak tighter about me and stand at the edge of the buyer's area, where I can watch the slaves in the corral without anyone noticing.

They're even more pathetic than the bunch I was with. A hunched old woman, a scrawny, red-faced kid with a bandage wrapped about his head, a one-eyed man in his thirties with skin almost as dark as Qito's, and a weathered fellow with sun-bleached white hair, probably a pirate. It's hard to decide which one Sactaren will despise more. The kid is out, of course — I would never subject a boy to the whims and perversions of that man. The pirate could take care of himself, and I doubt even Schaff would dare mouth off to the man with one eye. The woman, of course, would probably be safest, although she looks like she might have trouble managing all those stairs.

The auctioneer, his nose as red and swollen looking as ever, steps up onto the platform and clears his throat, motioning for the slavers to bring over the first item up for sale — the boy. Hauling the kid up onto the platform is none other than Erion. I clench my fists beneath the cloak. What I wouldn't give for ten minutes alone with that piece of filth. I might become a murderer after all. Erion gives the boy a slap across the face I can hear all the way back here, and leans down, saying something that makes the boy cringe.

"Well, well, well, would you look at this fine young man!" starts the auctioneer, but no one seems to be paying much attention. I don't blame them. This is a fishing village, a farming community, and the kid doesn't look strong enough to carry a chicken or skilled enough to scratch his own ass. He'd be snapped up in a second in a city — bathed, dressed, perfumed, and warming some rich man's bed before the sun set, but here... The auctioneer is scowling, asking a mere four laenes for the boy, but nobody's buying. Giving the kid a dirty look, Erion steps back up on the platform to take him away.

"Wait a minute." Every head turns as Lord Drumar struts forward, walking up to the edge of the platform and looking down his nose at the kid. "This thing isn't even human. I'll give you two laenes — the rope is worth something, at least."

The auctioneer looks to Erion, who scowls, but gives a slight nod. "All right, the bid is two laenes, going once. Two laenes, going twice—" He raises the gavel and I leap forward, reaching into my pocket as I shove my way between a couple of farmers. I pull out the bag of money and rip it open.

"One coin," I say, holding up the shiny gold piece.

Drumar turns on me, anger darkening his haughty features, and I draw further back into the shadow of my hood. "Two coins," he counters, his hand straying to the pearl handle of the dagger at his hip.

I clench my teeth and without a word I drop the open bag onto the platform, half a dozen coins spilling out, with at least that many still inside. A hushed murmur ripples through the crowd. The auctioneer turns a sickly shade of gray, raising his eyes from the money bag to me. I guess he recognizes the bag.

"S-sold, to the Traxen Mage," the auctioneer says, the gavel shaking as he thumps it down on the podium.

I glance at Drumar. He takes a step back and acknowledges me with a slight bow. I wonder what he'd do if he knew it was just me under here? I don't think I want to find out.

Chapter 19

People trip over each other trying to get out of my way as I lead the boy away from the slave market. I can't help but wonder just what Sactaren has done to make these people so afraid of him. Grown men shrink back and lower their eyes as I pass, casting looks of pity on the kid as he stumbles along behind me. I don't know why he's having so much trouble walking — he's not hobbled, and I'm certainly not walking too fast. I hope Erion didn't break his legs or something. I wouldn't put it past that man.

When we left Ventia, there was an old man among us slaves. When we docked at Traxen, there wasn't. Slavers like Erion are under contract to transport and sell government slaves — minor criminals, beggars, political dissidents, farmers who can't pay their taxes — and they have to take whoever the government gives them, even if it would cost the slavers more to feed and ship the slave than they could get at auction. So instead of feeding a slave that isn't likely to sell for more than a laene or two, like an old man, Erion lets his scumbag crew take turns beating the crap out of them, just for the fun of it. I tried to stop them and wound up thrown in the hold for my trouble, covered in the old man's blood. Slave ships always have rats, and rats are attracted to blood, so it was a rough five days.

Actually, I'm surprised the kid made it to Traxen in one piece, though from the look of his face, it wasn't an easy trip. He's covered in cuts and bruises, his skin raw and inflamed looking. I hope he doesn't have some sort of disease. I stop after we round the first bend in the road, the green hills hiding Traxen from view, and take a closer look at him. Drumar was right, he's not human.

He watches me with almost feral gray-green eyes and his jaws are elongated, more like the muzzle of an animal than a man. He's scrawny, thin as a scarecrow, and his head doesn't quite come up to my shoulder. His clothes are in unusually fine condition, pants that fall clear to his feet and a shirt with long sleeves and a high collar, patched and dirty, yes, but no holes or tears. His head is wrapped in strips of cloth, as are his hands and feet, making him look like a leper. Oh, shit, I wonder if that's what's wrong with him.

I take a step toward him and he dances back, light on his toes, keeping the lead rope taut between us. I allow myself a humorless smile. Who would've ever thought I'd be on *this* end of the slave rope? Not me, that's for sure. Raising my hands slowly, I push back my hood, the sunlight falling warm and golden across my face. His eyes narrow as he takes in my shorn head and the scars on my face.

"My name is Lark," I tell him. He doesn't respond, or give any sign that he understands. We regard each other for a moment, then I sigh and shake my head. "C'mon, let's go see if Sactaren can speak your language." Just my luck, I can't even talk to him.

I turn up the road, giving the rope a slight tug. He pulls back, almost jerking the rope out of my hand. I glance over my shoulder to find him staring back toward the village, his whole body tense and ready to flee. "What is it?" I ask, stepping up beside him, but even as the words leave my lips, I hear the rumble of hooves on the roadway, coming fast. I grab for my hood, but before I can raise it to hide my face, horse and rider have galloped out from behind the hill. I feel like I've swallowed a lump of ice. It's Drumar.

He jerks back on the reins, mud and rocks flying up from the horse's hooves as it skids to a stop. He scowls down at me, eyes like chips of stone. "I should have known it was you," he snarls, nudging the horse closer, driving me to the edge of the road.

I glance back, down into the ditch of muddy water, and clench my fists. "Don't forget who I belong to," I say, sidling out from in front of the horse. "My master will not tolerate this harassment."

"Your master," he says with a cold chuckle, "doesn't want you any more. As soon as he finds a replacement," he glances at the boy and his cruel smile widens, "you're mine."

My heart begins to pound in my throat. I impressed a lord, all right. I can still see the cut and a shadow of a bruise where I punched him. He turns his horse suddenly and I jump out of the way, right into the heel of his boot. Pain explodes in the side of my face as he kicks me, and I stumble back, dropping the lead rope.

"Better get used to that," Drumar laughs. "What little remains of your worthless life is going to be marked in pain and blood." My cheekbone throbs as I glare up at him, a trickle of blood slowly making its way down my face. "See you soon." Pulling his horse around, he gallops off toward the village.

"Son of a bitch," I mutter, using my sleeve to dab at the blood. It's not a big cut, as far as I can tell, but it's deep, and I know I'm going to have one hell of a bruise tomorrow. If I live that long. I should have known I'd never be lucky enough to get a decent master. Sad, really, that the kindest one I've ever had is also the one I'm most eager to escape.

"You're a slave, too?" I turn, raising my eyebrows at the sight of the kid halfway up the grassy hill, gnawing at the ropes binding his wrists. He snarls, hunkering down in the weeds and long grass, his sharp white teeth bared at me. "Stay back," he growls, though I haven't moved an inch.

"I'm not going to hurt you," I say, wincing slightly. Great, even speaking hurts now. "And yes, I am a slave. Like I said, I'm Lark." I wait, but he just goes back to chewing at the rope. "Do you have a name?" I ask finally. He snarls again, but I think it's at the tough rope, not me.

"My last master called me Kit," he says, looking hopelessly at the rope, which has barely begun to fray, "but that's not my name."

"So, what is your name?" I ask, taking a step toward him.

He snarls and scrambles further up the hill. "What do you care? You're a human, you're just like the rest of them."

"I am *not* like them," I say. "I've been a slave longer than you've been alive, and I've suffered more than you can even imagine, and if I was smart, I'd tell you to get the hell out of here, because once my master has a new assistant, I'm going to be sold to that asshole who kicked me, but if I do let you go, you'll just be caught and sold to someone else, someone who I can almost guarantee will treat you worse than Lord Sactaren, so really, I'm doing you a favor by giving you my job, even if it means a long and painful death for me, because I'm *not* like everyone else." I'm out of breath, and I'm not sure what I said makes sense, but it's close enough. I'm *not* just another human.

"If you go back, you'll be killed?" he asks after a moment, halfheartedly starting to bite at the rope again.

"Probably," I say. There's a chance Drumar was full of shit, but I doubt it.

"Then don't go back, you fool. Run away."

I sigh and shake my head. "So I can starve to death instead? No thanks. Drumar may not kill me quickly, but he'll get to it eventually." I watch the kid fight with the rope for another minute. "If you want, I can untie that for you."

Gray-green eyes narrow suspiciously. "You just want to take me to your castle."

"Fine," I say with a shrug. "Have fun chewing through it. I hope it tastes better than it looks." I turn and begin the long walk back to the castle. Behind me, I hear the kid spit, and then the grass rustles.

"Okay, hang on," he calls after me.

I stop and look back as he nimbly leaps the muddy ditch. He still hobbles when he walks, though. "What's the matter with you?" I ask, nodding toward his feet.

He glances down. "What? Oh." He flushes an angry red. "That slaver tied my tail to my leg to hide it. It makes me walk funny." A tail? I glance at his bandaged head. "Yes, they hid my ears, too," he says, scowling.

He stops about six feet from me, looking around like he expects me to have an army hidden in the ditch somewhere, just waiting to jump out and grab him. I just stand there and wait for him to come to me, which he does eventually, holding out his bound wrists for me to untie.

"Can't you talk to your master?" he asks as I pick at the knot. It's all wet with spit, the fibers swollen and tight. "Maybe if he knows what that man is going to do to you, he won't sell you."

"We're not exactly on speaking terms," I say. "The last time I talked to him was just after his eyes turned all red and he tried to...kill me." I don't think killing me was quite what he had in mind, but the kid is looking uneasy enough as it is. "It was my fault," I explain quickly. "I...I messed up, severely." It had been my fault, but I can't help but feel that Sactaren was looking for a fight last night. He'd been cold and snappish ever since the bath — no, before that. In the forest, he damn near bit my head off. I don't know what I did to deserve *that*.

I work the knot loose and unwind the rope from around the kid's wrists. He jumps back, ready to make a run for it if I try and grab him, so I just turn away and head up the road again. After a minute, he stumbles up beside me, walking just out of reach. "What's he like?" he asks.

"Well..." I remember Thadyn's answer to my question, and almost laugh. "You know, I don't have any idea. It's like he's a different person to everyone who meets him. The villagers hate and fear him, the one other mage I've met treated him with disdain, his wife won't have anything to do with him, the Spidersmith seemed to like him well enough, Schaff speaks about him with contempt and to him like they're old friends, and me...I find him very beautiful, and very frightening." I glance over at him, picking at the wrappings around his hands. He's having a bit of trouble. "I think you'll do just fine with him. Need some help?"

"No, I...I got it..." He growls and holds out one hand toward me. "Damn humans," he mutters.

The knots are tight, but the cloth is thin and old, so I just rip it. He jerks his hand back and uses his teeth to pull the bindings off. My eyes widen as his hand is revealed, thin and delicate, covered with short, silky hair. The back of his hand and as far up his wrist as I can see, is a dark silver color, almost pewter gray, while his fingers are a pale, sterling silver. He has no fingernails, but I think I can see stubby black claws hidden in the fur at the ends of his fingers, and his palm and fingertips are leathery black pads, like an animal's paws. Once one hand is freed, he's able to tear the wrappings from his other hand. "Quit looking at me," he hisses, and I realize I've been staring.

"Sorry," I say. "You just have beautiful fur."

"Let me guess," the kid says, "you like furry little boys to warm your bed, too."

I stop dead, appalled at the very thought. "No, never." He looks skeptical for a moment, then his features soften. I hope that means he believes me. "People have...done that to you?"

"They tried," he says, kneeling in the middle of the road and unwrapping his feet. "Did they try and do *that* to you, too?"

He glances up and I look away, out over the fields. "They did more than try. When I was younger than you, they did more than try."

He's silent for a long time. "My name's Kivixl," he says at last.

I force the ghosts of my past back where they belong — in the past — and turn to him with a smile. "Nice to meet you. Need any more help?" I jerk my chin toward his bandaged head.

"Thanks, but I got this." He reaches up and pulls the wrappings from his head, wincing as his large, triangular ears unfold from the awkward position they'd been stuck in. They're dark at the base, but lighten to white at the tips, and look softer than velvet. The rest of his head is sheared to the scalp, but I would guess that his hair is that dark gray, or maybe black.

"Maybe...maybe you *could* take a look at this, though. I can't seem to get it off." He begins unbuttoning his shirt and pulls back his high collar to reveal a thin band of silver metal encircling his neck.

I step closer to take a look and he tenses. "May I?" I ask, raising one hand ever so slightly. He hesitates, then nods his head. At first I just look, but I can't see any sort of hinge or latch, or even a seam. "I'm just going to turn it," I warn him as I reach up. I can't help but touch the fur at his throat, completely by accident, of course, and it's even silkier than it looks. I don't find a way to remove the metal collar, however. "Sorry," I say, stepping back, "it looks like it'll have to be cut off."

"Thanks anyway." He holds out his hands, turning them back and forth. "I guess I can stay like this a little longer. So, where's this castle of yours?"

"It's not *my* castle." At least, not for very much longer. "It's up on the mountain, there." I point toward Traxen Peak. "I think you can see Sactaren's tower from the top of the next rise."

"Well, let's go, then. I want to see." He starts hobbling up the road.

"Hey, Kivixl, don't you want to untie your tail?"

He slows, then stops, his head bowed and shoulders hunched. "It's fine," he mutters as I catch up. "I'll worry about it later."

"But, if it makes it hard to walk—" He says something I don't quite catch. I lean closer. "What was that?"

"They shaved it." He looks up at me, his hands clenched into fists. "It was too bushy to fit down the leg of my pants, so those damn humans held me down and shaved it. It's just skin and bones now; it looks horrible." He reaches up and gingerly touches his cheek, the skin scraped raw by a dull blade. "I look like hell."

"It'll grow back," I say, rubbing a hand over my own bristly scalp.

He lowers his eyes. "You don't understand," he grumbles. I sigh and place a hand on his shoulder. He shrugs me off. "You can't understand; you're human."

"Maybe," I say with a shrug. "I just meant, your fur *will* grow back eventually, while these…" I push up my sleeve and show him a criss-cross of scars on the inside of my arm, scars I've had since I was about his age. I can't remember why my master decided I needed to be carved up like a roast chicken, but I'll never forget how that knife felt slashing deep into my flesh as I tried to protect my face. "…and these…" I raise my shirt, watching him cringe as the sunlight hits the hard, knotted tissue on my left side. That one, I do remember. I spilled the basket of beans I had been carrying. For that, I got ten lashes. Nowadays, I could take ten and laugh, but this was years ago, and they didn't use a horsewhip on me, or even a bullwhip, they used a scourge, with seven leather thongs instead of one, and each one was tipped with a jagged, twisted piece of metal. It actually ripped hunks out of my flesh. I have to swallow a couple of times before I can continue. "These, I will have forever. And don't give me anymore of that 'you're human' crap. It was humans who did this to me, don't forget. Now come on, I'm hungry."

Chapter 20

"It's huge," Kivixl says in a small voice, his head tilted back to look up at the mage's tower. I keep my eyes on the ground. The last thing I want to see is my master watching me from his window. "And you said you have your own clothes *and* your own room? And all you have to do is sell people things?"

"Well, there's a bit more to it than that," I say with a chuckle. I fall silent as something occurs to me. "Oh, hey, can you read?"

His eyes harden, like he thinks I'm poking fun at him or something. "I'm a slave, what do you think?"

"Sorry." I decide not to point out that I'm a slave too, and *I* can read. As we pass under the arch and enter the courtyard, Schaff comes stalking across the stones, his ears plastered back against his skull and tail lashing violently. He does not look happy. I hear Kivixl growl under his breath and move behind me.

"Where in the hell have you been?" Schaff snarls. "We've been tearing the castle apart looking for you. You can't just go for a walk whenever you feel like it, you know. We had to turn customers away because—" He finally catches sight of Kivixl. "What is that?"

"My replacement," I say, stepping aside so he can get a decent look at the kid, "since you were never—"

The fur on Schaff's back stands on end and he hisses at the kid, his golden eyes narrowed to slits. Kivixl hisses back and takes a swipe at Schaff, his stubby black claws suddenly a lot more obvious.

I jump in between them, pushing Kivixl back. "What the hell is the matter with you two?" I shout as he tries to slip past me again.

Schaff turns tail and streaks back into the castle. "Naeven!" he screeches, his voice echoing down the hall as he heads for the tower, "Naeven, get down here now! Naeven, you can't let him do this to me!"

I turn to Kivixl. He's glaring after Schaff, a low, rumbling growl reverberating in his chest. "What in Maele's name is going on?" I ask, hitting him on the shoulder when he continues to ignore me. "Hey!"

"You didn't tell me Schaff was a machiran," Kivixl says, his voice still rolling with that deep growl.

"You got a problem with machirans, too? Humans, machirans, is there anybody you don't hate?"

Kivixl gives me a stunned look. "I don't—"

"What is this?" I stiffen as Sactaren's silky voice fills the courtyard. Kivixl glances past me and his ears drop flat. Slowly, I turn to face my master. "Lark, what happened to you?"

I start to raise my hand to my cheek, but gesture to Kivixl instead. "Nothing. M'Lord. This is Kivixl, my replacement."

Sactaren glides toward us, each step describing the fluid grace of a wave breaking on the shore, and I find my breath catching in my throat as I watch him draw near. His cold blue eyes remain fixed on me until he stops before us, then they shift to Kivixl.

"Kivixl," he says slowly, and I feel the boy shrink further behind me. "He cannot stay here," he says, bringing his eyes back up to me, his attention drawn once again to the cut on my face. "Schaff will not allow it." He turns away and starts back into the castle, like that's the end of it.

"*Schaff* won't allow it?" I say, my insides quaking but my voice steady. "I thought this was *your* castle."

He stops, but doesn't look back. "It *is* my castle," he says, his voice low and tight, "but I left this decision up to him. I trust his judgment more than your bleeding heart."

"You sure that's wise?" I ask, taking a step toward him. "After all, the last time you trusted his judgment, you wound up with me."

He whips around, his eyes flashing, and closes the distance between us without ever seeming to take a step. One moment, he's almost to the door, the next, he's in my face. I swallow hard, but refuse to be driven back.

"Schaff outdid himself when he found you," he hisses, and I shiver as that steely voice slides down my spine. "You...you were perfect, you...*are* everything I never thought I could have, and you just...you can't *stand* to be near me. Tell me how that is Schaff's fault."

The heavy scent of him surrounds me and it's like I'm back in the hall again, his body pressed to mine, his hands clutching at me, lips brushing against my throat. I gasp and stumble back, heat rushing to my face as I feel the beginning of an erection straining against the front of my pants. Damn him!

"It's *not* Schaff's fault," I say, speaking breathlessly around my wildly beating heart. "You have no one to blame but yourself."

He stares at me a moment, then squares his shoulders and raises his chin. "On second thought, I believe the boy will make an adequate replacement. Excuse me. I have to send word to Lord Drumar that his slave is ready to be picked up."

He stalks toward the entrance to the castle proper, the sunlight bringing out the gold in his hair as it fans out behind him.

I watch him go, feeling cold and scared, until Kivixl nudges me in the back.

"Tell him," he whispers. He's got to be kidding. I'm supposed to ask for a favor now, after what I just said? Sactaren will laugh in my face. "If he says no, it's not like you've lost anything, right?"

I unfasten my cloak and thrust it at Kivixl as I take off after my master. I do nothing, I get sold to Drumar. Sactaren says no, I still get sold to Drumar. Nothing to lose... So why am I trembling as draw up beside him? "M'Lord, you-you can't sell me to Drumar."

He slows, then stops, his eyes like old ice carved from the deepest crevasses on the highest mountains as he looks over at me. "You are mine," he says quietly, "I can do anything I want to you."

I suddenly realize that we're back in the hall again, just outside my room. I hesitantly wet my dry lips, watching his eyes for any sign of that horrible crimson as I speak. "I-I know, M'Lord, what I meant was...if you knew what he's going to do to me—"

"Oh, believe me, I know," he says, and the bottom drops out of my stomach, "but I don't see how it's any of my concern." He leans into me, his lips brushing against my uninjured cheek as he whispers, "You have no one to blame but yourself."

He walks away, leaving me standing in the corridor, staring after him. He doesn't care. I'm going to be tortured and killed, and he doesn't care. I shuffle back out into the courtyard and lean against the wall beside the doorway.

Kivixl hobbles over, my cloak draped over his arm and clutched to his chest. "Well? Did you tell him?" I nod, slowly. "And?"

"He doesn't care." I cross my arms over my chest. "It's no less than I expected from a cold, heartless man like that. I don't know why I even bothered. No one has ever given a shit about me, why should they start now?"

"The gods help me," Schaff growls as he stomps out into the courtyard, "if you don't stop your whining and moaning, I'm gonna give you something to whine and moan about. You think you're the only one who's had a shitty life?" The black fur between his shoulders stands on end as he hisses at me. "So you're a slave, and you were *abused*. Join the fucking club. And *you*," he bares his teeth at Kivixl, "this is *my* territory, you got it? If you want to stay, you keep the hell out of my way."

"Bite me," Kivixl snarls.

"Don't tempt me," Schaff barks back. "Now come on, Naeven said to give you a room."

Kivixl glances at me. "Go on," I tell him, "this is your home now; you better check it out. I'm just going to...wait here for my new master."

"Damn it, Lark, why didn't you just talk to him?" Schaff hisses. "You could have spared us all *this*." He shoots a dark look at Kivixl then stalks back into the castle, the tip of his tail just a white streak as he lashes it from side to side. I watch Kivixl follow after him, then sink down onto the cold flagstones, drawing my knees up to my chest and wrapping my arms tight around them. I stare out toward the main gate of the castle and watch the distant clouds sail in and out of view.

Everything in my head, and in my heart, so loud up until now, has gone silent, leaving me in a kind of peaceful fog. I know I'm going to die, a horrible, painful, lingering death, but it will have to end, eventually. And then all of this will be over.

Chapter 21

The sun is sinking into the west when I finally hear the clatter of hoofbeats on the rocky ground outside the castle. Good, I was starting to get stiff and cold, sitting on the damn ground. I groan and climb to my feet, brushing the dust off the seat of my pants as Sactaren comes gliding through the doorway, shrouded in a cloak of darkest burgundy, his face hidden in the shadow of his hood. He neither speaks nor looks at me as we wait, and I return the favor. I think if I did look at him, something inside me might break, and the dull pain that pushes against the inside of my ribcage might become something harder to bear.

My shoulders tighten as Drumar rides through the arch, his haughty expression taking on a hint of cruel joy at the sight of me. He pulls his horse to a stop and dismounts, bowing low to Sactaren before stepping closer and raking me with his eyes.

"Very nice," he mutters, his lips twisting into a smirk as he eyes the cut he gave me. He grabs me by the chin, trying to open my mouth to look at my teeth, but I jerk my face out of his grasp, balling my hand into a fist and raising it like I'm going to punch him again. He steps back and nods once to Sactaren. "Just what I've been looking for," he says, pulling a bag of money out of an inside pocket of his cloak.

Sactaren holds out one claw-like hand, with thick scales and sharp talons just like Thadyn had, and Drumar pales slightly as he hands over the money. I feel like I've been kicked in the stomach. Drumar reaches up and takes down a coil of rope looped over his saddle horn. I stare straight ahead as he binds my hands in front of me, refusing to wince as the rough rope bites into my wrists. "Many thanks, Lord Sactaren," Drumar says as he swings back up into the saddle and urges his mount toward the gate at an easy walk.

I can feel Sactaren's eyes on my back, but I will not turn, I will not give him the satisfaction of seeing the tears that silently streak my face. After we pass beneath the main arch, Drumar turns in his saddle, smirking down at me. "Not so tough now, are we?"

"Go to hell," I say, and spit at him, but my mouth is so dry, I ought not to have bothered. Drumar laughs and jerks on the rope, nearly pulling me off my feet. I hear a high whistle, and then a sharp *thwack* as he smacks me across the side of the head with his riding crop. It stings, and there's a ringing in my ear, but I clench my jaw and glare up at him, ignoring the pain. "Is that all you've got?"

He draws back his arm for another blow, then lowers it, smiling down at me instead.

"It's almost ten miles from here to my castle," he says, letting out about five feet of slack in the rope and then tying it off at his saddle horn. "A man gets dragged that far, even his own mother won't be able to recognize him, so you'd best not trip."

I cast one last look back at the castle, my eyes seeking out Sactaren's tower, expecting to see him framed in the window, watching me be dragged to my death, but I'm not surprised to see Schaff instead, the white tip of his tail flicking back and forth as it hangs over the edge of the sill. He's there but a moment before he disappears. I turn back to find Drumar smirking at me.

"Missing him already? Don't worry, I'll make you scream just as loud as he did." He digs his heels into his horse's ribs and she takes off at a brisk trot.

I don't wait for the rope to pull taut, liking my shoulders too much to let them be dislocated again, but chase after him, my bare feet flying over the packed mud of the mountain trail. Drumar glances back, scowling when he sees that I'm keeping up, and urges his horse into an easy gallop. The rope grows tight and I feel myself being pulled, my feet pounding hard as the feeling begins to leave my legs. I can't breathe, and it feels like someone's stabbing me in the side with a knife. Each step is barely more than an desperate attempt to stay on my feet, because I've seen what happens when a horse drags you, and I'll be damned if I let him kill me like that.

"Great Maele!" Drumar shouts, reining in his horse.

I crash into the beast's sweaty flank and fall into the mud. She turns a nervous circle, nearly stepping on my legs several times. Gasping for breath, I flounder on the ground, trying to get back on my feet before Drumar takes off again. I stagger upright, the muscles in my legs knotting up and burning, my knees like water, but somehow I keep from falling again. Behind me, Drumar's horse whinnies softly, a thin, fearful sound, and I glance down the road to see what has spooked her. I'm expecting a snake, or maybe a wolf, but certainly not the large black unicorn walking slowly toward us, each step powerful and deliberate, his rider hidden beneath a burgundy cloak.

My heart leaps. He's come to rescue me! I quash it down. That might not be it at all, and I can't afford to be torn apart by false hope. I watch him, my face schooled into a hard mask as the unicorn walks past me.

Drumar's mare flares her nostrils and paws at the ground, but he holds her steady, fighting to regain his own composure. "Is there a problem, Lord Sactaren?" he asks.

"I changed my mind." The voice that issues from within that hood would be better suited to a demon, or a dragon, than to the beautiful man I know to be under there. A clawed hand flips Drumar's sack of coins back at him. Drumar nearly drops it, sputtering indignantly.

"I... You can't... We had a de—"

He falls silent as Sactaren draws a long, shiny sword out from under his cloak, the blade glinting black, gray, and orange in the last rays of the setting sun. With a single stroke, Sactaren slices through the rope binding me to Drumar. I stagger back as the unicorn steps between us.

"Yes, well..." Drumar clears his throat. "We're both reasonable men. Do keep me in mind when you *do* grow tired of him. Good day, Lord Sactaren." His horse shies away from the unicorn as he spurs her forward, and he gives me a look of purest loathing as he rides by.

I stand in the road, still trying to catch my breath, arms aching and legs shaking just from the effort of keeping them under me, watching Drumar sullenly disappear around the bend.

"You didn't tell me he wanted to kill you," Sactaren says, a touch of anger coloring his voice as he swings down from the unicorn and slides his sword back into the scabbard belted to the unicorn's saddle. The big beast turns his head toward me, nosing me in the shoulder and nearly knocking me off my feet.

"I tried," I tell him, pushing the unicorn away with my bound hands. "You said you didn't care."

Sactaren grabs the rope in his taloned hand and jerks on it, almost pulling me into him.

"I meant I didn't care if he...if he used you," he says, drawing a slim dagger out of his belt. "And I was just angry; I didn't mean it." He cuts the ropes binding my hands and puts his blade away.

I absently rub at my wrists. "*Used* me?" I say quietly. "Is it easier to stomach when you put it that way?" He turns away, resting one clawed hand on the unicorn's shoulder as he stares at the ground, but I have this tight knot of words in my throat that refuses to be swallowed down. "Because I would hate to offend your delicate sensibilities, but I don't feel used, Your Lordship, I feel molested, sodomized, brutalized, raped, and *fucked*." My voice echoes down the valley, like the cawing of ravens in the twilight. "And I'm tired of it. So if you're just going to sell me to someone else, someone who *will* use me, I'd rather you give me back to Drumar and let him end it." He doesn't respond, just stands there stroking the neck of his unicorn with one grotesque, taloned hand. "Better yet," I hiss, "why don't you fucking end it yourself!"

"That's enough!" I jump as he whirls around and grabs me by the front of my shirt, but I stand my ground. "Damn it, Lark, can't you see..." He gives me a small shake, then lets go, turning away with an exasperated sigh. He reaches up and shoves back the hood of his cloak, his talons vanishing like smoke in the wind and his fine, white-gold hair dancing about his face as he turns back to me. "Look, I was angry and I took it out on you, and that wasn't fair. It was your choice not to assist me, and I had no right—"

"What choice?" I ask. "I wanted to keep helping you and you said I couldn't."

He frowns at me. "No, I didn't."

"*Schaff said—*" I say in the same breath he does.

We stare at each other in shock. "Schaff did this," I whisper, looking over the unicorn's back at the castle, the high tower rising up against the purple and gray face of the mountain. After a moment, I look back at Sactaren, who has moved off to the edge of the road and is standing silhouetted against the platinum sky. "M'Lord..." My voice falters. I don't know what to say to him. "I-I-I'm—"

"I know," he says softly. "So am I." He crosses the road, his eyes shadowed by a deep frown. "More than you will ever know." He sighs. "Come on, let's get back and see what Schaff has to say for himself." He motions for me to mount up first, and I look up at the saddle on that unicorn like he's asking me to scale Traxen Peak itself. I grab the saddle horn and raise my weary leg almost halfway to the stirrup. That's about as far as I can go; I'm so tired. With a sigh, I step back.

"It's not far," I say. "I can walk." It can't be more than half a mile. On these aching legs, it might as well be a thousand. Still, walking I can do — riding, I'm not so good at. I start up the road, and wince. The bottoms of my feet hurt, cut or bruised on the stones in the road. I don't bother to check which; it doesn't matter. On the bright side, it means that the feeling has returned to my legs.

"Thank you," Sactaren says suddenly, and I glance back. "You were magnificent, as always." He strokes the unicorn's face as he speaks, and for a moment his eyes are gentle and his lips curve in a joyous, peaceful smile, and he's more than beautiful, more than seductive and frightening and powerful — he's someone I would like to serve, someone I would like to know. He glances at me, and his expression becomes guarded again. "Return to Qito," he tells the unicorn. "I shall mark another day off your debt." The beast nickers and noses him in the shoulder, then turns and trots past me, his tail waving like a plume of finest black silk.

"M'Lord," I say as Sactaren climbs the rise toward me, "you shouldn't be walking in this mud."

He arches an eyebrow as he draws abreast of me. "I thought I asked you to call me, Naeven," he says. He scuffs one black suede boot against a rock. "I'm no stranger to mud, you know. When I was your age, I walked from one side of Panteri to the other, eight thousand miles of mud and swamps and mountains and deserts. I think I can make it up this hill."

We begin to climb, neither speaking for several minutes, but I keep stealing glances at him. Is everything okay, just like that? All those things I said, the things I did, forgiven? I don't understand him.

"M'Lord," I say, ducking my head as he gives me a pointed look. "I mean, Naeven," I whisper, "I was wondering, I...in the forest, after we caught the salamander...what did I do? To make you angry, I mean."

He sighs, a sound of sadness and regret. "You didn't do anything," he says. "I was — I was angry at myself, for not checking if you were susceptible to the salyr a'havon, and for not taking better care of you. You shouldn't have had to suffer through that. And I was angry because I knew what I would have to do to you, and I just knew you would hate me afterward. Which you did. I made sure of that."

"I didn't hate you," I say after a moment. "I was confused and angry, and-and ashamed. I'm sorry, I should never have touched you like that with these hands." I look down at my calloused palms, so rough, so hard.

"It wasn't your hands," he tells me. "I just — I know what the salyr a'havon can do to a man, how it can compromise his better judgment, and I didn't want you to do something you might regret later. I like your hands," he adds. "They're strong and real."

"Clumsy and inept," I mutter, feeling my neck burn as I remember my awkward groping of him in the hallway. "I *didn't* know what I was doing."

"That wasn't what I meant, either," he says, tucking one of his thin platinum, black, and burgundy braids behind his ear. "I guess I should have said, 'you don't know what you're doing *to me*.' You have no idea how much I wanted you, how much I *needed* you at that moment, just to touch me, just to connect me to something real." He sighs. "Magic is a cold mistress, driving us to seek comfort in the arms of others. Be glad you're not a mage, Lark; it is as much a burden as it is a blessing."

We reach the plateau that the castle is built on and pause to catch our breath. I have just one more question, but I can't seem to find the right words. I don't want it to sound like an accusation.

"It's a beautiful castle," I say into the silence, taking in the high tower, the lower turrets, the battlements, the arched gateway, all that smooth, dark gray stone. I want to ask him about the spell, ask him why he would cast it on me, because this man, the one I see before me now, wouldn't have done it. He wouldn't have. Which would mean... Suddenly, I can't breathe. Suddenly, I don't want to know.

"It is beautiful," Sactaren says, looking down at the ground, "but even after all these years, it still reminds me of pain and ugliness." I want to ask him what he means, but he clears his throat and gestures for us to continue. "So, when you said you wanted to keep helping me, shall I assume you meant that before...all this happened, and that you've since changed your mind?"

"If you do," I say slowly, "you'd be mistaken, M'Lord." I can feel his eyes on me, but I stare ahead at the castle.

"You do realize that, as easily as you were taken by the magic, it will probably happen again. Frequently."

I swallow hard, my mouth suddenly dry. I can't tell if that's a threat, or a promise.

"M'Lord, as long as I'm not more trouble than I'm worth, I would like to be your assistant again, with everything that entails."

"With everything that entails?" he repeats, arching an eyebrow at me. "I see someone has been furthering his education."

I feel my face color and look down at the ground. "There hasn't been much to do in the evenings lately, except read."

"You are truly amazing," he says, and I glance up to see who he's talking to, forgetting for an instant there's no one here but us.

He raises his hand to my face and I tense but don't pull away as his fingertips graze my jaw, his touch cold as ice. He leans toward me and I feel a surge of panic: he's going to kiss me. I've never been kissed. My heart begins to pound. What do I do? I can't breathe. He shouldn't be doing this; masters don't kiss their slaves. Beat, rape, maim, and kill, yes, but they don't kiss them. I swallow hard.

"Damn him," Sactaren whispers, raising his hand to gently touch the cut on my cheek. I wince, but am relieved. "Sorry. We should probably wash that out before it gets infected." He steps back, a slight frown on his face. "Did you really think I would let him kill you?"

"You were so angry," I say softly. "I didn't want to think so, but..." I look toward the castle and sigh. "I suppose I owe Kivixl my thanks."

"Kivixl, why?"

"He told you what Drumar was going to do. That's why you rode out here to save me."

He shakes his head. "I was already leading Raem out of the stable when Schaff came racing down from the tower, shouting at me to go after you."

"Even before you knew..." He wanted me back. Not just to save my life. "Wait, Schaff?"

"Yes, Schaff. I guess his little joke got away from him. He's lucky it *was* him who told me. It's the only reason I'm going to give him a chance to explain himself. And he had better have a damn good explanation, or I shall personally wring his furry neck."

Chapter 22

Schaff meets us in the courtyard, his golden eyes reflecting the dancing torchlight as he glances back and forth between us. "I see you two finally had a talk. About fucking time."

"You have a lot of nerve," Sactaren says between his teeth. "Lark could have been killed."

"Not my fault," Schaff informs us. "If either of you had bothered to start a simple conversation, it would never have gotten this far. I tried to tell you," he says to me.

"When?" I demand. "You never told me anything, except how fucking stupid I was."

He rolls his eyes. "You men and your selective hearing. This morning, I tried to talk to you, remember, but you already knew; you'd been eavesdropping, remember?" He glances at Sactaren. "Something the two of you have in common. Rats, my fuzzy ass. Do I look like a housecat to you?" His fur is standing on end and a low growl threads through his words. "Damn it, both of you, fucking this up at every turn. You!" He turns to Sactaren. "You insecure, hot-tempered, spiteful martyr." He rounds on me. "And you, stubborn, brash, pathetic coward. I gave you two every opportunity to work this out, nudged you in all the right directions, and *still* you couldn't fix the problem."

"If it hadn't been for you, there wouldn't have been a problem!" I shout at him.

"You so sure about that?" he asks with a smirk, sitting down on his haunches and beginning to wash his face.

"Schaff," Sactaren says in a cold, warning voice.

Schaff looks up at us, a hint of scorn on his sharp features. "You asked me to ask Lark if he wanted to keep helping you. Hello! Of course he's going to say yes, he's your slave and he wants to please you. He knows helping you will make you happy, so he'll do it regardless of what he wants."

"But I *did* want to help," I say.

Schaff blinks at me. "I know. Good for you. Now shut up. Naeven, you gave him a choice he would not say no to. You could ask him to do anything, and he wouldn't say no, because he's been trained to follow orders; it's been beaten into him until he can't do otherwise." He cocks his head to one side as his eyes shift to me. "Although, giving Drumar a fat lip really shocked the shit out of me. I really expected you to march your scarred ass upstairs and tell Naeven off after that."

"Will you be reaching a point any time soon?" Sactaren asks, standing with his arms crossed and his brow furrowed, but in thought rather than anger. *I'm* still pissed, though.

"The point is, unless this was clearly Lark's decision, he would resent you every time the magic took him." Sactaren opens his mouth to say something, but Schaff doesn't let him. "Every time, Naeven. Don't argue with me, I had a feeling about it. Of course, I expected him to fight for what he wanted, not sit around and whine, and I didn't expect you to be so damn emotional about it, yelling at him and throwing things." He jumps to his feet, his fur fluffing out again. "And what the fuck were you thinking — phoenix ash? We both know there are easier ways of removing scars, ways that don't involve high magic. You know how dangerous it is. You swore—"

"I know, okay?" Sactaren says, flinging his hands to his sides and pacing a few short, angry steps across the courtyard and back again. He looks at me, his eyes dark and troubled. "I know. It won't happen again."

"Right, that's what you said *last* time, but the first piece of ass that comes your way, you—" He jumps back as Sactaren brings his boot down a hair's breadth from Schaff's nose. "Hey!"

"You will *stop* referring to him like that," Sactaren says, no voice tricks, just pure fury.

Schaff takes several slow steps away from him, his tail slung low. "Of course, My Lord," he says calmly, but I think he knows he overstepped his bounds at last. I don't know what made Sactaren wait this long. He's needed a swift kick in the tail for some time. "Anything else?"

"Get out of here before I turn you inside out." Schaff nods respectfully to him, glances at me, then turns and pads silently into the castle. Sactaren watches him go, then sighs and runs a weary hand across his face. "He's probably right, you know."

"M'Lord, I can make my own decisions," I say. "He did this for the fun of it."

"Maybe," he says, and motions for me to follow him as he heads into the castle. "I want to talk to you about the boy. He can't stay here."

"I-I know you don't need another slave, M'Lord, but...he's just a kid. Please."

"Schaff will not tolerate him. Machirans are very territorial."

"He didn't seem to have any problem with me," I say.

Sactaren laughs. "You're not a machiran."

"Neither is... Wait, is that what Kivixl is? He...he doesn't exactly look like Schaff."

Sactaren comes to a stop outside the door to my room and leans against the wall, his hands in his pockets. "You saw that metal collar he wears? It keeps him in humanoid form."

Ah, that's why he said, "I guess I can stay like this a little longer." I glance at the door, just wanting to go inside and pass out for the next eight hours, but I can feel that there's something else Sactaren wants to say to me. All the more reason to slip off quickly.

"Well," I say, sounding slightly out of breath, "thanks for not letting Drumar kill me. Er... I'll see you tomorrow?" I didn't mean for it to sound like a question. I fully intend to see him tomorrow.

He pushes himself away from the wall and takes one of those gliding steps toward me. I try in vain to swallow my unease. There's just something about the way he looks at me...

"I don't suppose you'd like to wake up in my bed," he says, and my knees go weak. He takes another step, and it's all I can do not to back away from him. I watch his eyes, waiting for that crimson stain to bleed across them. "What do you say, Lark, do you want to sleep with me?"

Maele help me, I never expected him to come right out and ask. I know he wants me, and I would be extremely ungrateful if I said no, seeing how he did save my life, but I'm not sure gratitude extends to letting him hurt me. I mean, I can't see him being as rough and sadistic as some of the men who've had me, and I know he wouldn't hurt me on purpose, but I can't help it — having another man inside me hurts. That's how it's always been.

Looking at him, though, and remembering his hands moving across my bare skin, his arms wrapped so tight around me, I imagine after the pain, falling asleep in his arms, waking up nestled against his chest, being something more than a tight hole to violate. I've never had that.

I take a breath to answer, but hesitate. I'm scared. That's the long and short of it — I am afraid. I'm also taking too long to answer, and I glance at him, hoping he's not angry at the lack of decision, but he's just watching me, not waiting, really, but studying me, and the reality of his question hits me like a kick to the chest. He's testing me.

"That's not fair," I say quietly, looking him dead in the eye for a moment before turning away. "Good night, Lord Sactaren."

I slip into my room and shut the door without a backward glance. Damn him! It was just a test, to see if I *could* make my own decisions. I stalk into the little bathroom, stripping off my shirt as I go. I'm completely spattered with mud from running along behind that horse. I grab a washcloth off the linen shelf and pour a basinful of water.

A test. And not a very good test, at that. He's assuming my personal choice would conflict with his own. If I want to say no, but I know he wants me to say yes, then it proves if I can make my own decision. But is that what I want? Would I have said no? Suddenly, I'm not so sure.

I shake my head and begin to wash up, remembering too late about the cut on my cheek. The rough cloth snags the scab and rips it away. Fresh blood trickles down my face and I grimace. I lean toward the mirror and dab at it with the corner of the cloth. Oh, yes, it's turning a lovely shade of purple already. I can't wait to see what it looks like in the morning. I frown and look closer. The edges of the wound are red and puffy. Great, it's infected.

I glance down to rinse out the washcloth, but pause. Something's not right. I raise my eyes back to the mirror and slowly turn my face a little to the left. The burn scar on my jaw, where one master shoved a guttering torch into my face, is gone. I frown, trying to remember... Outside the castle, when Sactaren touched me, his hand was freezing. It wasn't that cold. But why would he—

"You're right, that wasn't fair." I jump and spin around. Sactaren is standing in the doorway, his burgundy cloak gone and the top few buttons of his loose, ivory shirt undone, exposing a narrow triangle of smooth golden skin. I swallow hard, at a loss for words as he continues. "I thought I could prove something, to you, to me. I wasn't sure, but all I proved is that I've underestimated and undervalued you. And even though I meant that question in the most literal sense, I won't ask you again, as a test, or otherwise."

"Thank you," I say after a moment, though I'm not at all certain that I mean it. Honestly, I'm a little disappointed. When I saw him in the doorway, I had thought he'd come back to ask me for real this time. I feel out of breath as I realize what my answer would have been. I'm staring at him and quickly lower my eyes. "Is-is there anything else, M'Lord?"

"How is your face?"

I glance in the mirror, at the scar I know is there but cannot see. I'm almost starting to look human. "Very good, M'Lord, thank you."

He steps into the room, a ghost of a smile on his lips. "I meant that cut." He stops beside me, his fingertips warm on my jaw as he turns my head to one side. "You should have told me Drumar did this; I never would have let him take you."

"I didn't think you'd care," I say, wincing slightly as he touches my cheek.

"I care very much," he says, then blinks and shifts his eyes to mine. "I cannot allow anyone to abuse my property. It would make me look weak."

"Of course, M'Lord," I say, lifting my chin slightly and pulling away from his touch. Property. I am property. I can't help but feel bitter about it, though. He treats me so well, it's easy to forget that all I am is something to be bought, sold, and owned. "Is there anything else you want of me?"

He regards me for a moment, then hands me a small glass jar of lavender salve. "This will stop the infection and speed healing." He turns toward the door, then looks back over his shoulder, wisps of pale gold falling into his eyes. I swear he did it on purpose. "And if anyone from the village asks, tell them I was the one who hit you. Good night."

He sweeps across my room and out the door before I can ask him why. Why would he want the villagers to think he beats me? Why would he want them to fear and hate him even more?

I dab the salve on my face and finish washing up, shrugging into a light, clean nightshirt before stepping out of the bathroom. I pause at the bookshelf, looking for a title I haven't read yet. There aren't many left. I finally pull down a thin volume on the five tribes of North Coast selkies.

"That book is mostly crap, you know."

I turn and scowl at Schaff, who is curled up on my pillow. "Get out," I say. I stalk to the table and jerk out the chair, sitting with my back to the bed and Schaff.

"Look, I'm sorry you didn't catch on sooner," he says. "I really expected you to confront him, and then I'd say, 'Oops, my mistake,' and he'd know that you really wanted to keep helping, and you'd know that he'd really let you go if you wanted, and everyone would be happy."

I twist around in my seat. "And what gives you the right to decide what makes us happy?" I ask. "What if I'd rather he didn't know I wanted to help? I mean, Maele only knows what he's thinking now, when all I want is to grind herbs and feed the draklings."

"Are you sure that's *all* you want?" Schaff asks. I turn back to my book. I'll never admit, especially to Schaff, that I would have gone to his bed tonight. "Because I've seen the way you look at him," he continues, apparently unable to take a hint, "and when a man looks at another man like that, he wants to grind more than herbs."

"Stop being perverse," I say, closing the book with a snap and pushing it away. "I'm his *slave*."

"You know, Naeven isn't real big on the whole master/slave thing. He'd give you your freedom in a minute — all you'd have to do is ask."

"Do you really think I'd fall for another of your tricks?" I ask, standing up and shoving in the chair. "Oh, yes, wouldn't it be funny to see him laugh in my face? No master would *ever* free their slave. The only freedom I'll ever find is death."

"Naeven would," Schaff insists. "He freed me. He freed Thadyn."

I walk over and slump down on the end of the bed, crossing my arms over my chest.

"I don't believe you."

He shrugs his tail. "You don't have to. You'll see, if you haven't already. Underneath his demons, of which he has a few, Naeven is a good man. He tries very, very hard to do what's right. He would love you, if you would let him."

I think I would like to let him, but I am so afraid. "I know," I say softly.

"I don't think you do, or you wouldn't be down here talking to me." Schaff gives me a pointed look. "I told you there weren't many men like him and I meant it." He jumps down onto the floor and sprawls out, rolling onto his side and yawning. "You've been with a lot of men?" he asks. I look down at the floor and nod. A lot is an understatement. "Always against your will?" I nod again. "You've never been with someone you wanted?"

"No," I say, scowling. "Why would I want someone to hurt me like that?"

Schaff regards me for a moment, the white tip of his tail twitching back and forth across the flagstones. "Naeven won't hurt you," he says at last.

I laugh humorlessly. "How do you know? Have you ever been with him?"

"Yeah, a few times."

I feel the expression bleed out of my face. "But-but you're a...you're...not human."

He flicks an ear back and smirks. "Nice save. You were going to say 'animal', weren't you? I'll let you in on a little secret. The Great Council defines an animal as a creature incapable of rational conversation, complex emotion, and higher thought. So I guess your six-legged rat and his friends are off the menu now. Thanks a lot." He pauses to wash behind one ear, then smirks at me again. "Remember that assistant I told you about, the one who got taken by magic all the time? He may have stopped assisting Naeven, but that doesn't mean he left the castle."

"You? But...but..."

"Here's another secret, one I would have thought you'd discover on your own, considering the state of the little fleabag you brought home with you today. We machirans are shape-shifters."

He stretches again and my eyes go wide as his legs begin to lengthen, his paws stretching out into hands and feet, and his pointed muzzle shrinking back into his face, until he looks like Kivixl, only dark red instead of silver gray, and with all his fur intact. With a crooked grin, he props his head up on his fist. "Ta-dah."

"You...you're... So that's how you got to my pie."

He rolls his eyes. "Among other things." He looks down the length of himself, running his fingers through his thick, bushy tail. I wish I could do the same; it looks so soft. "So, you can see why Naeven had to find himself another assistant," he says softly. "I'm not exactly his type." He sounds almost sad.

"Schaff, do you...miss being his assistant?"

He snorts and shifts back to his regular form, rolling to his feet and giving his coat a good hard shake to settle it back down again. "Me, miss all that work? Are you kidding? I stay like this all the time just so I won't have to help with the dishes."

He pads over to the closed door and gives me an expectant look. I start to get up, but then sink back down on the edge of my bed. "Are you planning anything else to 'help' me?" I ask.

He shrugs. "Nothing specific," he says, "but I'll let you know if something comes up. Now, you want to open the door?"

I get up and let him out, watching him as he slips away down the shadowy corridor. Is he right — about anything — or is he just having a laugh at my expense? I shut the door and walk back over to my bed, falling heavily upon the quilt and staring up at the ceiling.

I would have slept with him. Even after all the anguish and pain he caused me, I would have said yes. And if he asks again? He said he wouldn't, but...I lick my lips, my mouth suddenly dry, and roll onto my side, gripping handfuls of the quilt tight in my fists.

I don't want to wait for him to ask. I sit up, pulling my knees up against my chest and wrapping my arms around my legs. *Is* it a spell? Did he do this to me with his magic? I should have found out! Using magic on me would be unforgivable, but the alternative...that I — that I want to—

"Maele, help me," I whisper, squeezing my eyes shut. And then I see Sactaren, that small, gentle, *real* smile softening his exotic beauty, making him human, making *me* feel warm and safe and at peace. Can magic do that? Can magic make me think of him, and dream of him, and want to be with him? Maybe, but I don't think so.

I slowly unfold myself and rise to my feet, my hands shaking as I reach out and turn the lamp down to the barest bronze glow. I take a steadying breath, square my shoulders, and head for the door. I'm not going to wait for him to ask.

Katica Locke lives in Western Oregon's Willamette Valley with her family, pets, and unruly imagination. *Magebound* is the first volume in her homoerotic fantasy romance series.

CPSIA information can be obtained at www.ICGtesting.com
Printed in the USA
LVOW080409030212

266875LV00002B/149/P